CONSTANCE & ENZO'S TEA TIME WITH PEYTON

A Novel By

Theresa Dale

ISBN Print: 978-1-989897-07-2
ISBN eBook: 978-1-989897-06-5

For my readers.

CONTENTS

Chapter 1 - Tea

It was four o'clock. Tea time.

The heavy drapes were pulled aside, each held in place by delicately-wound, silvery rope weighted at each end with generous tassels. Sunbeams filtered through the tall western window, filling the room with that just-before-sunset quality of light, still full and bright, but beginning to wane as it travelled slowly downward toward the horizon. The white, periwinkle blue and silver tea room would change as their daily ritual progressed, reflecting the twilit sky not just through colour, but through the lengthening shadows of its objects and occupants alike.

Constance had instructed Cook to modify the timing of their tea according to the season, and judging from her view from the fourth-story loft, winter was finally giving way to spring, Peyton thought. They'd be meeting later before long.

Peyton trusted this was the case, based on her conversations with Constance and Enzo. She'd never seen Constance interact with Cook – or any of the staff, for that matter. In fact, she'd never seen the staff, full-stop. Constance kept her a mystery. Peyton wasn't sure exactly what they'd been told, but Enzo was confident they'd follow any instructions from Constance to the letter.

The staff were paid generously by Constance and Enzo's mostly absent father, who was tenth in a long line of successful London businessmen. The Everleigh name was an institution here – one need only walk the streets of London's finer neighborhoods to see evidence of that. Wineries in Knightsbridge and Notting Hill, several residential properties in Chelsea, and golf courses – Peyton couldn't remember how many – throughout the further reaches of England.

Apparently, though, none of that really mattered. Family money had been funnelled down as generations passed on and the line had dwindled enough to ensure those who remained, remained in the type of comfort they were accustomed to for the remainder of their years.

Peyton was quite sure the staff did Constance's bidding for another reason, too. She had a temper like a spoiled toddler. Nobody wanted to be on the receiving end of *that*.

Peyton surveyed the afternoon's fare, her eyes drinking in the gorgeous spread as they did each day. She delighted in discoveries both familiar and new, her palette slowly becoming familiar with each day's delicacies after several weeks' experience.

The table was set with exquisite elegance, as always. The pale blue and white china and flawlessly shined silver complimenting the colours of the room. Intricately patterned damask napkins were the focal point of each setting, having been carefully folded into varying origami-like designs and centered on each plate. Today there were two three-tiered serving stands: one boasting a colorful variety of tea sandwiches and pinwheel wraps and the other displaying desserts almost too beautiful to eat. Peyton often wished for her camera – or even better, her paints and canvas – just to capture the visage of the desserts alone. To her, the experience of their taste was a separate thing entirely from the experience of their beauty. To be able, somehow, to capture that duality would be immensely satisfying.

"And how are you today, Peyton?" Constance asked, her voice high and prim.

Peyton put a small smile on. A *polite* smile, Constance called it. Just a hint of an upturn at the corners of the mouth as you made eye contact with your company. "Very well, thank you. And yourself?"

Constance was fascinated by Peyton's awkwardness in social situations. She'd made it a priority to teach her how to behave properly in company, even if it felt wrong to Peyton (and in spite of the fact that she'd only ever had the company of Constance and Enzo since she'd arrived). Peyton had tried to explain it to her once, but her Asperger's diagnosis seemed of no consequence to Constance. She expected Peyton to act a certain way, and so she would, regardless of the effects that being on the spectrum rendered.

Constance was of the opinion Peyton's affliction was, in fact, a blessing more than a curse, though Peyton had tried endlessly to persuade her hostess that Asperger's was not the reason that she was able to commune with the dead.

Regardless, Constance saw the world just exactly how she wanted to see it. Enzo said that translated to Constance getting her way all the time. *Every* time, regardless of what she had to do to make it happen.

"Everything looks lovely!" Peyton exclaimed, having learned that compliments were appropriate after having sat down, and before one began to consume the provisions.

Constance surveyed the table. "Yes. Cook's outdone himself once again! Let's enjoy, shall we?"

Peyton paused. This was awkward.

Enzo leaned back to observe her hands, still tied tightly behind her back, and rolled his eyes. Peyton sent him a questioning look, which he answered by shrugging, a wicked twinkle in his eye.

I'm glad this is entertaining to you, Peyton thought, wishing she could put the words in his head as he was able to do with her, but failing. As always.

"Well?" Constance raised her eyebrows at Peyton.

Peyton usually served at this point. She felt a familiar seed of panic deep in her belly, threatening to take root. She couldn't serve, but she couldn't question Constance in any way, either. Sweat beaded on her forehead as she looked at Enzo again.

"You're just going to have to tell her," he said.

Constance glanced in the direction of Peyton's gaze. "What's he saying?" she asked, a quiet desperation flashing briefly in her eyes.

Peyton snapped her eyes back to Constance. "He says he'd like the pink petit-four," she managed, revelling in Enzo's reaction.

"What? It's not fair you're able to decide what I'm saying at your own whim!" he protested.

Peyton merely raised her eyebrows at him.

He rolled his eyes. "Fine. Just stand up. Show her your hands as though it's part of the routine. Like you always do it this way."

Peyton nodded almost unperceptively, then stood. "Tea?" she asked, smiling.

Constance nodded, placing her napkin in her lap.

Peyton approached her, then turned, her back to Constance. Enzo watched his sister, his anticipation evident on his raptly attentive face.

Constance had started talking before Peyton had reached her. "It's absolutely gorgeous outside these – *oh!*" she started. She cleared her throat delicately, then continued smoothly as she untied Peyton's hands. "I've always said spring is a messy, slushy season, but it's been so lovely this year that I've had to reconsider!"

Peyton tittered dutifully as she reached for the silver teapot. It took everything not to rub her wrists, get the blood flowing again. She sent a grateful look to Enzo, then carried on. "Have you seen any spring flowers yet?" she asked, breathing easier now that her hands were her own.

Constance brightened, as Peyton had hoped. The woman loved gardening. Not *actually* gardening, mind you, but *talking* about it at length was a favorite pastime for Constance.

"Oh, ever so many! There are fields of snowdrops throughout the countryside, of course -"

Peyton finished pouring for Constance, then snuck a look at Enzo. He rolled his eyes, folding his arms over his chest. He was wearing a sailor-style sweater today: deep blue with a white collar and stripes around the cuffs. Peyton wondered for the millionth time why he continued to dress as his mother had dressed him when she was alive. She poured tea into his cup, leaving room for the cream and sugar.

Remembering herself as Constance continued describing local daffodils and alpine meadow, Peyton nodded politely. "How wonderful!" she commented, hoping, as always, that Constance would give away some detail – anything, really – about exactly where they were. It hadn't mattered yet, but maybe someday it would.

"Enzo always loved tulips," Constance lamented quietly, then took a dainty sip of her tea.

"It's true," Enzo confirmed, sounding wistful.

Constance sighed heavily.

"Would you like me to serve your sandwiches?" Peyton asked as she replaced the teapot on its tray and straightened, folding her hands primly in front of her.

"No, thank you, Peyton. I'll take my time choosing

today."

Peyton nodded, then started toward her own chair.

Constance cleared her throat loudly.

"Oh!" Peyton exclaimed, turning to Enzo. "I'm so sorry, Enzo. Would you like me to serve your sandwiches?"

Enzo smirked.

Peyton raised her eyebrows.

Enzo gave her the finger. Peyton couldn't help it; she giggled.

"Well?" Constance demanded.

"I'll take the pink petite-four, please, Peyton," Enzo smiled, his eyes sparkling again.

Peyton cleared her throat, glancing at Constance, then back at Enzo. "Would you care for a sandwich first, sir?" she asked.

Constance giggled. "Dessert first, again?"

Peyton sighed.

"Yes, please!" Enzo enthused, his smile taking over his face.

Peyton remembered what had happened the last time she'd served Enzo dessert first. Constance was laughing now, but Peyton's memory of her reaction last time won. She took the tongs from the sandwich tray.

"Ah, cooperating now, are you, Enzo?"

"Don't you *dare* give me a sandwich!" Enzo growled.

Peyton sucked in her breath and chose a pretty cream cheese and chive pinwheel.

Enzo stood.

She paused, considering.

His reaction certainly couldn't be as bad as Constance's would be if she made a different choice.

Could it?

She placed the pinwheel in the center of Enzo's plate.

Enzo roared.

Peyton let her breath out slowly, replacing the tongs on the serving tray and hardening herself against the dark energy that emanated from him.

"You weak, pathetic *bitch!*" he hissed. Peyton took note of the tendons standing out on either side of his neck.

"There, now. Shall we?" Constance smiled coldly at Peyton, then reached for the tongs.

Her hand froze in midair, her attention taken by Enzo's sandwich, which had darted to the edge of his plate.

Peyton's eyes widened as she watched Enzo gather every ounce of energy he could before trying again. He'd never succeeded in actually moving anything before.

But like his twin, Enzo, too, suffered from a very bad temper.

"FUCKING STUPID SANDWICH!" he hollered, then swatted at it powerfully. Peyton jumped as he made contact, sending the pinwheel flying across the room.

Constance squealed, her hand still frozen in midair. "Enzo!" She cast a look that was somewhere between confusion and horror at Peyton.

Peyton stood, panic taking hold of her with a strength she hadn't felt since she'd first arrived on the estate.

"What's happening?" Constance wailed, her eyes shining with tears.

Peyton tried desperately to get hold of herself, but she could feel her resolve crumbling. It was all too much. A swarm of bees buzzed in her head. Lights flashed behind her eyes. She realized she was pulling her own hair, her fists balled up on either side of her head.

Hair tangled around her fingers.

Enzo was laughing hysterically. He seemed to have forgotten his rage as he exclaimed to Peyton, "Did you see that? I did it! I fucking *did it*, Peyton!"

Every syllable pulsed within her head as though it was being pounded in. She squeezed her eyes shut and heard herself whimper but hadn't the strength to stop it.

"*Peyton!*" Constance said her name so shrilly it was as though it sliced through her brain.

She cried out.

"Oh, no you don't," Constance said now, her footsteps quickly approaching Peyton, who had sunk heavily to her knees. "You hold it together, missy!"

"Oh, shit. I'm sorry, Peyton. I didn't mean to freak you out. Shit. I'm sorry I called you a bitch. I didn't mean it, of course! I love you, you know that, Peyton!" Enzo was next to her now, his words like an endless stream in her ear.

She tried again to come back to herself. Took a deep breath.

"That's right. Just breathe, Peyton. You're OK," Constance crooned.

"Oh, God. Please don't be mad!" Enzo sounded desperate, on the edge of tears.

"Shut *up!*" Peyton screamed, then gasped.

Enzo gasped, too, but giggled afterward. "Oh, shit. You've done it, now."

She cracked an eyelid. Constance's lips were set so thin it seemed like they'd disappeared completely.

"I'm sorry!" Peyton wailed. "I was talking to Enzo, not you!"

"How *dare* you talk to *either* of us that way!" Constance spat, her face a dangerous shade of red.

Peyton squeezed her eyes shut and bit the insides of her cheeks.

It was silent for a moment, and then there was a distinct *pop!* as Enzo disappeared.

Peyton took a breath and cracked her eyelids. To her amazement, Constance was still sitting beside her. Even more strangely, she reached out to wipe Peyton's tears away. She steadied herself against the nearly overwhelming urge to recoil. With monumental effort, she looked into the hazel eyes of the other woman.

"I know he can be difficult," Constance said, and it was almost a whisper. "But he's all I have."

Peyton nodded. "I'm sorry. Can we go back to tea?"

Constance nodded, then waited for Peyton to rise before offering her hand. She took it, helping Constance up. It was strange standing so close to her. She was nearly a full head shorter than Peyton.

"Where is he?" Constance asked.

Peyton scanned the room and, though she expected to find Enzo gone, was startled to find him. He was different, but he was there. She pointed.

Constance followed her gaze. "In the corner?"

Peyton nodded. She didn't like it when Enzo got like this.

"Tell him to come back to tea," Constance said, her eyes still riveted on the corner.

"E-Enzo?" Peyton stammered, and the mercurial embodiment of him shifted. Peyton saw two tendrils – arms – rise to compress the place his throat might be. She squeezed her eyes shut again. "I'm -" she swallowed hard, "- sorry, Constance," she choked past an empathetic tightening of her airway.

"No! Enzo!" Constance was crying. "I just wanted us to have tea! Why do you have to be like this?" she moaned. "I'm sorry! I'm sorry, OK?"

Peyton got images of a hayloft in her head.

She'd seen this before. It was dark. An older woman with shining blonde hair cascading in waves down her naked back. The feeling of jealousy, of hurt.

Of rage.

She opened her eyes again. He was gone, now. She exhaled.

Constance threw her arms around Peyton, her sobs shaking her body. Peyton stiffened, then mindfully relaxed her muscles, one by one.

"I just wanted us to have a nice tea," Constance cried into Peyton's armpit.

"I know," Peyton said.

Just like that day, she thought.

That day you killed him.

Chapter 2 – Intro To Science & The Supernatural

"Think about it," Margot said as she stepped toward the edge of the stage. She met the eyes of as many people she could as she paused. "Science and the supernatural don't have to be separate things at all. *Can't* be! In fact, throughout history, humans have leaned on the supernatural to explain the unknown. Think of a religion, any religion. What is that religion founded on? Are gods not used – some would even say created – to make sense of the questions we have?"

Margot took a step back. "I get a lot of flak for saying things like that. Those who are religious accuse me of attacking their faith. Scientists laugh at me for believing in ghosts. And believers in the supernatural scorn me for my theories on how science and the supernatural relate."

She paused.

"I get trouble from all sides!" she exclaimed, throwing her hands in the air, and the audience laughed politely. Margot smiled, too, and walked the stage, tossing the remote for the dropdown screen from hand to hand. It was still early in their first session, but the feel of the auditorium changed, relaxing as Margot and the audience relaxed.

She stopped at stage left, looking into the faces of the crowd. "Fairies to explain an infant's illness. Strange tales of beasts – the Loch Ness Monster, the abominable snowman, Sasquatch - to put a name to sightings of otherwise unidentifiable creatures. The wrath of the gods to explain famine. The blessings of Mother Nature to explain a plentiful harvest."

She placed her hands on her hips.

"The first experience of anything unexplained."

She started toward stage right. "Imagine seeing the northern lights for the first time with no previous knowledge of them," she continued as she gestured to the ceiling. She stopped again, turned to the crowd. "The first reaction is fear. Then overwhelming amazement. Later, as we ponder our experiences again and again, we search for meaning. It's our nature, right? 'Why did those lights appear to me on that night? Was it a message for me? A sign?'" Margot laughed. "To be a little self-centred is in our nature, too."

The audience murmured in agreement. Several people chuckled.

"But eventually, we humans decide that there is a much better way to tackle the unknown. We figure it out. We discover. We learn *why*. And voila! We have science. Certainly, the northern lights can be scientifically explained. What about the Loch Ness monster?" Margot pointed her controller at the screen, clicking. A photo of a massive creature stretched across several men filled the screen. "Have you seen this?" Margot raised her eyebrows at the audience.

"Nessie!" came a theatrical voice from the back of the room.

Margot smiled. "You aren't wrong. This is a giant eel. It could explain 'Nessie', and it's only one of many possible explanations." She turned back to the screen. "But *look* at that thing! I challenge you with this: just because we've given that monstrous thing a name and we can relate it to something we already know, does that mean it's not an impressive, unusual, even terrifying creature? *I* wouldn't want to go swimming with that thing!"

The audience laughed.

Margot walked to the podium, then turned to face the class, resting her forearms on it and looking thoughtful. "And what about 'miracles'?" she asked, quietly. "Acts of God? Angels? Divine intervention?"

The room was silent.

"Scientists explain these things very logically, right? Some of the time, at least? Sometimes, it takes a bit longer, but modern science had done an incredible job of explaining much of these previously inexplicable events. So now they're not supernatural experiences; they're cold, hard scientific facts. The unknown becomes the known."

There was a pause, and then someone raised a hand. Margot nodded toward him.

"This is all very philosophical, isn't it? I mean, I'm not complaining!" The audience tittered. "I just wonder, without any spoiler alerts," another appreciative reaction from the audience, "but are we going to be able to walk away from this class actually *knowing* anything?"

Silence again, with a palpable nervous edge to it.

Margot smiled, sighed, then straightened. She grasped the podium on both sides and surveyed the faces of her new students. Remembered the group who'd asked her this last year, and the year before. Remembering how grateful they were at the end of it all. Let her confidence show.

"That's an excellent question," she said, finally, and the room warmed again with a collective exhale. Margot smiled. "You might not like the answer," she continued.

A woman entered the room from the door to her left. Margot glanced at her. She was older than most of her audience. Perhaps another professor? It wasn't uncommon for her to have drop-ins from parents, professors, or even strangers who'd heard of her course. Science and the Supernatural was only taught at one University, after all. Except for speaking engagements, Margot devoted her time to her students at Acadia. This campus, these students. She'd created the class, not just to expand the perspectives of young minds, but as a personal bid to continue learning, to reach out for like-minded souls, to figure it all out. She nodded to the woman, who backed up to stand against the wall, her face disappearing into shadow.

"The truth is that if you walk out of this class thinking you know all there is to know about science and the supernatural, you weren't paying attention." Margot surveyed the faces before her. "My goal is to open your minds to the possibility that we, as beings subject to various limitations – our vehicles, otherwise known as our physical bodies – our circumstances, our influences – I'm sure you've all heard the term 'nature versus nurture?'"

Nods from the audience.

"I won't argue that case either way," Margot shook her head as she stepped around the podium and walked toward the front of the stage. "But I will have you consider them as constraints – methods of shaping our knowledge, our experiences, our very *reality*." She pointed to the boy who'd asked the question. "And your reality may be very different from, say," she moved to point to a girl in the front row, "hers," she finished.

The girl she'd focused on looked confused. "How does that help us in any way?"

"Also a fair question. Listen, guys. I'm sure a lot of you are taking this class as an elective. I'm also sure we have a very unusual coming together of students in this room. What program are you in? Theology? Science? Philosophy? There are students from all those areas and more. I'd venture to say we even have some students who are here *only* to take this class, because they're curious. Or because they've had experiences they can't explain, no matter their background or their specific set of boundaries."

She strode back to the podium, then regarded the audience. "Personally, I am a scientist. I also believe in a greater... being? Consciousness? God? *And* I'm also someone who made friends with a ghost when I was fourteen."

"Tell us about Bird!" someone called from the crowd, and a cheer rose.

Margot shook her head. "Sounds like you already know about my ghost," she smiled, and the room filled with relaxed laughter. "And I *am* known for telling ghost stories, but not today."

Margot raised her hand to a collective sound of disappointment.

"I will, though. In time. But I will also devote an entire to class to reported 'acts of God', as well as several classes to the scientific answers to many of the historical events that, when they were first reported, were considered otherworldly. I'm not biased! I don't have all the answers. And that's the key." She looked at the young man who'd raised his voice. "I want you to consider that we simply don't know everything. And that it's possible that in the future, science will be able to explain the supernatural, or various aspects of it. And when that happens, ghosts won't be so scary, will they? Because we'll understand."

She looked at them, breathing. Waiting.

"The unknown will be known."

The room filled with both the sounds of agreement and of derision. But Margot saw it; what she looked for in every group she engaged. Those few whose eyes brightened as they experienced an epiphany.

She looked at the clock. "That's all for today. See you

next time."

She always left them wanting more.

In her first year of teaching, she'd been heavily criticized for her oft-theatrical flair. She'd also been told she wouldn't last the semester. But she challenged everyone who opposed her to come to her class, during which she unfailingly won their interest, at the very least. She never claimed to know the answers; she presented information without bias, as she'd claimed, and almost always achieved her goal of at least opening student's minds to the ongoing fact that we simply don't know everything.

It was a topic both celebrated and criticized, and either way, the University delighted in the attention. Thus, she ran two packed classes every semester and the waiting list was bordering on ridiculous. When asked if she was satisfied, however, her answer proved to be complex.

She loved being the conductor of her own orchestra, so to speak. Her success as a student and a practitioner before she started teaching was well known. She was a pioneer, and for the most part was allowed to conduct her classes as she wished. But as exciting as it was to open people's minds, Margot had grown tired of the constant backlash. There were always those she challenged who refused to attend a class or even hear her point of view. It got tedious, and her commitment to being unbiased restricted her arguments.

It also took up much of her time. She had the biggest auditorium on campus, and it was brimming with students. She'd had to devise creative ways to test and grade them. It was simply impossible to follow the traditional method of marking students. Luckily, she'd been raised, and in fact, homeschooled by brilliant minds. Both her mother and father had taught her that learning had no limits, and sometimes the best way to succeed in teaching was to step outside of conventional methods. She took pride in teaching with these concepts in mind and at heart.

In the end, though, when she crawled into bed at night, she was lonely. Her methodologies and perspective weren't new, but widespread acceptance still retreated into the distance. Her students went away enlightened, but she still wallowed, mostly alone, in the deep end of her own pool of thought. Being different had always meant a bit of loneliness for Margot. It had always been OK with her, until suddenly she found herself in her early thirties, her lifelong ideas of family – a partner to share life with, children of her own – having taken the back seat and still eluding her.

She theorized that her propensity to assume she was different – and consequently meeting people with her guard up – certainly had to do with where she'd ended up.

Even Chris, who'd gone through so much with her, had in the end become distant. Not necessarily with the intention of having less contact with Margot, but rather finding himself drifting away on the tide of his own life as hers went in another direction entirely.

They were still friends. They still shared a love that couldn't be broken by circumstances or time. But their time together had faded into the past.

Margot had packed her things and greeted several new students by the time the room had emptied out. She'd learned to defer deeper discussions to her office time after spending much of her first year speaking with students that hung behind. She'd loved those "mini-lecture" sessions and still indulged after the more profound classes but had learned to respect the need to take care of herself, as well.

She watched the last of the stragglers leave with a smile on her face, but let out a gasp as the woman who'd joined the class late emerged from her place in the shadows.

"I'm sorry!" the woman exclaimed, looking mortified at

having shocked Margot. "I didn't want to scare you; I was just waiting my turn to talk to you!"

Margot, catching her breath with a hand on her chest, let herself laugh a bit. "No, don't apologize! I'm often so caught up with whatever's going on in my brain that I lose touch with what's happening around me! I saw you come in, and then forgot you." She walked toward the woman now, her hand outstretched. "I'm Doctor Margot Francis."

The woman looked relieved. She took Margot's hand with a smile, but Margot noticed the whitening of her knuckles as her free hand gripped the strap of her purse with a touch of unease. "I'm Jane Hale. I believe you and my daughter Peyton knew each other in school?"

Margot smiled, placing her free hand on top of Jane's so it was sandwiched. She hadn't spoken to Peyton in so long. Too long. "Jane! It's wonderful to meet you. Please call me Margot."

The woman nodded, but no joy touched her eyes.

Margot frowned. "I hope everything's alright. I really enjoyed my friendship with Peyton, but I haven't spoken to her in quite a while – "

Jane bent her head, emotion changing her features. "I'm afraid she's in trouble." She met Margot's eyes again. "She's missing."

Chapter 3 - Jane

Margot's eyes widened as she inhaled sharply.

Jane fought back tears. There'd be more time to cry later. Now it was her turn to add a comforting hand to their already three-hands-strong greeting. "I'm sorry to shock you," she murmured quietly. A tear did escape her eye, then, despite her efforts. "Peyton spoke so highly of you – your kindness to her – I – I don't know where else to go!"

Margot released Jane's hands to embrace her, and Jane allowed herself a moment to be comforted. She was afraid that if she didn't, she'd break down entirely.

"Don't apologize. Of course, you're going to try every avenue to find your daughter," Margot said as she stepped back, leaving a hand on Jane's arm as she gestured to a seat in front of the stage.

Jane sat. She dug a tissue out of her purse and pressed it to her eyes, then her nose. Margot seemed to be giving her a moment. Jane tensed at the look of concern on the tall, attractive woman's face as she sat across from her on the stage. She crossed long pantyhose-clad legs below a pale yellow skirt, sat back and regarded Jane coolly. It was a look that would have been uncomfortable, if it weren't for the kindness in the woman's eyes. "Thank you."

Margot only nodded.

"I'm so sorry to come unannounced; I couldn't find a way to contact you."

Margot sighed. "That's my fault. I was getting calls and messages at all hours of the day when I first started teaching –

and not just from students. I had newspapers, talk show hosts, and frankly far more people needing help with their ghost issues than I was able to handle."

Jane looked mortified. "Oh my God. I'm just adding to it!"

"No!" Margot reached for her again. Her short-sleeved navy blazer bunched a bit at her shoulder as she gripped Jane's arm for just a moment. "I'm so glad you've come! I DO have contact information out there. I've just made it more difficult to find." She sat back, shaking her head. "My interests lie in considering the supernatural from a different perspective. And I'm a scientist at heart. My abilities are limited in both fields, though. Even though I've had what I refer to as 'irregularly accurate intuition' over the years since my experiences, my 'medium' days ended with my first ghost, who I - met – when I was fourteen."

"I understand. Peyton said you could understand much of what she was going through, but it was more of a one-time thing for you."

Margot nodded. "In my travels – I do hands-on research for my classes, books and speaking engagements – I've met some incredible people. But none of them had the type of gift that Peyton has – "

Jane put her face in her hands. "It's so hard for her," her words were muffled in her hands, so she removed them. "I've always said she needs a mentor, but she's never found anyone that even understands what she's going through, much less be able to *teach* her!"

"And if I remember correctly, finding people – meeting new people, I mean, asking for help, was all really hard for her?"

"Yes. We always used her Asperger's diagnosis to explain her 'quirks'," Jane used air quotes as she described her daughter, "but I don't think an accurate label exists for who Peyton is, and why."

"Exactly. I agree completely."

"And now – she's gone. I don't even know how long she's been missing!" Jane sobbed into her hands again.

"Can you tell me what happened?"

Jane nodded, fishing for another tissue. "I don't know if you're aware of what Peyton did after University?"

Margot nodded. "I attended her first vernissage for her paintings. She had that show in Halifax. Incredible work."

"Right. She got a job illustrating for a graphic novel, and even taught classes for a while."

"She graduated before I did, but we tried to keep in touch. Things got harder when my career took off." Margot paused, her brow furrowed. "I should have tried harder. Made room for her."

"Don't be down on yourself. Peyton was busy, too. I only talked to her once a week, if that. And visits had dwindled to holidays and events, mostly. Which is why I'm not sure exactly how long she's been gone." Jane got a faraway look in her eyes. "Her father and I depend on her brother to keep tabs on her." She met Margot's eyes again. "But he's been studying abroad since the new year. He and his sister lived in the same condo building in Halifax," she explained.

"Spencer, right?" Margot asked.

Jane nodded.

"He's around the same age as my brothers," Margot smiled.

"Oh?"

Margot nodded. "Peyton talked about him all the time."

Jane smiled now. "They're such good friends. Spencer is taking his doctorate, doing his residence overseas."

"That's incredible!"

"I'm sorry. I'm taking up too much of your time."

Margot glanced at her watch. "I have a meeting in ten minutes. Would you like to walk with me?"

Jane rose, nodding.

The air was crisp, but the sun was bright. Winter was finally melting away, though the campus still showed evidence of the waning season – dirty snow piles left where parking lots had been plowed, and fields flooded here and there, bright green blades of grass poking up through the boggy earth between the pools of melted ice and snow.

Jane talked faster as they walked, her mind on Margot's valuable time.

"I'd been trying to get in touch with Peyton since the end of January. I hadn't heard from her for a couple weeks. I just got her voicemail, so I figured her phone was dead and I'd try the next day. She's eternally forgetting to charge that thing." She shook her head.

Margot looked sideways at her. "When did you realize something was wrong?"

"A couple days later when I still couldn't get her, and I decided to drop in on her art class that evening."

"Let me guess: she didn't show?"

Jane shook her head. "They said she'd been there the week before, though."

"So, she disappeared sometime during the week in between."

"Yes. I called the police and met them at her condo. I

have a key, but they asked that I wait for them. Anyway, she was just gone!"

"Was anything missing?"

"That's the strange thing. Only her jacket and one pair of shoes was missing, as far as we could tell, but the knapsack she took everywhere is gone. And there are no records of her travelling. The police have checked every avenue."

"So, she didn't take her clothes, but she took something." Margot slowed, gesturing to the tall building beside them. "This is me."

Jane faced Margot. "I scoured the place. Peyton is a creature of habit. Routine. I knew what she'd take if she was going somewhere: her art supplies, her books, and her scrapbooks. She keeps records – newspaper clippings, her own notes, pictures she's received from families – of the people she's helped."

"They were gone?"

She nodded. "So was the picture of us – the family – she usually kept on her bedside table."

"What about a laptop? Phone? Tablet?"

Jane shook her head. "That was strange, too. All of her electronics were together on her dining room table, which is where the laptop always was. She was always online." Jane finished, gazing up the steep incline of the road with a faraway look.

"What do the police think?"

Jane brought her gaze back to Margot. "They're confused. They're exploring everything. But yesterday, they called to let me know that some of her art students saw her talking to a woman after the last class she gave. The woman wasn't a student, but seemed really interested in Peyton. She was short -"

"Ah, there you are!" a male voice greeted them from the entrance to the building. Jane's anxiety heightened as she realized Margot had to go.

"Hi, Syd, be right in," Margot waved to her colleague, but didn't budge. She looked back at Jane. "How can I help?"

"I know you have contacts. Like you said, people like Peyton. And I know you're her friend. The police are working on the case exactly as they're supposed to, but -"

"- but you want to try every option available," Margot finished for her.

Jane could think of no better words to express her need. She looked into Margot's eyes, willing her to feel it instead. She was desperate.

Margot took her hand again and fixed her eyes on Jane's. "Give me a few days. I – this is going to sound strange, but my mother called me last week. She was talking about a woman that's recently come to live on the same street as my childhood home. I got this feeling when I was listening to her."

Jane's bewilderment was evident on her features.

"I'm sorry. I'm not making sense, but something tells me this woman might be able to help. I need to go home and find out."

A glimmer of hope shone in Jane's eyes. "Your parents live in Greenwood, right?"

"Greenwood Square."

Jane's brow furrowed. It sounded familiar, but she couldn't put her finger on why.

"I have to go, Jane. Here," she pulled her phone out of her leather satchel, "let me take your number."

Jane recited her cell number and her husband's. "If you can't get either of us, or you feel like contacting Spencer, too, his number is crazy; here, let me put his contact in for you."

Margot handed her phone to Jane. Jane perceived the woman folding her arms, but she didn't feel hurried. She glanced up. Margot's expression was unreadable. Her gaze was fixed on some point behind Jane, her eyes clouded and brow furrowed. She'd heard more about Margot than Peyton had told her; although viewed as eccentric, Margot was heavily lauded for her brilliance. She remembered Peyton saying, once, that her friend never stopped thinking. Jane understood that statement as she regarded Margot now.

"Thank you so much, Margot. Even if you're not able to help, thank you for your time. And for being Peyton's friend." Jane handed Margot's phone back, tears shimmering in her eyes again. It felt wrong to reassure this woman that it'd be OK if she couldn't help. It felt like giving up. Truly, she felt like falling to her knees right here on the sidewalk as students milled about them, and begging Margot to help her find her daughter.

"I'm going to do everything I can," Margot said as she retrieved her phone. "But if you learn anything new, please keep me informed." She pulled her card out of her bag. "You'll have no problem contacting me now," she smiled, then grasped Jane's hand again, squeezing slightly as she smiled. "Until then, take care."

Such a clichéd sentiment, but in that moment, with her nerves raw and her heart exposed, Margot's words were a balm. "Thank you," she said, then turned to go.

Chapter 4 – Peyton
And Enzo

Peyton woke slowly, becoming aware of warm sunlight on her face. She stretched.

It wasn't unusual to find Enzo regarding her from the neighboring pillow to hers as she awoke, but today she dreaded seeing him.

She opened one eyelid, just a sliver.

He wasn't there.

She exhaled and stretched again, this time allowing herself to luxuriate in the warmth of the heavy duvet and the silky softness of the sheets. She may be here against her will, but Constance had spared no expense to make her comfortable. Enzo said it was force of habit for his sister to buy only the best, regardless of the reason or the recipient.

She sat, arms raising straight above her head and lacing her fingers together and show her palms to the ceiling, then letting them drop to the bed on either side of her. She looked around.

It really wasn't a bad spot to wake up in. The loft was rectangular and larger in itself than any place – house, apartment, or condo - Peyton had ever lived. It was entirely open and bright, windows lined all of the walls except for the eastern-facing one, which hosted the locked door, instead, and Peyton's canopy bed. Flanking it were oversized bedside tables topped with lamps and stacks of books, much to Peyton's relief. Besides tea time, she spent all of her days and nights within these four walls. Books were both a refuge and an escape. She wished for her paints, too, but though she'd been allowed to bring some, Constance had frowned daintily when she'd gathered the courage to ask where they were.

"Such a mess though, Peyton," she'd remarked casually, waving the subject away as though it were a pesky fly.

Bookshelves took up the parts of the Western wall that weren't dotted with windows in the living area to her right, and a chaise lounge occupied the corner, lit generously by windows on both sides. A gorgeous handmade quilt was draped over it invitingly, and a pink and cream chenille throw made it irresistibly comfy. It was a favorite spot for Peyton, whether she was reading or simply looking out at the quiet world beneath her.

An oversized couch and chair set further separated the living area from the rest of the space, an intricately-patterned Persian rug pulling the whole area together. Heavy shades were available to cover the windows, but Peyton rarely used them. It was one thing to accept a place as a cage, but another entirely to enclose it by covering the windows. Then, it was a prison.

The other end of the loft was comprised of a kitchen area as well as a little dining space, boasting a comfortable corner table with plush bench seats. Peyton would often stretch out there, a tea on the table and her eyes riveted toward the river beyond the property.

Despite the generous windows, the landscape was unchanging, except for the slow transition from winter to spring. Though beautiful, it certainly wasn't enough to keep one occupied for long, unless they had a fantastic imagination...or, as in Peyton's case, a rare aptitude for communing with the dead. But though her strange visitors helped stave off boredom, they weren't always the most pleasant company. And they were quieter than usual too. Peyton was sure Enzo had something to do with that.

Ghosts are needy, she thought. And if Enzo had been anything in life like he was in death, his excessive demands on her made sense.

The Estate was vast, but the house, the stables and the gardening shed were the only buildings upon it that Peyton knew of. Then there were the woods, the fields, and the river. From her vantage point, the only residents aside from the family, their servants, herself and the horses were either dead or wild. The 'wild' category, though largely made up of bird, bug and beast, would sometimes overlap with the 'dead' category, be it through the death of a creature or through the particular attributes of the dead.

Aside from what she could see, Peyton knew precious little about the Estate. Its exact location, she was sure, would be a snap to find online, but she was bereft of electronic devices that could allow her access to the internet. It was a purposeful exclusion, to be sure. One could do anything on the internet nowadays, calling for help included.

Or reporting a crime. Or two.

Diagonally from the bed and beside the bookshelves was the door to the bathroom, toward which Peyton padded in her sock feet now, pulling a pink velour housecoat over her nightgown as she did.

All things considered, if I have to be imprisoned, it could be far worse, she thought, not for the first time. She missed her family (or at least the choice to see them) and she missed her own home, but there were perks of being locked away in an enormous mansion, an entire floor of one wing to herself.

Solitude had never been a negative thing for Peyton. Nor had lack of conversation with the living. And the routine was comforting, somehow. She had the entire day to herself until tea, and then again until bed, and she'd crafted her routine to be both relaxing and fulfilling. Her morning consisted of waking with the sun, breakfast, and books. Then lunch and a nap. Then tea, then writing. In absence of her paints, Peyton had found writing to be a surprisingly satisfying outlet. Constance had even allowed her a typewriter and an endless paper supply, after some persuasive words from her brother.

Each evening, after tea, Peyton would be escorted back to her loft, her hands tied with ribbon behind her back. Soft ribbon, tight knots. And she would find her stocks replenished and her living area cleaned. She detected clean, crisp bed linens twice per week – Mondays and Thursdays. The fridge was well stocked, with fresh eggs, milk bottle refilled, and produce refreshed every day. Her cupboards were filled with melamine tableware, her utensil drawer with plastic cutlery, wooden spoons and rubber spatulas. On the days she'd neglected to wash her dishes or make her bed, she'd return to find someone else had done those tasks for her, as well. It was an odd sensation to have her needs attended to in such a ghostly way, when the perpetrator wasn't a ghost at all.

The bathroom sparkled, always. Peyton glanced at herself in the mirror. She was pale. Her eyes looked large and dark, surrounded by sallow skin and worry lines. She was thirty-six. Thirty-six years old, and she'd never seen a spark of recognition in her own reflection. The face was familiar, but strange. Doctors had different names for it, but they didn't mean much to Peyton. All she knew was that when she saw herself as a reflection, it felt as though she was seeing an acquaintance. Even worse, a stranger, but one that lurked. Judged her. Scorned her for her failures. Laughed at her inadequacies.

Her relationship with herself was just fine away from the mirror, but it was like catching someone you trusted breaking a promise when she regarded her reflection. As if her own outward appearance betrayed her true self, and Peyton hadn't a clue how to fix it.

She rubbed her face and padded toward the kitchen.

A timid knock at the door made her jump as she placed ingredients for a breakfast sandwich on the island.

She froze. The only person who'd ever knocked at her door was Constance – and even then, it was only done as a courtesy before she unlocked the door and let herself in.

Nobody else was supposed to come to her room. Her floor, really.

She went to the door. Stood, her hand hovering over the knob even as she remembered it was locked from the outside.

The knock came again and she gasped, jumping back.

The panic was coming again, churning low in her gut. *If it's Constance and I don't answer, she'll either be glad – if she's testing me - or furious, if she isn't. If it's anyone besides Constance, I shouldn't even acknowledge.* She grimaced, bringing the hand that had frozen over the doorknob to her mouth.

"Peyton, it's me," came Enzo's disembodied voice.

She frowned. "What -?"

He laughed from behind her, and she whirled to find him leaning back against a bedpost, arms folded, legs crossed, and looking well entertained.

She looked toward him, mindfully taking a deep breath. "Why knock today? You usually just show up in bed, or in the bathroom." She made a dismissive sound, her annoyance clear.

"I thought I'd be nice today, considering how I treated you before," he smiled, but his eyes still sparkled with mischief.

"And then you tricked me by appearing behind me?"

His smile faltered. "I'm sorry. I was always told I wasn't very good at apologizing."

Peyton rolled her eyes and went back to the island, muttering, "You know I couldn't open the door for you if I tried."

Enzo was suddenly beside her. He was getting better at being dead.

"I *am* sorry," he said quietly. Peyton bristled at the nearness of him. "It *was* you who taught me that I could – what did you call it? – interact? – with things on your plane."

She looked at him sideways. "Not so you could throw things! Especially when we're with your sister!"

He disappeared, then reappeared on a stool across from her, his elbows on the counter, chin resting on his folded hands. "Why, then?"

She took some things from the fridge and gave him a look. "Besides sandwich swiping? You really can't think of another reason besides that?"

He looked thoughtful. "To... touch?"

Peyton shrugged. "A lot of ghosts like to touch their loved ones, or move something of significance, to let them know they're around. It can be really comforting in some circumstances." She frowned, then added, "But not all."

Enzo's eyes brightened. "Hey! If I wanted to *really* touch somebody – "

Peyton squinted at him, her knife paused halfway through a slice of swiss cheese. "Please don't finish that thought, Enzo. Please."

Enzo laughed.

"You're a pain in the ass," she muttered, which only made him laugh harder.

She continued preparing her sandwich in silence.

"I really am sorry," he said.

She looked at him. Nodded. "I know."

He rose and walked to the window. He placed his hands on the upper sill, leaning downward and toward the glass.

"I don't feel like comforting Constance," he muttered.

"I know that, too," Peyton said.

He turned back to her, hands going to his pockets. "Game of chess?"

"Sure. You can practice," she answered, giving him a grin.

"You mean you want me to move my own pieces?"

"Only if you promise not to throw any!" she said, her voice escalating at the end.

He smiled. "I promise."

She cut her sandwich in half. "And," she looked up at him, more serious, "you have to promise me that if I keep teaching you, you won't use it like that in front of your sister again."

His face darkened. "You don't want me to use my powers for evil?"

Now Peyton laughed. "Exactly!"

He smiled again, then saluted. "I promise to use my powers for the light side only, sir!" He smiled when she did. "Thank you for being so patient with me."

Enzo could be very kind when he wanted to be. Even in death, there was something more *real* about him, when compared with his live twin.

Peyton carried her sandwich to the table and got herself situated in the corner where she could look outside. "My patience would be even more impressive if I had a choice," she said, then turned her eyes to Enzo.

"Hey, don't look at me for answers about your predicament," he said, his palms facing her.

She looked at her sandwich, pondering silently.

"You know, if I get really good at it – at touching and moving things – I could help you get out of here."

Her gaze moved quickly to his.

"I like you here, but I don't want you trapped, Peyton."

She gave him an appreciative smile. "Thing is, I don't want you trapped, either."

"How do we fix that, though?" he asked, his hopelessness transforming his features.

"You look like a little boy," she whispered.

"Is there a way?"

Peyton nodded. "There always is. Sometimes it just takes time to make itself known."

Chapter 5 – Margot
Goes Home

Margot's mother put a cup of tea in front of her daughter. Margot tore her eyes from the paper she was reading with some difficulty and smiled up at her. "Thanks, Mom."

Mom nodded toward the paper. "What do you think of that?"

She looked back at the article. It was in a local newspaper, and the subjects of the front-page feature were homegrown, too, but were currently touring Europe, giving lectures on their most recent work. Margot shook her head, smiling. "They sure have come a long way from wiping their boogers on my leg," she remarked, and Mom snickered.

"The three of you – Dad and I are very proud, you know."

"We learned from the best," Margot raised her eyebrows. "Where *is* Dad, anyway?"

Mom swatted her with a dishtowel. "Smartass!"

Margot giggled, but as she gazed again at the story, she allowed herself to be proud of her brothers, too. Their work in biology and chemistry was cutting edge; their partnership and sense of competition both motivated and pushed them forward. Each always trying to outdo the other, but ultimately doing their best work when they came together. The fact that they'd both grown into handsome and charismatic men – and were even more entertaining as a duo – had ensured they'd be in high demand as long as they were willing to share their brilliance with others.

Their talks were captivating. They, like Margot, delighted in opening the minds of their audiences, but their focus was possibilities for the future rather than normalizing the mysterious now. Not so different when you looked at it, really. Unlike Margot, though, they had their partnership to boost their confidence and to buoy them when they met with doubters. And their talks came off as well-planned, even choreographed, shows. Most of their viewing audience hadn't a clue that their "show" depended largely on their connection with each other. They'd always had those uncanny twin quirks that had fascinated Margot and her parents – not to mention neighbors, friends, employers, and now audiences around the world.

"'Aaron and Mason Francis make kids want to grow up to be scientists, and challenge adults to reconsider everything they think they know. Everything is possible, according to this dynamic duo, and to prove it, they've set out to prove it to the world with a series of talks geared at making science fun again,'" Margot read from the article with a dramatic flourish.

Mom took a forkful of carrot cake into her mouth, then shook her fork at Margot. "Oh! Read the next bit; you'll laugh."

Margot frowned, then looked back at the article. "'Older sister, Dr. Margot Francis, is also known for challenging minds, but ventures headlong into the unknown, mixing science with the supernatural. Her trailblazing ways have earned criticism and praise alike, but none can question her success. Her twin brothers have it much easier when it comes to public opinion. T – the two seem to gain fans rather than supporters. Even those who don't buy into their theories can't seem to say a word against them.'"

"Ha!" Margot finished, and Mom laughed.

"Told you."

"Good thing I don't need things to be easy, hm?" Margot

asked, folding the paper and holding it up. "Can I take this?"

Mom nodded. "Your father bought more than we'll ever need or use, even if we wallpaper the place with them."

"Aw, he's proud," Margot smiled. She put the paper in her bag, carefully. "I am, too."

"He's proud of you, too," Mom said, her fork pausing midair as she looked at Margot.

Margot looked up. "I know!"

Mom went back to her cake.

"He never liked me talking about Wren," Margot acknowledged.

Mom raised her eyes. "Not because he doesn't believe you."

"But because others don't," Margot finished.

"He's just worried about you."

"He's worried I make everything I say less credible by including my experiences, but that's why I do it, Mom. I need to make people consider the possibilities."

"Just like your brothers," Mom cut her off. They'd had this conversation before.

"Yeah, yeah. Just like my brothers, but with 'ghost stories'. Dad doesn't like that I open myself up to criticism."

"He likes to fade into the background. You've never been afraid to draw attention, though, if it's what you need to do to stand up for what's right." Mom always made sure Margot knew she understood where Margot was coming from. It *almost* disguised her own doubts about her daughter's methodology.

It was ironic. Her parents had been rule-breakers when it had come to teaching their children. And now that Margot was emulating them, they were cautious. Worried. Concerned about what people thought. Her brothers, at least, were loyal supporters. *If only they were around more!* she thought.

"Speaking of drawing attention, can you tell me again about your new neighbor?" Margot changed the subject.

Mom sat up. "Oh!" she said, excited. "Right! You should hear the rumours going around."

Margot frowned. "About the woman?"

Mom shook her head. "Not just about her. Remember the old abandoned place at the end of the road? You and Chris were always hanging out there."

She rolled her eyes. "Of course I remember, Mom."

"Just making sure! Yeesh." Mom swept a stray curl of hair out of her eyes. "Anyway, you should see the place, now!"

"Oh, my God! Did they finally tear it down?"

"Yeah. Apparently, they found the owner. He sold the place to Maggie Ridgewood's brother."

Margot shook her head. "I can't believe Jack is back at his old house."

"You should go say hi," Mom said, then sipped her tea. "Oh, that's good."

"Nah. I haven't seen him in forever. It'd be awkward."

"Don't be silly, Margie-Mae."

"Anyway -" she prompted, urging her mother to continue with an impatient hand gesture.

"Right. Anyway, apparently the owner – Kotova, I think is his name, though when he was here it was Maplestone – long story. Anyway..."

"What does any of this have to do with the woman?"

"I'm getting there, Margie!"

"Sorry." Margot sipped her tea, then left her lips on the mug to prevent further outbursts.

"Apparently there was some connection between the Ridgewood property and the Maplestone one, Something about the past owners. And the woman who just moved into the old farm helped them figure it all out."

"What kind of connection?"

"That's not as clear, but it was something to do with the Maplestone mother – Rose? I guess she'd had another child, but it died, and her husband buried it back in the woods -"

"*What?*" Margot's eyes widened.

"I know!" Mom's eyes sparkled. "Our little community is more interesting than we realized."

"How did they figure all of this out?"

"Strange things started happening at the Ridgewood's, I guess. So, they talked to this new woman – this Charis – and she helped them." She leaned toward Margot as though she was worried someone was eavesdropping. "The rumour is that she's a psychic."

"Huh." Margot was non-committal. She liked to wait until she had all the details before deciding anything about anyone.

"You know, I wouldn't necessarily call this part of the province, well, progressive. We have our ways and we like 'em. But people seem to like her, Margie. I never hear a negative thing said about her."

"You haven't met her yet?"

Mom shook her head. "You know Dad and I are intro-verts. But I know she and the Browns have an agreement about the farm. They take care of the goats and the rest of the land is for her and her family. She's got four kids, I think, though I've only seen the older ones. She seems very busy. Truth be told, I don't want to introduce myself just to have her think I want something from her."

"What was her name again?"

"Charis. Interesting, isn't it? You don't hear that, much."

Margot frowned, her eyes distant.

"What?"

"Peyton used to talk about a Charis when we went to school together. I'm sure of it."

"Really? Well, I don't know how she would've known about her then."

Margot snapped back to herself, turning her gaze to her mother. "Peyton knew everything about anyone who could see ghosts, Mom. She was on a perpetual search for people like her."

"I remember you talking about Peyton. She was the one with Asperger's, right?"

"Yeah, and she saw the dead just as easily as she could see the living. I've never met *anyone* quite like her."

Mom shook her head.

"What?"

"Well, it's the skeptic in me, I suppose, but – how do you know it was real?"

"I never doubted her, which is probably why she opened up to me. But as I got to know her, I learned more about what she saw. And for the first time since Wren, I was glad I've never seen another."

Mom raised her eyebrows.

"It was such an overwhelming part of who she was,

Mom. Just imagine it – half the people you interact with, no-body else can see. And even when you work hard to help them, there's little to show for it in a tangible way."

"Huh," Mom said now. Her forehead creased as she con-sidered this. "I can't imagine, honestly."

"She had a rough time of it. She was always trying to find people who could understand – and now she's missing. It scares me. What if someone's taken advantage of her?"

"What do you mean?"

"She's too trusting, Mom. Sometimes she just can't see the dangers that are right in front of her."

"Kind of makes sense, considering what she must've been seeing all her life. I mean, didn't you see a train blow right through Wren? Didn't he show you how he died?"

Margot nodded, her eyes filling with tears. It was strange – she included him in her lectures (with a fake name, to pro-tect him and those involved, of course) without batting an eye. But his name – and her own mother bringing him up – it reminded her that he was real, not just some story she told her audiences.

"And you've seen one ghost. Imagine seeing them every-where. How might that have changed you?"

"I can't even – I don't know," Margot answered.

Mom wrapped her hands around her mug.

"I just hope she's OK."

"Well, it sounds like they're doing everything they can," Mom said.

"Maybe that's not enough," Margot looked toward the dining room window and out to the street. "Do you know if this Charis is home?"

"I haven't seen her car. I know she goes back to Ottawa now and then."

"I'm going to write her a note, just in case," Margot said, her face changing with her determination as she rose to find a pen.

"Here," Mom said as she dug a notebook out of a drawer in the island.

Margot took it, then leaned over the counter to peer into the drawer. "Got a pen?"

Mom fished around, making a sound of annoyance. "I have tons. If only your father would put them back where they belong..." she trailed off.

Margot sat and opened the notebook, her eyes seeking the view from the window again. She could just see a hint of the old Brown house, across the street and diagonally to the right. She thought of little Stevie Brown and neighborhood baseball games. What an amazing time she'd had here as a kid. Somehow, it had taken growing up and moving away to see it.

"Ah!" Mom triumphantly brandished a pen, then held it out to her.

Margot took it, then got to work, her head bent low as she wrote.

"Aaand I've lost her," Mom said, taking the dishes to the sink.

Margot wrote on, but spared a chuckle for her Mom. "Love you, Ma," she muttered, but didn't listen for a response.

Dear Charis, she wrote.

Chapter 6 – Charis

Dear Charis,

Welcome to the neighborhood! I grew up here, so even though the house across the street from you is not my current home, it's still my always-home. My parents still live in that house! They're self-proclaimed introverts, but they're working up the courage to come say, "Hi."

But today, I'm writing you for another reason. One I'm sure you're used to – I hope it's alright. If it's not, just ignore this. I won't be offended.

If, though, you're still reading, I hope you'll give me a call. I'm going to fold my card into this note and cross my fingers, but I won't expect to hear from you; you owe me nothing!

I have a friend, you see. Her name is Peyton, and she's like you in some ways, or so I've heard. But she's in trouble. She's missing, and your insight would be wonderful to have, in addition to everything the police are doing. It's not in the news; her parents don't want to spook kidnappers, if that's indeed what's happened, or spook Peyton herself, if this absence is her way of taking a break. She's taken smaller breaks in the past, but usually lets her folks know so they don't worry.

So, they are worried, and so am I. Peyton doesn't see people as most do. I honestly think she'd rather help a kidnapper than escape without trying. It's not because she's not clever; she's just different. She thinks differently… sees differently, in many ways.

I know what it's like to be hounded by needy people. But I also know there are some that come to you because you're supposed to help them. I'm supposed to help Peyton. Only you can decide whether you are, too.

Yours sincerely,

Margot Francis

Charis frowned.

Doctor Margot Francis? If it was one and the same, her close friend Maggie had attended a talk by her, noting that Jack, her husband, had grown up with her. Had been really impressed with the woman, apparently, so Charis's interest had been piqued. She'd even done a bit of research and had been impressed by what she'd found.

Charis knew she would call her as soon as she'd seen the name, "Peyton," but was even more intrigued now that she'd read the signature. She looked at the card that had fallen out of the note and onto her kitchen counter. Interesting. And weird. The way the universe brought things back around never failed to amaze her.

Peyton had contacted Charis years ago, asking to meet. Asking to have a conversation. Asking, really, if she could learn from her. Charis had dismissed her, but not unkindly. She simply hadn't the time to mentor anyone. Her life was overfull. But she'd never forgotten the name. Nor had she been able to shake the twinge of guilt that would grip her whenever she remembered Peyton's plea. Some of what the girl had written had seemed completely familiar to Charis, but some had been foreign, as well.

Still, although she couldn't have answered some of her questions, she knew she could have helped the girl to control her gift. She remembered responding to Peyton's email with a reference to her regular class times (for she'd been teaching as well as working at the time), as well as with her home phone number, should Peyton feel desperate for a sympathetic ear.

But she hadn't encouraged her to call. She had, in fact, made it clear that she was overwhelmingly busy.

And now it seemed Peyton was back and needing her again.

Charis wasn't going to miss this second chance to help her. This time, she'd make things right. For Peyton, and hopefully for herself, too.

Because she really could do without that little twinge of guilt.

Chapter 7 – Two Lessons

Enzo's focus intensified as he brought his face almost to the tabletop, his hazel-green eyes narrowing on the little white feather they'd retrieved from Peyton's duvet.

Peyton giggled. "Your eyes are crossing."

Enzo remained singly engaged in his task.

Peyton sucked in a breath and pursed her lips in silent support.

Enzo inhaled, then blew, his gaze never faltering, and though the feather remained on the spot they'd carefully placed it (which was the same result as the first and every attempt that had followed), it fluttered, ever-so-slightly.

Peyton gasped painfully, her lungs already full of held air, then cheered on a giant outbreath.

Enzo peered up at her, a light in his eye. "Did you see that?"

Peyton nodded, and Enzo cheered, too, jumping up and dancing around the room.

"You did it!" she exclaimed, hopping a little on the spot in a rare moment of unfettered joy. But a familiar feeling stirred beneath the excitement, too, as she watched Enzo whirl about the room, his form leaving trails as it zipped too fast to be solid, too smoothly to be trapped inside a body that was tangible.

Apprehension.

For Enzo's progress meant something more than an improvement to his mood and endless possibilities insofar as his freedom was concerned. It also meant an enhanced capacity for the types of tricks and teasing that Enzo loved - and Peyton would surely pay for, should Constance catch on.

But even more ominous was the fact that Enzo's hair-trigger of a temper would experience a dangerous boost in potential outlets.

He was happy now, but Peyton knew him well enough, even after only a few months of acquaintance, to predict a shift back to resentment – or worse – boredom, as soon as the novelty wore off.

Enzo whooped as he spun again, then darted back to the table. Peyton watched, a small smile still playing at her lips as she tried not to ruminate on the darker implications of his success. But instead of refocusing on the feather, which *had* moved in the wake of their celebrations, he jerked his gaze to the windows. "It'll be time for tea soon," he murmured, his voice low.

Peyton scanned the line of windows along the western wall, then looked down at herself, her heart starting to race. "Oh, no!"

She'd been so busy with Enzo that she hadn't even dressed for the day, much less for tea.

Enzo observed the frenzied flurry of activity that followed with an amused smirk.

"Can I have some privacy, please?" Peyton asked, her voice high.

He picked at his teeth, then looked at her lazily, his eyebrows raised. "Hm?"

"Enzo! I need to get ready!"

He rolled his eyes. "You *know* I could watch you dress anytime without you having a clue."

Peyton threw her hands into the air, the dress and tights she clutched flouncing dramatically. "Can we please keep up the *pretense,* for my benefit, that I'm able to *believe* nobody is watching me *dress?*" she exclaimed, punctuating the sentence with several little stomps, like an overstimulated toddler.

Enzo bent to the table again, his eyes on the feather.

Peyton feared she might explode. "Enzo!"

He ignored her.

She shut her eyes, inhaling. Willed her heart to slow and her blood pressure to stabilize. She blew out, regarding him again as she concentrated her angst on the clothes she grasped with clenched fists. "I've spent a lot of time helping you in the last week. The whole time I've been here, actually."

Enzo raised an eyebrow in her direction.

Peyton shuffled her feet a bit. She loathed confrontation, but had found herself challenged by it more in her short time with Constance and Enzo than she'd ever found at any other time of her life. And that was saying something, given the very things that made her different. "Enzo, please."

Empowered by her gift or not, Peyton was ever-aware that she was at the mercy of the twins. And if Enzo was angry with her and refused to cooperate, Constance would know. And she was fully capable of acting on her whims, being alive and all. Peyton hung her head.

"Oh, don't be so dramatic," Enzo lamented, but something like satisfaction laced his words.

Peyton clenched her jaw.

Suddenly he was in front of her and she froze. It was hard being this close to *anyone.*

"You're so weird," he voiced, and it hurt her more than anger could have, because it was true.

She glanced again at the trees, the sunlight dipping behind them, making them into silhouettes. "Fine," she whispered, tears welling in her eyes as she begun to remove her shirt.

Enzo giggled. "Don't be indecent!"

Peyton, pressed onward by the anticipation of Constance's arrival, did not pause.

"Ugh," Enzo sighed, then snapped his fingers and was gone, just like that.

Peyton did pause, then. "That was new," she muttered.

He was back before Constance arrived, though, popping back into existence as soon as Peyton was dressed. *He* was *watching!* she internalized with a frown as he sat beside her on the bed.

"She's late," he said.

Peyton nodded. "Do you know why?"

Enzo shrugged.

Peyton studied his features. "You do, don't you?"

He smiled as he studied his fingernails. "She's had a visitor." Something darkened his expression, even as he feigned indifference.

Peyton paused, then ran to the window. "That car's here again," she remarked, mostly to herself. It was a black Bentley, and she'd seen it once before, but had missed its owner. She whirled on Enzo. "Whose car is that?"

He regarded her darkly.

"A friend?"

He laughed.

"Family?"

His smile faded.

"Is it your father?" she tried, but knew it was wrong. He wasn't due to return for another week.

Enzo shook his head. "If it were, we'd be at tea now. He's not here even when he is."

Peyton looked down at the car again.

"You've seen her before," Enzo hinted, but the teasing tone she'd usually have expected was apparent.

She frowned again. *Her?* "I've only ever seen you and Constance," she retorted. "Unless -" she gasped. "Oh!"

Enzo watched her, waiting.

"You know what I've seen?"

"Who do you think's been showing you?"

She shook her head. She'd never quite understood just how the dead communicated. The methodologies escaped her, though she heard them, loud and clear. It wasn't just conversation, though. The give and take of that was easiest to comprehend, but more difficult for *them*. Dreams seemed easiest, and visions came in as a close second, but there were so many more ways. Her thoughts turned to the one constant she'd seen in her head since Constance had approached her after her last art class: the stables. The hayloft. The blonde woman, naked and straddling the bodily form of the ghost who watched her, now.

"Her?" she asked, and the word was met with a single nod, Enzo's eyes hard. She looked back down and as if by some miracle of timing, she was there, walking toward the car in a smart skirt and blazer, her hair pinned into a French twist. Peyton leaned forward until her forehead met the cool glass, straining to see details and failing as the woman lowered herself into the driver's seat smoothly. She watched the car turn and fade down the driveway, then looked over her shoulder for Enzo. She jumped back, having found his head just behind her, disembodied and gazing out the window over her shoulder.

"Sorry," he muttered as the rest of him materialized.

She shook her head. "Who is she?"

"My mother," he replied without hesitation, all traces of mischief erased from his comportment.

Just for that moment.

And then there came the sound of a key in the lock.

Chapter 8 – Progression

Peyton froze as the lock clicked.

There was a pause, then the door opened just enough for Constance to peer around it. Peyton unwittingly compared the effect to Enzo's disembodied head from moments earlier.

Constance's hand appeared around the door, then, and pointed to the spot where Peyton should have been waiting.

"Sorry!" Peyton cried as she raced toward the door.

"Good heavens!" Constance muttered, but said nothing more as she wound the ribbon around Peyton's wrists.

Peyton watched the windows silently, her thoughts racing.

"Is he here?" Constance asked, and Peyton turned to scan the room

She found him with a start, the visage of his lower half sprawled on the bed. Peyton frowned and leaned to see past Constance and found his upper half, but this time, his head was missing.

"Well?" Constance demanded, hands fisted on her hips.

Enzo's head materialized slowly, a purplish mass appearing first and then oozing into its proper shape, Enzo's arms going to this throat as his features became apparent.

Peyton fought the urge to cry out at the sight, meeting Constance's gaze, instead. "M – mostly," was the only answer she could manage.

Constance manufactured a prim expression and put her nose in the air. "Well, tell him it's time for tea."

Peyton paused.

"My word, Peyton! You're slower than usual tonight!"

"I'm sorry. It's just that I don't need to tell him. He can hear you."

Constance averted her eyes as she pressed her lips together.

It wasn't the first time Peyton had reminded her of the fact, but somehow it became more difficult each time, as unsure as she was of Constance's disposition from moment to moment.

"Right, then. Shall we?" Constance was blushing. Peyton could see red blotches on her neck, as well. Her skin seemed as temperamental as her mood, flaring in tandem. A red flag.

Peyton nodded, muttering a hurried, "Of course," before stepping lightly past the shorter woman and into the hallway.

Constance peered around the space once more before joining her, then started down the hall, nose in the air again.

Peyton frowned, but followed, taking in every detail as they went. Constance sometimes forgot to remove her constraints, but forgetting to put her blindfold on was new. She knew she should speak up – her reaction to the revelation would no doubt sting less than the discovery of it after Peyton had seen too much and held the knowledge back – but she found herself unable to dislodge the words from her throat.

There wasn't much to see; the hallway was short. One wall was decorated by large tapestries and a single painting of riders on horseback, hounds at their feet. A simple side table adorned with a massive, empty vase was displayed midway down the opposite side. But as they neared the stairs, Peyton's eyes widened as her view did. Several paintings lined the descending wall. She recognized the one of the twins first, though their captured images looked back from younger faces than she was accustomed to, and another of Enzo, alone. He was dressed in riding gear, one foot on an overturned barrel and his opposite arm bent to hold a riding crop over his shoulder. His pose spoke pridefully, but Peyton saw sadness in his eyes.

As they continued down, the largest of the paintings caught her attention. It was a dignified-looking older man with Enzo's eyes and a stern-looking woman with thin lips and tightly pulled-back hair. "Who's *that*?" she mumbled aloud, then gasped, inwardly cursing herself for having gotten so distracted by her surroundings that she'd forgotten to keep quiet about it.

"What?" Constance turned as the reached the bottom, then uttered a high-pitched, "Oh!" as she pulled the thicker ribbon from her sash. "Why didn't you tell me?" she growled in Peyton's ear as she tightened the knot at the back.

Peyton grimaced at the pressure on her eyes and the way the knot pulled at her hair.

Constance tapped a flat hand on her cheek, urging her to speak. It wasn't a slap, really, but it made her jump, nonetheless. "I'm sorry!"

"You say that so much!" Constance growled. "And rightly so; you're such a fuck-up!"

Peyton recoiled at Constance's rare use of profanity. Heavy footsteps retreated downward then and she pictured a smug look on her captor's face. When she heard no more, she considered her options. She'd never navigated the stairs blind without Constance's guidance, and the simultaneous restraint of her hands did Peyton no favours. "Constance?"

Silence answered her.

"I -" Peyton faltered, noting the odd sensation of tears trying to well in her eyes, which were so tightly compressed in their sockets she felt they may implode. "I don't want to fall," she finished, her words sounding pathetic to her own ears.

A warm hand gripped her elbow and Peyton exhaled in a rush, relief flooding her. "Thank you," she muttered as she continued downward. She became aware it was Enzo helping her when she reached the landing and Constance took her opposite arm roughly.

"My brother likes to oppose me," the woman fumed.

Peyton turned her head to see him, reminded of her blindfold after the fact. "Enzo?"

Constance tugged on her arm with a growl of irritation. "If I'd known the two of you would gang up on me, I'd never have brought you here!" Her fingers dug into Peyton's upper arm as she accentuated her words with violent yanks.

"Oh!" Peyton cried as her shoulder sent out a bolt of pain.

"Shut *up!*" Constance spat, pulling Peyton down roughly so she could yell into her ear.

Peyton was quickly forgetting the rules of social etiquette she'd worked so hard to gain. She sucked in a breath and made an effort to concentrate only on walking, using Constance's lead regardless of the pain it caused.

"*Bitch*" Enzo's voice came from her left, and Peyton fought the urge to turn toward it again. "She's such a baby," he added, childishly.

Peyton knew the irony would be funny later, but it felt too dangerous to laugh at, now.

The smells of tea and cakes filtered through the air as they stepped onto hardwood floors, and Peyton realized with a sense of dread she'd forgotten to put her shoes on. She bit the insides of her cheeks, throwing a prayer out to whomever could hear her. *Please don't let her see.*

She was shoved unceremoniously, her knees meeting something solid quite painfully. She didn't cry out, though. She stayed still instead, hoping Constance would remove her blindfold quickly so her eyes could return to their proper homes.

"Oh, did you hurt your knees?" Constance crooned from behind her.

Peyton bit her lip, wanting to be anywhere else. Wanting to be sleeping. Wanting to be *gone*.

The blindfold loosened, then was torn from her head. Peyton was aware of the stinging pain of some hair being torn out with it, but focused instead on the overwhelming relief of having the pressure removed from her eyes.

But what she saw tossed her in another direction, entirely.

Enzo was on the table, squatting over a tray of sandwiches, a huge smile beaming in Peyton's direction.

Peyton struggled to remain calm as her wrists were freed from their restraints, but she couldn't look away.

His pants and underwear were puddled around his ankles, but Peyton could see that nothing on the table had been disturbed.

He made a feather flutter, she reminded herself. *There's no way he can take a crap on the sandwiches.*

Still, her appetite had waned considerably.

Peyton cleared her throat and looked at Constance. "Shall I serve your tea?"

Constance fumed. "I'd like an apology, first!"

Peyton worked to steady herself as Enzo whispered, "Should I do it?" then broke into a fit of laughter.

"I apologize about the blindfold. I didn't realize until we were already walking, and then I saw the pictures and got distracted."

Constance looked regretfully appeased, her eyes still flashing angrily.

"How old were you and Enzo? In that one with -"

Constance pointed a finger at Peyton's face, the heat of her fingertip palpable between her eyes. "*Don't* ask questions about things you shouldn't have seen!"

Peyton lowered her gaze. "I'm sorry."

Enzo, apparently bored, stood and pulled his pants up. "You're no fun," he muttered, then jumped off the table and disappeared in midair.

Constance marched to the head of the table and sat, her dress fluffing out at the sides. The woman was short, but she wasn't slight.

"Serve," she demanded.

Things were quiet while Peyton served Constance. She'd deigned to let Peyton choose everything for her this time, seemingly distracted. Then she made up a plate for Enzo, though he hadn't reappeared.

Peyton served herself last, and had to hold herself back as her appetite returned with a vengeance. Chicken salad sandwiches with little slices of sweet pickles were her favorite of all the sandwiches served, save perhaps the cream cheese and swiss croissants with cucumber and tomato. She ate in grateful silence, watching Constance warily. But the woman's eyes were clouded over.

Finally, she said, "He's not here, is he?"

Peyton froze mid-chew, then shook her head as daintily as she could.

Constance sighed heavily, her eyes going to the windows and out into the darkening evening. "She doesn't ever stay long, but I know her visits upset him."

"Who?" Peyton asked before she could stop herself, her heart suddenly pounding hard.

Constance sent her a withering look. "For your information, our stepmother was here today. She stays in the city when father is away on business." Constance said in a rush, her eyes going to her plate. "Oh, brownies!" she muttered, and Peyton's eyes widened as Enzo's laugher seemed to come from all sides of her.

She squinted toward Constance as the woman brought the chocolate confection to her mouth, desperately trying to remember whether she'd served her brownies or not. Relief rolled over her when Constance closed her eyes, saying, "Mmm!"

Enzo popped into his chair at the opposite end of the table. He was still laughing. "You actually thought I did it!" he pointed at Peyton.

"I didn't realize your father remarried after your mother's death," Peyton said smoothly, proud of her lack of reaction to Enzo's tricks as she looked back at Constance.

"It's not your place to realize that," Constance replied, but there was no force behind her words.

Peyton sipped her tea.

"The truth is, if father wasn't so busy with work, they'd be divorced already," Constance said, reaching for her tea.

"Pfft," uttered Enzo, who'd crossed his legs as he lounged sloppily. "She's always been so jealous of her."

Peyton knew he was talking to her, but his eyes were on Constance.

"Why?" Peyton asked, then sucked in her breath, looking at Constance.

Constance frowned. "Because she's hateful!" she said, replying to the question Peyton had meant for Enzo, in some twist of luck.

"Because she loved me best, just like mother," Enzo whispered, and it tickled Peyton's neck, for he was behind her, now.

And she was momentarily distracted from both of them, caught up in the feel of his breath on her skin. Remembering the warmth of his touch on the stairs. And finally, envisioning the fluttering feather from that afternoon.

He was progressing remarkably fast.

This could be bad.

Chapter 9 – Mutual Admiration At First Sight

Margot watched as Charis went through the file she'd brought on Peyton's disappearance. That's what they were calling it, now. And, as Jane said, if it wasn't as good as "kidnapping," it was a step up from "runaway."

"You got all this from her mother?" Charis fixed a brown-eyed gaze on Margot, one of her eyes partially obstructed by an unruly blonde curl.

Margot nodded. "Except the notes in the front, of course; those are my thoughts."

Charis straightened in her chair and stretched.

They were sitting in Charis's modern farmhouse kitchen, the only sounds providing accompaniment to their visit the drips of melting snow on the windows and the occasional giggle leaking into the hallway. Her two youngest were doing a puzzle, apparently, the seven-year-old watched by his teenaged brother.

"Do you just have the two?" Margot asked, cocking a thumb to the hallway.

Charis smiled, her pretty mouth stretching unselfconsciously. "The two you hear are only half of them."

"Four?"

Charis nodded. "Do you want more tea?"

Margot hadn't touched her first one. "Whoops! Let me drink this one, first."

Charis stood, bringing her own mug to the counter. "Yep! Four boys," she said, turning to talk over her shoulder. "But the oldest lives in residence at the University of Ottawa, and the nineteen-year-old has a full-time job."

"He doesn't go to University?"

Charis came back to the table, but didn't sit. "He graduated early; he's kinda scary-smart."

Margot smiled, now.

Charis frowned. "I wanted to home-school the kids, but before we moved here, I had a really demanding job with the government. I only do that part-time now," she smiled, her cheeks pinking.

Margot frowned, unable to get past her first words. "Why'd you mention homeschooling?"

She shook her head and waved the question away. "Sorry; I forget people can't hear my thoughts, ugh," she started toward the hallway. "I'm just going to peek my head in on the boys."

Margot was still frowning. This woman was – fascinating. She was relaxed and kind at the same time as being scatterbrained and ridiculously intuitive. And so pretty – but looking just at her build would have you thinking she was fragile. Her comportment was built on strength, though. Just one look from her and Margot saw it.

"So much for the puzzle," she sighed as she came back into the kitchen and sat. She regarded Margot with a smirk. "Video games."

Margot smiled. They'd never been her thing, though her brothers were avid gamers.

"You *were* homeschooled, right? I see you and two little boys at a table with lots of natural light. There's a patio door that leads to the back yard and an island between the -"

Margot held up a hand. "Whoa."

Charis laughed and leaned forward slightly. "You know what I can do, right? I mean, isn't that why you contacted me?"

Margot laughed. "Yeah! I just – I didn't expect it so – soon?"

"I can hold back, if it makes you more comfortable, but I think we need to have all our cards on the table if we're going to work together to find Peyton."

"Wow. This'll take some getting used to."

Charis smiled. "It's a conversation for another day, but you're no stranger to knowing things you shouldn't."

Margot seemed unable to avert her eyes; Charis held her gaze intently, a small smile at her lips.

She cleared her throat. "Uh – do you have time? To help find Peyton, that is?"

"Of course," Charis muttered, rifling through the file, again.

"My parents – across the street?"

Charis nodded, pulling Margot's notes from the file.

"They tried to come say hello, but you weren't here. I imagine you're very busy..."

"I thrive on chaos," the petite woman laughed, meeting Margot's eyes again. "The kids aren't so dependent anymore, and when nobody's here to play with Demi, I have family – friends – to take care of him."

"Demi?"

"Dmitry," Charis smiled. "After his great-grandfather." Seeing Margot's puzzlement, she waved that away, too. "Long story!"

Margot nodded. "You're lucky to have support nearby,"

she gazed out the window. "I remember Steve Brown when we were kids – and Jack Ridgestone, next door, was only a couple of years older than me." She smiled back at Charis. "It was a wonderful place to grow up."

Charis narrowed her eyes, studying Margot. "I'd like to hear more about your childhood, when there's time."

"I'm sorry," Margot blushed, "I shouldn't be talking about myself."

Charis shook her head, her curls bouncing. "No, I mean it! It's very cool to meet you, knowing you grew up with someone I'm so close to, now. He and Maggie are family to us!" she gestured toward the hallway. "And – I'm curious to know whether you ever went to the abandoned property at the top of the hill."

Margot's skin broke out in gooseflesh.

"I think you have?"

She nodded. "You're very good at what you do."

Charis shrugged. "Just a part of life for me. Besides, when I told Jack and Maggie I'd be meeting you, Jack remembered you and talked about your experiences with Wren," she held her hands out, "with respect, of course! He knows you prefer to keep names and details private."

Margot laughed. "If you can call publishing the story and using it to help students explore my theories, you could say that."

"He says you helped him."

Margot nodded. "I haven't seen another ghost since."

Charis's eyes darkened. "Do you want to?"

Margot paused, her pulse quickening, then noted a twinkle in Charis's eye as she grinned. Margot laughed. "I'm not sure!"

Charis sipped her tea, still smiling. "It's a choice for some."

Margot's smile faded. "For me?"

Charis nodded.

A flurry of activity had them both looking toward the hallway, where a sprightly little boy was barrelling toward them, squealing as he was chased by who Margot assumed must be his brother.

Charis received a hug from the little one with a laugh. "What's going on?"

The boy pulled away slightly and looked at his mother with eyes so dark they could be liquid. "Sasha says he's gonna eat me."

Charis smiled at the older boy, who Margot judged to be fifteen or sixteen. "I'm guessing you guys want a snack, then?"

The older boy nodded, then looked at Margot. "Hi, I'm Sasha."

"Hi, I'm Margot," she gave a little wave, amused.

"Margie-Mae," he smiled, and Margot gasped.

"How -"

Charis leaned forward as she lifted Demi off her lap. "He's like me."

Margot shot her a look.

"But, uh, more so."

"More like you than *you*?" Sasha laughed, then started rifling through cupboards.

Charis smiled at Margot. "I think the first order of business is to get in touch with her brother."

Margot shook her head a bit. She wasn't used to feeling

one step behind, but everything about this woman – her family, the house itself, what she'd said to Margot about her past – had her off-balance.

"Do you want me to do that? Or, I could do some digging where she taught her art classes. I feel like that'd be best. Have you met Spencer?"

Margot absently rubbed her temples.

"Sorry; what were you thinking? Next-steps-wise."

Margot looked up at the woman, her forehead in her hands. "Uh – exactly what you just said, actually."

Charis smiled. "Good! And you're fine with talking to her brother?"

Margot nodded.

"OK. Call me when you've talked to him. I can go over to the center where she taught tonight."

"We'll meet again, then?"

"Depends," Charis sat back in her seat, folding her arms and looking thoughtful. "As soon as we know enough, we'll have to go to Europe. Not sure where, exactly, but England or Scotland feels right."

Margot shook her head.

The boys dashed back into the hallway, Sasha with a box of crackers in his hands. "Bye, Margie!" he called over his shoulder.

"This is going to take some getting used to," she muttered, and Charis smiled, sipping her tea again.

"Everyone says that," she replied absently as she frowned into her mug.

"What is it?"

"Something about tea."

Margot frowned. "Huh?"

"She has *tea* with her captors?" Charis said it like she was talking to a ghost. Margot scanned the room, her neck tingling. "Nobody's here," she placed a flat hand on the table to get Margot's attention. "I just see it." She shook her head. "Beautiful house. An old plantation."

"But you think she's there against her will?"

Charis nodded, frowning. "Yes."

"And you pluralized 'captors'."

She nodded. "It feels like two, but in truth, only one did the kidnapping."

"Shit. Are you sure?"

Charis looked at her, her eyes dark. "I knew as soon as I read your note. And we have to hurry; there's a death coming."

Margot stood suddenly, the backs of her knees hitting her chair and sending it scraping backward.

"Don't panic; we have time to find her. And it's not her death." She frowned again. "I don't think -"

"Peyton is my friend!" Margot cried, getting angry now at the woman's apparent nonchalance.

"Do you want me to hide what I see, or include you?"

"What?"

"I'm saying it casually because it's *normal* for me, Margot. I'm scared, too."

Margot sat back down and Charis reached for her hand. Depleted, she reached, too.

Charis placed her free hand on top of Margot's. "I want to find her, too."

Chapter 10 – Pillow Talk. Sort Of.

Enzo liked to lay in bed with Peyton; he said he felt most *solid* when he was there. Tonight he was quiet though, laying on his back and making shadow puppets on the ceiling by the warm light on the bedside table.

Peyton wondered at the science of it. While Enzo continued to make progress when it came to interacting with material objects on her level of existence, she didn't quite comprehend the manifestation of his shadow. Did he manifest as a solid being when he lay with her, even if unconsciously? She pondered his weight on the bed; how she could feel him there.

She remembered something Margot, an old friend from university, said about Peyton's experiences. Maybe it was *her* who allowed the ghosts she saw to interact in material ways. Perhaps her own perceptions stretched the possibilities – merged two levels of existence by faith alone? Or by some unexplained skill?

She wondered if anyone else would be able to see Enzo's shadow crow, flapping its wings in slow motion.

Maybe only some could. Maybe Charis, the woman she'd learned of through searching online for people like herself, would perceive the shadows, and Enzo, himself.

But maybe it was only Peyton.

Regardless of whether the notion was true, she *felt* alone. And here, in the gilded prison that had become her whole world, she was.

Enzo let his hands drop, but his eyes remained on the ceiling, where his shadow-bird still flew, fading into nothing as it flapped its wings.

Peyton frowned. *How could science ever explain* that?

He turned toward her, his back to the light and his eyes dark. Peyton suffered terrible anxiety when she felt her personal space was being breached. It often only took the meeting of a person's eyes to activate the feeling of being suffocated. But Enzo was such a familiar energy, now. It was almost comfortable having him near.

"What are you thinking?" he asked, his voice almost a whisper.

Peyton grinned. "You have an accent even when you whisper."

He rolled his eyes. "You thought I'd cease being British if I lowered my voice?" he smiled.

"No," she whispered back. "It's just – interesting."

He frowned, but the corners of his mouth remained slightly upturned. "You *are* strange."

She nodded. "I know."

They fell into silence again, each tethered to the other's gaze, thinking their own thoughts, until Peyton realized her own eyes were getting heavy.

She opened her mouth to talk, but he did, first.

"Have you ever done it?"

She frowned lazily. "Huh?"

"You know. What two people do when they're in bed together."

She was suddenly wide awake, but did not reply.

"You know," he said again, "sex!"

She focussed on breathing. On keeping eye contact, lest he take her breaking it as embarrassment, or some other indication of an unspoken answer that he could tease her about.

"I only ask because you're different," he explained, his voice still low. "I know you have problems with – people – and I just wondered if it extended to acts of intimacy," he finished, quite serious, then giggled. "You don't have to tell me."

She pursed her lips, then shook her head. "It's not that I haven't had the – opportunity," she started, choosing her words carefully, "I've been in relationships. And it's not that I don't get, uh..." she faltered, and did break eye contact, then.

"Horny?" he offered, his eyes bright, even in the shadows.

She giggled but rolled onto her back as she felt her cheeks warm in a blush.

"Urges?" he tried again, but without laughing.

She turned her head to meet his eyes again. "I think I'm just too anxious about it. It seems so chaotic. So messy!"

Enzo laughed. "Ah, that's the best bit," he said as he rolled onto his back, too, his eyes on the ceiling again.

Peyton rolled toward him again, encouraged by his docile mood, maybe. "I fantasize sometimes, and it's..."

He turned his head expectantly when she didn't finish.

"Well, I'm pretty sure everything *works* – physically," she finished with a smile, her cheeks burning anew. When he only continued to probe her eyes, she went on, "But then I start to imagine the logistics of it and the draw of it sort of... fades."

Now Enzo laughed heartily, but didn't turn from her. "Peyton, I don't think you're supposed to consider the *logistics*."

"I know!" she cried. "And I won't blame my being on the spectrum. I know lots of Aspies who love sex. I'm pretty sure I'm just extra-weird."

Enzo shook his head, his hair rubbing against the pillow, and looked puzzled. "It's too bad. Sex is fun."

She frowned. "Do you miss it?"

He shrugged. "Maybe, but only in a sort of nostalgic way. Things are different, now." He looked down at himself, so Peyton did, too, and noticed his legs faded into nothing at the knees. Enzo laughed. "I can't even be *whole*, most of the time. And sometimes, even when I'm trying, I'm something entirely different than this."

"Why does that happen?"

He frowned, seeming to will his legs back into existence. They reappeared briefly, then faded as he looked back at Peyton. "It's like I have a harder time remembering my body as time goes on," he said. "And sometimes I get scared because I feel lost when I'm not in this form. Or maybe I just feel different and that – unfamiliarity – scares me into thinking I'm lost." His eyes lit up a bit as he went on, "I got lost in a department store once. Not lost, actually. I only lost sight of Mummy for a few seconds, but her absence threw me into an entirely different world – one in which I was alone and terrified. Everything looked intimidating, every person looked threatening. And then she walked around the corner, scolding me for getting distracted, and everything was right with the world, again."

Peyton nodded. "Do you know where you're supposed to go, now that you're - untethered?"

He shook his head. "I don't look for that way, not yet."

"Because of how you died?"

His eyes darkened. "Not just that."

Peyton waited, expecting flashes of his memories to assault her, holding her breath in preparation, but nothing came.

"I was killed more than once before I really died," he murmured, and it was he who averted his eyes.

"I'm sorry, Enzo," she whispered.

Something about him wavered, his form rippling as he swiped at his eyes, which Peyton had seen tears well in before he moved.

"Do you want to tell me about it?"

His form solidified again, but he still didn't meet her eyes. "Not tonight, but you'll have to know, I guess, before this is all over."

Her heart sped up again.

"I'm sorry, Peyton. I want you to know that, even though I'm glad you're here, I never would have taken you. Constance has always had less – self control – than I."

"What did you mean, about this being over?"

"*Me*, of course. You know I don't belong here anymore, regardless of whether Constance wants me here or not."

Peyton nodded. Full of questions, but tired, too. And unwilling to sacrifice such rare moments of peace for the chance to learn more about her situation.

"We're alike in that way, aren't we?"

She didn't answer. Her eyelids fluttered as she tried to focus on him.

"Neither of us should be here. I just hope *you* get out alive."

Chapter 11 – Charis
Does Some Digging

It was a Tuesday night and Charis had a lot on her mind as she circled the Community Arts Center in Halifax, where Peyton had taught classes before she disappeared.

The kids were fine; Demi and Sasha were at the Wolfville house with Ashleigh and Greyson, much to the elderly couple's delight. She would have preferred to have them at Max or Maggie's on a school night, but Greyson happened to call that morning, begging for a visit, and she gave in. Wolfville was on the way back, anyway. She'd pick the boys up before going home.

She wanted to visit the Center on a night that Peyton would have been there. Sometimes the absence of someone allowed for information to fill the empty spot in. She hadn't called first; she found face-to-face meetings were best when she was digging. A friendly face did a lot to relax whomever she was questioning.

So, it wasn't the visit to the Center that was furrowing her brow. There was something tugging at her from her subconscious, refusing to surface fully. And she couldn't help but go over and over Peyton's plea for help that time. And reliving the sick feeling of guilt over and over, too.

She inwardly chastised herself for not sharing that little tidbit with Margot when she'd come to see her. She couldn't put her finger on it, but something about the woman had her holding back, just a little. It wasn't that she wasn't approachable, or even friendly. Margot Francis was known for being kind as well as brilliant. Perhaps that was it. There was something about her eyes, as though they were portals to an ever-turning systems of cogs, thinking a myriad of thoughts at any given moment. So, when you looked at her, you felt she was *learning* you while she smiled quietly.

It probably wasn't something everybody would notice, but Charis had a sensitivity to being scrutinized, even inwardly. And though she'd abolished the idea of having to prove herself long ago, she found herself hoping for Margot's approval – something she hadn't felt in a very long while.

There was something else, too. Charis found herself wanting to learn Margot, too. Granted, Margot had only interacted with a ghost during a short period of her life, but from what Charis had read, it had been a full apparition, so close to life it took her several encounters to realize he was... different. And after she'd solved the mystery of him, she'd never seen a ghost again. But she believed. She'd seen. And beyond being smart, she was clearly more intuitive than your average person. It called up questions in Charis that she'd been dogged with for years.

Could *she* have stopped her own gift, too? Could she have ignored it, or changed her perspective so that ghosts would let her be? And what about the other things – the *knowing* of things when she shouldn't? The seeing of people in shapes and colours, symbols and patterns? The flashing images and auras and smells. Was it all a part of one gift?

What could Margot see now?

How different was she from Charis?

And how was she similar?

It was a rare thing for her to feel compelled to let someone in. Her hectic life had been relieved greatly when she'd moved to Greenwood Square, what with her new, extended family living on either side of her and her choice to stay home more to be with people she loved. Greyson was a big part of that, but not forcefully so. His involvement was as much due to the fact that Charis loved him and Ashleigh as surrogate parents as it was due to the fact that Demi was Greyson's son.

But she wanted to open up to Margot. Let her in.

"Ah!" she exclaimed as a sedan pulled out of a spot on the road across from the Center. She slowed and pulled in, smiling triumphantly.

It was easy enough to navigate the building. Easels with hand-written directions for each class were at the four corners of the busy lobby, and though Peyton hadn't taught a class in several weeks, her name was still at the top of one of the sheets, an arrow pointing toward the right with the number "401" written atop it. Charis paused at the easel, first gazing down the hallway and then scanning the room. She wasn't pulled to the hallway, yet, so she opened up for guidance. If she'd been asked what she was opening *to*, she probably would have said something expansive, like, "The universe," but in her heart of hearts, she knew she was just letting herself work. Trusting.

Faith is a critical factor in divination.

She thought it often, but rarely said it aloud.

I could say it to Margot, she thought, then frowned, unsure of the reasoning behind her own sentiment.

The room buzzed with chitchat and new arrivals. Charis smiled at other visitors, noting the cheerful atmosphere with some relief. A side table set up with drinks and plates of cookies lined the wall to her left, and her eyes met those of the squat, older woman behind it. The woman smiled, then gestured to the cookies.

Thrilled at the invitation, Charis beelined for the table.

"You looked a little lost," the woman smiled, her velvety cheeks pudging out charmingly.

"I was. Is it a special evening?"

The woman laughed. "Nope! Just like any other Tuesday – or Thursday, to think of it! Folks who come for classes come to socialize, too. We're like family, here. Cookie?"

"Huh? Oh!" Charis laughed and chose a gingersnap, using the moment to consider how to proceed. Another glance at the woman's face and she went with the usual: the truth.

"Are you here to join a class?"

Charis hesitated, then took a moment to look back at Peyton's name on the easel. "Actually, I'm here because I've been asked to help find someone. Peyton Hale?"

The woman's eyes registered recognition before Charis had finished saying her name. She reached out to give Charis's arm a gentle squeeze. "Just terrible, isn't it? Peyton was a very popular teacher. Her classes were in high demand!"

Charis nodded, hoping for more.

"People loved the way she taught. She made everyone feel special, even with her – different – ways, you know? Due to her Asperger's?"

"Yes, I understand she was quite high-functioning."

The woman leaned forward and lowered her voice. "Personally, I don't go in for those labels. If you ask me, Peyton's the perfect example of how everybody wants to put labels on things they don't understand."

Charis was taken aback at the woman's candor, and impressed, too, at its progressive nature. She gave a laugh. "I guess it's safer when we can categorize things."

The woman straightened up. "I have the feeling *you're* not so easy to compartmentalize, either."

Charis raised her eyebrows and took a bite of her cookie.

"Mmhm, avoidance." The woman winked. "I wish I could give you some insight on Peyton's whereabouts, but I've told the police everything I know already – which is largely about her performance here, mind you." The woman frowned. "Who did you say you worked for? You one of those private dicks?"

Charis nearly spit her cookie out at the term, but managed to get the back of her hand to her mouth before her sudden laughter accomplished it.

"Guess nobody says that nowadays!" the woman laughed too, eyes twinkling. "Coffee?" she smiled at a man who'd approached the table and poured him a cup.

"I'm actually – well, you were right when you said I'm hard to categorize," Charis smiled. "I know the police are doing everything they can, but Peyton's family is just trying to do everything they can. Have you heard of Margot Francis?"

The woman's eyes clouded as she shook her head.

"Hm. Well, she's a brilliant scientist, but happens to be into the unexplained as well – the supernatural?"

The woman nodded. "And you do, too?"

Charis smiled. "Yes. One could say I have a bit of skill in that area."

"But what does that have to do with finding Peyton?"

Now Charis leaned forward. "I'm just digging around to see what I can find; I might see something the police don't, you know?"

The woman folded her hands over her ample belly, then scanned the room.

"The only information I have, beyond the fact that Peyton was a wonderful member of the Center, is that she was seen speaking with someone after the last class she taught.

Someone nobody recognized."

Charis made an effort to disguise her excitement at learning something new. "Did *you* see her talking to the person?"

The woman's jowls trembled as she shook her head to the contrary. "'Fraid not. But Pete over there did, and so did Jewel, that woman in the burgundy dress?" She pointed toward the doors, where a rather large man stood with a fistful of cookies, laughing along with a friend, and then to the opposite corner, where a woman stood alone in her pretty dress, looking unsure. Of anything.

"I'll go talk to them; thank you very much, um -" Charis reached out to shake the woman's hand. It was a habit, and a useful one. She used it as a final gauge of a person's sincerity. There was no hiding energy when they deigned to be touched.

"Clara," the woman smiled and took Charis's hand in turn.

There's something else, Charis knew when they touched, but she knew she wouldn't unearth it, not this time.

She started toward the woman named Jewel instead, but the woman caught sight of her and quickly walked in the opposite direction, down the hall whose sign boasted a pottery class and a showing of "Old B&W Movies."

Charis frowned and turned back toward Clara, but the woman was already engaged with eager coffee-drinkers.

She shrugged and turned toward the doors. A bell sounded as she reached Pete and his friend.

"Oh!" he said, then smiled at Charis absently as he started toward the hallway where Peyton's class used to be taught.

"Excuse me, Pete?" Charis stepped in beside the man, though his long legs were much faster than hers.

He looked sideways at her, only slowing slightly. "You coming to class?" he asked.

She nodded, then shook her head, discombobulated. "I was interested in Peyton's class, actually - Miss Hale?"

He stopped, then. "Well, that's where I used to go at this time, too, but now I go to Asian Cooking." He shrugged. "I liked painting much more, but cooking is a sort of art too, isn't it?" He shoved his hands in his pockets, smiling.

"Clara -" she gestured toward the table, where the woman was starting to tidy up, "- mentioned you'd seen Peyton talking to someone after her last class? I don't want to keep you from your class too long, but could you tell me what you remember about the person?"

Pete glanced over his shoulder, then looked back at Charis. "Come on, let's go to the paint room. It's empty now, and I don't mind being late for cooking if it could help Peyton." He started off again, then stopped with a frown. "*Will* talking to you help her?"

Charis smiled. "I really hope so."

Chapter 12 – Unlocking Secrets

"Peyton!"

A weight brushed her shoulder, then took hold of it and shook her.

She groaned as she rolled to her back, aware of Enzo's form above her only as a further darkening in the night. She propped herself up on an elbow, her eyes on the windows. "It's the middle of the night!" she whispered, exasperated.

Tea had been particularly long that evening. Enzo had been distracted, and Constance seemed in need of extra attention as she pondered her father's return the following day. She'd gone over instructions for Peyton – most revolving around her being extra careful not to make noise in the loft, and backup plans, should the man perceive a presence and discover her.

"He never goes up there," she waved a hand dismissively, but went right back to her instructions, revealing the depth of her concern.

"What was it used for – before me?" Peyton ventured, making an attempt to be casual as she refilled Constance's teacup.

She gave a small laugh. "Enzo and I used to play there. Sometimes, we'd stay for days; Cook bringing our meals and mother peeking in now and then." The smile melted away as she got a faraway look in her eyes. "One would think it was because she cared – that's what Enzo thought, anyway – but I'm pretty sure she was just making sure we were still alive." She seemed to catch herself and raised her eyes to Peyton's. "She and father ran the businesses together; they were very busy."

Peyton pondered the words, sneaking a peek at Enzo, who was picking at his nails listlessly, his eyes on the sunset.

"It's good you had each other," she said, finally. "Was there someone to take care of you? A nanny?"

Constance shook her head. "Only when we were very young. I thought Father might hire someone after Mummy died, but I guess he knew the reality - that we'd been taking care of ourselves for a long time, even when she was alive."

"May I ask -" Peyton paused, her stomach somersaulting uncomfortably.

"You may ask, but I may not answer," Constance twittered, her eyebrows raised slightly.

"How did she die?"

Constance didn't miss a beat. "She got sick."

Peyton held her gaze. "I'm sorry."

Constance shrugged. "We had a stepmother very quickly, and she treated us pretty much like Mummy did, so the loss was less impactful, you might say."

Enzo made a sound of derision.

He's not so distracted, after all, Peyton realized, and then they were back to preparations for the impending arrival of Mr. Everleigh.

"I was thinking at tea tonight, that tonight is our last chance to try an escape before Father is home," Enzo said, his voice frantic.

"Escape?" Peyton bolted upright, her mind already on packing, on running. On finding her way to civilization, and then back home. And realizing she hadn't contemplated it before with a frown. *I am* strange.

"Yes! If nothing else, from this room! You need to learn the house, learn the traps before you can get out!"

"Traps? What traps?" she muttered as she reached for the light on the bedside table. She gasped when Enzo was revealed, in full shape, but not in colour. He was a shadowy mass, limbs and head separate blobs, though indistinct. "Why are you like that? Come back!"

Enzo's shadowy form seemed to filter slowly into color. "Sorry; guess it's easier not to think about how I look at night," he muttered, his hand outstretched as it became more – *there*.

Peyton watched as he materialized into something more relatable, noting his facial features were last, this time. She exhaled when he smiled at her, eyes clear.

"Better?" he asked, and she nodded.

"What's going on?"

He leaned toward her, a hand outstretched. "I've learned something new!" he said, barely able to contain himself.

Peyton took his hand, impressed at the solidity of it, and allowed him to pull her up and toward the door. "What time is it?" she wondered aloud.

"Late…or early, I guess," he answered absently. "Open it," he said then, releasing her hand and pointing at the doorknob.

She made a face. "What?"

He smiled. "I unlocked it."

Peyton paused, and then inhaled sharply. "Really?"

He held his hands up in surrender. "No tricks, promise."

She reached for it gingerly, Enzo doing an impatient dance beside her. And when she turned it, there was no resistance. She looked at Enzo. "Holy cow!"

He nodded. "Open it, silly!"

Peyton pulled, but gently. Enzo was doing well. He'd even been friendly lately – consistently so! But she remembered his mischievous ways. He'd been a bully, too. "Why?" she asked, suddenly doubting him.

"To *learn the house*, stupid!" he rolled his eyes, clearly exasperated, and Peyton recoiled, her hand shrinking back from the knob.

But the door followed her retreat with a slow, creaking swing. It was already done.

"I'm sorry for calling you stupid," Enzo said, "but only *you* would hesitate to run after being held captive for so long," he shook his head, his eyes angry.

Peyton stepped backward, her eyes on the hallway. "If Constance catches us – me! -"

"She *won't*! You forget I can see her, too. She's dead to the world, snoring not-so-prettily. And starting tomorrow, you'll need to worry about getting past Father, too. And Constance's wrath is *nothing* compared to his."

Peyton sucked in a breath.

"Go," he said, giving her a little push. Little, but firm.

So, she went.

The hallway was familiar, at least. Constance hadn't forgotten the blindfold again, but Peyton had memorized what she'd seen.

Wallpaper, tapestries, painting of riders with hounds at their feet, then stairs. This time, she stopped by the picture of the twins' mother and father.

Enzo appeared at the bottom of the stairs, motioning

her forward with some impatience. "Come *on!*"

Peyton pointed at his mother. "How long ago did she die?"

He growled quietly, throwing his hands in the air, but Peyton didn't move.

"It doesn't matter," he said, his annoyance barely restrained.

"I'm interested in your life – before," she pressed, aware of the dangers in doing so, but compelled, regardless.

"She was never a mother to us, really." He shook his head and studied the painting with distaste. "She was only interested in the business, and gaining Father's attention," he muttered. "Constance is a lot like her, except she only ever wanted *my* attention." He turned and paced the landing, his form flickering in his agitation. "And unfortunately, neither of them got what they wanted," he gestured to the ceiling, then stopped. "And two deaths were the result," he finished, his eyes on Peyton's darkly, now.

Peyton stepped to the landing. "Your mother's and – yours?"

Enzo nodded, his jaw set.

"Were both by the same hands?" Peyton asked boldly, holding his gaze.

"You could say that," Enzo replied, then averted his eyes, looking into the darkened rooms off the landing.

Peyton pressed, but made her voice soft. Gentle. "Constance?"

Enzo laughed and gave her a dark look. "No." He shrugged. "Who knows? She left, Peyton. This place was a prison for her, too. For all of us," he said, turning his back to her and walking in the direction of the tea room.

Peyton tiptoed down the rest of the flight, whisper-calling, "*Wait!*"

He appeared in front of her, arms folded, and she let out a squeal, her hands flying to her mouth.

They both froze, waiting, but there was no sound in reply.

"I don't want to go to the tea room!" she whispered, leaning toward him. "I want to find the door."

He shook his head. "You can't, not yet." He turned again, but she stayed put.

"*Not* the tea room!

He disappeared around a corner, and still she hesitated. She scanned her surroundings. Stairs behind her, tea room somewhere ahead, and who knew what else lay in the other direction, beyond the darkness. She leaned into the hallway in front of the stairs. A room opened up across from where she stood, and immediately to the left, the last flight of stairs which would lead to the first floor, she presumed.

"Peyton!" Enzo called from behind her, but she started toward the stairs, with some urgency in her steps. Enzo appeared halfway down, looking incensed. "What are you *doing*?"

"You're right!" she whispered, her control starting to fade. "I *should* get out of here! Why explore the second floor – why *learn the house!* – when I could just leave it behind!"

Enzo ceased looking angry. "You can't, not without the password for the alarm system. And, there's something else. Something *I* need you to find..."

Peyton made a sound of frustration, tears welling in her eyes. It was true she hadn't pondered her escape until that night, but now that the possibility lay before her, stretching out for the taking, it hurt to consider any other alternative.

"The code is in Constance's diary," he added, his words hurried.

"And the other – thing?"

"Locked in a closet," he replied, perhaps a bit quickly. "And the key is in her room, too. I think."

Peyton made a face. "You *think?*"

"I sorta missed that part."

Peyton rubbed her temples.

"You'll have to excuse me. I was a bit distracted just after I DIED," Enzo hissed, his face altogether too close to Peyton's for comfort.

She backed up a step, effectively rendering herself at an advantage where height was concerned. She steadied herself, then put her nose in the air as she'd seen Constance do many times. "If you're going to treat me badly, I don't want to do *anything* you say."

He raised his eyebrows, either impressed or surprised. Maybe both. Then he took a step up, too, and was taller than her again. Peyton glanced downward, puzzled. He shouldn't be *that* tall. She pursed her lips, finding his semi-transparent feet hovering rather than meeting the stair, then looking back at him, a bit afraid.

"If you set off the alarm, you can't leave anyway," he grinned smugly, eyes dark.

Peyton shrunk back.

"I'm not stopping you, Peyton. I'm trying to *help*. But I need you to help, too."

Something rose in her – weeks of pent-up resentment, as-yet unspoken, or even acknowledged, and she lowered her head, unwilling to let him see her face crumple as her eyes filled with tears.

"Hey," he said, but she wouldn't look up. "I'm sorry," he added.

"I don't want to be here anymore," she cried, and the words were the last step in her release. She put her face in her hands, suddenly overwhelmed with sadness.

"I'm sorry," he said again, and she felt him move closer, but he didn't move to touch her.

She looked up, caring little if he saw her red-faced and awash with tears. And his expression made her stop.

There was something like fear in his eyes, and regret. Something she'd never seen in him before.

"What is it?" she asked. "The thing you need me to find."

"Evidence," he said, his voice wavering. He seemed at a loss to say more, so instead he raised his shirt, revealing a wound in his chest, open and red, his still heart revealed beneath smashed bones.

Peyton recoiled again, so quickly that she stumbled and landed hard on a step, her tailbone sending lightning shocks of pain down her legs. She recalled in passing having injured this part of herself before and squeezed her eyes shut, overwhelmed.

Enzo squatted in front of her. "She tried to save me when she realized," he cried, and Peyton opened her eyes to meet his tearful ones. "Everyone loved me most," he smiled sadly.

Peyton shook her head. "What does that mean?" She wiped her own tears, and then his, but touching him felt strange.

"Jealousy, money... doesn't it always come to that?" he answered, but he was flickering.

Peyton stood and reached for his hand, but she went right through him, that time. "Come on. I'm sorry; of course I want to help you. Let's go."

He looked up at her, doubt clouding his expression, and then he was gone, before she could say more.

She gasped, then froze, listening. Waiting for him to return.

When he didn't, she did the one thing she hadn't considered earlier: she went back up the stairs, then up the other flight, and down the hallway to her room. Then she sunk to the floor, her eyes on the doorknob. "Enzo?" she tried. Her voice was high, but quiet. "Please lock it again!" she cried, the tears returning in her desperation.

When there was no reply, she went back to bed and stared into the darkness for a long time before letting go. Waiting for a click. Just a little reassurance that Constance wouldn't have an excuse to fly into a rage that night before tea.

And falling, finally, to sleep.

(blank page follows)

Chapter 13 – Exchange Of Information

Charis leaned forward, squinting into the rainy night in an effort to pick names and numbers out in the dark.

Your destination is on the left, the GPS chirped, and Charis sighed. There was no shortage of cute coffee shops in the university town of Wolfville, but the road was too busy for her to drive slowly enough to read the signs.

She spotted a gap along the side of the street and pulled in without hesitation, glad for the bit of luck, and resolved to find the café by foot, despite the rain. She thought regretfully about the umbrella gathering dust at home - always ready, and just as consistently forgotten – as she pulled the hood of her jacket over her curls.

She scanned the windows of the shops that lined the street with interest. Many were darkened, but an impressive variety of restaurants - from a sub shop to a high-scale French restaurant - were still lit and doing brisk business, judging by the full tables and crowded street. She wondered how things would change in the summer, when students left town and tourists flooded in.

"Similar numbers, probably," she muttered. Maggie – her closest friend and neighbor - had professed her love for the town when she'd come to watch Demi. She even seemed to wish she was coming with her, but Charis had giggled, reminding her of the Wolfville cottage they all visited regularly.

"Oh, but that's way out there by the wineries," she'd said, waving the comment away. "It's different."

She's right, Charis thought as she reached a four-way-stop and pressed the walk button, her eyes on the corner café across the street. A wooden sign hung above the door, rocking back and forth in the wind. Margot had called the place, "The Merchant," and said it was on the corner of Main and Axemen Way. *That's got to be it.*

She was relieved when the sign confirmed her suspicions, and even gladder to find Margot just inside the door, bent forward and studying the dessert selection intently. She looked up when Charis approached.

"Oh, good; you made it! I hate to make you drive here on such a rainy night!" she exclaimed.

Charis felt for a moment that the woman might hug her, but Margot smiled and lightly touched her forearm, instead. She smiled back. "Wolfville doesn't seem to mind the rain!" she gestured toward the window.

Margot looked toward the street. "It's a unique destination – the Town has strict rules about what businesses can operate, and even what the storefronts look like, but that's tempered by the variety and convenience offered. Business is good," she looked back at Charis, who nodded. "I am sorry I couldn't come to you, though. I had a late meeting with the board."

Charis shook her head and remembered her hood. She pushed it back and her curls sprung from their trap. "Oh, my God," she muttered, patting it down. "It's huge, isn't it?"

Margot laughed. "Don't worry. You look on-trend - natural is the way to go these days.

Charis rolled her eyes. "It's a good thing. I don't have any control over this mess!"

Margot laughed again, then pointed at the desserts. "You need baked goods."

Charis frowned at the taller woman.

"What? They fix everything!" When Charis only grinned, Margot gestured toward the confections again. "Come on, it's my treat. And you'll be doing me a huge favor, because then I won't have to eat a giant piece of that black forest cake alone!"

Charis gave in with a giggle, and Margot clapped her hands, her eyes sparkling charmingly. "You'd get along well with a friend of mine, I think," Charis smiled, thinking of Maggie's brother, Max.

Once they had their mugs, they sat at a corner table by the window. Margot's eyes were on the server behind the cash, obviously eager for her cake.

"Long day?" Charis wondered.

Margot flicked her gaze toward her, then back to the counter. "Yeah, but I did get the chance to call Spencer." She looked at Margot again, folding her hands on the table as if to contain herself. "Peyton's brother?"

Charis nodded.

"He's doing a year in France," she went on, then frowned as she looked out the window, "Biology, I think," she shrugged. "Nice guy, and really concerned about Peyton. He says she's far too eager to please, especially when it comes to strangers." Margot paused, sitting back in her chair while the server placed her cake on the table, then followed suit with Charis's brownie.

They both dug in, moaning their approvals simultaneously, then laughing.

"This is amazing," Charis muttered.

"Told ya!" Margot beamed, then forked another bite into her mouth, a spot of whipped cream falling to her chin.

There was something so genuine – so real – about the woman. Charis felt herself relaxing in her company. "What else did he say?"

Margot paused, her fork still at the ready, and took a sip of her coffee. "He was planning on coming home -"

Charis interrupted with "No!" before Margot finished.

Margot raised a hand, smiling. "I told him to stay for now. I remembered what you said about having a feeling about Europe."

Charis exhaled. "He'll be of more use to us there."

"I thought so, too, though I do have the feeling we'll be joining him before this is resolved."

Charis paused. *She* is *intuitive!*

"What?" Margot knit her brows as she plowed back into her cake.

Charis shook her head. "It's just – refreshing – not to be the one making predictions all the time."

Margot smiled. "It's refreshing that you don't look at me like I'm nuts when I do make predictions."

Charis's curiosity piqued again, but she pushed it aside, determined to focus on business so she could get back to the farm with its stone hearth and her family. "My visit to the Center was interesting," she started, and Margot raised her eyebrows. "I spoke to a man who took Peyton's class. He described a short, well-dressed woman who approached Peyton after class. Apparently, she wore a hooded jacket, though, with a fur-trimmed hood. He was distracted enough by it not to note her features.

Margot frowned. "What would someone – especially a well-off woman – want with Peyton?"

"That's not as difficult to fathom as you might expect."

Charis pulled her phone out of her jacket pocket and scrolled through her open apps. "All you have to do is search for 'psychic medium' and you'll find Peyton Hale." She flipped it over for Margot to see when she found what she was looking for. "She has a prominent online presence."

Margot's eyes widened. "Oh, right! I did some online stalking of her after her mother came to see me. From what I could see, her search for others like her was an open one, and very public."

Charis nodded. "I stuck around to talk to another witness, named Jewel – she's on the spectrum too, incidentally – and she said a lot of Peyton's students had found her online. She had quite a following; not only by those interested in her gifts, but for her unique art, too."

"She's incredibly talented," Margot nodded, her cake seemingly forgotten for the moment, "and apparently sought-after by artists and art dealers, sure, but by a huge group of the general public as well, because her subjects are so... unusual."

"You don't hear of artists whose forte is drawing the dead very often," Charis grinned.

"Much less one who claims to draw from actual experiences with the ghosts themselves," Margot nodded, then paused, her eyes straying to the window again.

"What is it?"

"I wish I could have helped her more," Margot said quietly.

Charis sighed. "At least you were her friend."

Margot sent her a questioning look.

"I didn't even do that for her," she admitted, her cheeks heating up with shame.

Margot shook her head. "You knew her?"

"No, but I could have – *should have,* maybe. She contacted me, hoping to meet up so she could learn from me, and I turned her down," Charis lowered her eyes to her brownie, which seemed less tempting, now.

Margot patted her hand. "I'm sure you get those requests a lot. You can't blame yourself for assuming she was just like all the rest, probably wanting more from you than you had to give."

Validated, Charis met the woman's eyes again. "Thank you."

Margot smiled, pulling her hand back to her lap. They sat in pensive silence, Charis sipping her tea.

"Did they say anything else – the folks at the Arts Center?"

Charis nodded. "The woman – Jewel – she said Peyton would draw new people all the time. She'd sketch people she just met right away and kept a collection, like a visual story of personal interaction."

Margot perked up. "Yes! She drew me more than once while we were in school! She said it was part of her effort to get more comfortable with communication - a way for her to get to know people through her art." She frowned. "Do you think she could have drawn the woman?"

Charis shrugged. "I don't know, but it did raise that question and more."

"Right, like when *exactly* she disappeared. Did she even have time to draw?"

"And there's something else – the woman who worked there - they said she managed the place on weeknights when classes were in session - seemed less than eager to talk to me when I started asking tougher questions."

"Like what?" Margot folded her arms across her chest.

"Like when she locked up that night, and whether the place was empty or not when she did."

"Huh."

"She told the police the same thing, and her assertion that she couldn't exactly isn't suspicious, really."

"But you think she's hiding something?"

Charis nodded. "Her energy was buzzing when I talked to her that second time, and I had to *find* her. She made herself scarce after the first time we spoke."

"OK. Might be worth a second visit."

"I was thinking of visiting the cops, actually. Might be a more direct way to get the facts. Do you think you could convince Peyton's mother to pave the way for that?"

Margot nodded. "Maybe they – or Jane, herself - could help us look for any drawings she might have, too."

Charis smiled. "Exactly."

Margot nodded brusquely, then picked up her fork, her interest in her confection renewed. "I'll call her tomorrow."

Charis nodded. "There's more."

Margot looked up from her cake.

"I've been getting flashes. Pete, one of the students I talked to, mentioned that the woman had a British accent, so I'm not entirely sure I'm not projecting, but I've been hearing whisperings in my ear..."

"British?" Margot raised her eyebrows.

"Yep. And something else – it's a male voice I'm hearing." She glanced out the window, perplexed. "I don't see a woman at all."

"Your gifts are different than Peyton's. She talks to ghosts like they're here with us all the time, but doesn't make predictions. Not like you."

Charis waited, unsure of where Margot was going with this.

"But you see the dead, too."

Charis nodded. "Not quite as – *easily* - as she seems to, but yes. But I know they're ghosts. They appear differently, *feel* different than live people do."

"Whereas to Peyton, they're nearly interchangeable. She was *twelve* before she even knew they were spirits... and she's a smart woman." Margot said.

Charis frowned. "So?"

"The male voice you're hearing. Is it from someone dead, or alive?"

Her face cleared. "Dead. I never hear the living that way."

Margot smiled. "Then maybe there was someone else talking to Peyton after class – someone besides the short woman."

Charis folded her arms, now, impressed. "You're very clever."

"So they say," Margot let out a laugh.

"But how does that help us, besides opening up to the possibility that a woman *and* a man were involved? We don't even know the woman had something to do with her disappearance!"

Margot gave her an exasperated look.

"OK, *we* know, but that doesn't mean much when you're dealing with cops!"

"Every bit of information counts, Charis," Margot leaned forward again, her forearms on the table. "No detective could have solved the mystery of the only ghost I've ever hung out with."

Charis shook her head, still confused. She wasn't used to feeling behind. It was – refreshing.

"Let's find everything we can," Margot continued, her voice hushed, "and use it in ways no-one else can. If we're looking for *two* drawings, and find them, we have twice the information to give to Spencer, for example."

Charis exhaled, finally. Getting it. "If we know what they look like, what their surroundings look like – any aspect of their lives, he could do research there!"

Margot nodded. Her dark eyes shone. "Surely, when ghosts are involved in a crime, foresight and intuition are just as important as material evidence." She sat back, looking pleased.

"Not to mention the ability to interview *all* the suspects!" Charis giggled. "Dead or alive."

"So, we work with Jane to get access to Peyton's things. I can do that," Margot said with a decisive nod. "I want to update her, anyway."

"And we find out what we can from the cops. I know a couple," Charis nodded back, noting the satisfying sensation of puzzle pieces snapping into place.

Margot picked up her fork and held it upright. "To foresight and intuition," she smiled.

Charis was charmed. A little ball of excitement started a spin in her chest. "I don't think I've ever felt matched when – working," she wondered aloud, an unabashed smile on her lips. Then she raised her own fork, tapping it against Margot's. "To finding Peyton our own way."

Margot dug back into her cake with a fervour and shook her head. "My life is so weird."

Charis laughed, surprised once again. "Mine too," she muttered.

"At least we're not alone," Margot replied, her lips covered with cake.

And Charis felt, for maybe the first time ever, that the sentiment was true.

Chapter 14 – Double Dream

Charis realized she was dreaming right away. She was in an unfamiliar place and, worse, a body that was not her own.

Dreams orchestrated by ghosts weren't her favorite. Though they often taught her much, she had so much less control over the interactions when she was asleep. But finding herself in another body entirely was hands-down the worst. She was relegated to an observer; unable, for the most part, to make decisions at all. Save one – she could wake herself up, and she wouldn't hesitate if she had the inclination.

For now, though, I'll wait and see. If Peyton could benefit in any way...

She considered her surroundings as the person whose body she travelled in stepped forward – it was a barn of sorts – stables, if her nose proved right, but it was the fanciest animal shelter she'd ever seen. The scent of hay and horse was strong, but the floor was impressively clean and aside from the occasional stomp (no doubt from a hooved resident), the place was pleasantly quiet.

She halted at one of the gated corrals and watched a male hand reach out to touch a chestnut mare. The name "Oaken" sounded in her head as his lips whispered it. She felt it, but did not perform the action. The horse whinnied, seemingly pleased at the attention.

Charis focused on the hand outstretched in front of her. It was male, yes, but delicate, with long fingers immaculately kept. *Piano fingers*, she thought. A breeze from whence she'd come brushed over him, making his tawny arm hairs stand on end as his skin prickled with gooseflesh. Suddenly Charis had a view of the wide-open stable doors, through which walked a woman, smiling into the eyes of the body Charis inhabited with comfortable familiarity. Her movements were confident, lithe, and her smile was kind. As she moved closer, though, her eyes revealed something else – something which caused a heat to ignite deep in the man's body, and Charis's for the moment. And as the hand reached out in front of her again, this time to touch the woman's face, Charis knew it was desire.

The odd sensation of a body part she was, for the majority of the time, bereft of, hardening and straining against the man's pants had them holding their collective breath.

Huh – I do *have a bit of control,* she mused, wondering if the man's arousal had afforded it. And with that, she was suddenly ejected from the body, her gasp echoing off the walls as she travelled through the air, coming to a stop by the doors again, but above them, this time.

Neither the man nor the woman flinched as she gathered herself. "Hello?" she tried, her voice timid, but continued to go unacknowledged, though as the young man whose body she'd been thrown from embraced the blonde, Charis could have sworn his eyes flickered to hers over the woman's shoulder.

"Hello, love," the woman muttered, kissing him and then laughing, her hair waving in a gossamer sheet down her back. "Hmm, you're ready for me," she muttered, and Charis saw her reach behind the man, presumably to press him harder against herself.

The man groaned low in his throat and took her lips. When they parted slightly, he leaned into her ear and whispered something Charis couldn't make out, but this time, she was positive his eyes met her own.

"Who are you?" Charis demanded, but the man only continued to stare as he moved his mouth to the woman's throat.

The woman answered instead, unwittingly. "Oh, Enzo."

Charis frowned, aware in the moment that she was floating. An observant presence, it seemed, but one detectable by Enzo, whoever he was.

You know more than you're letting yourself realize, a voice inside her said and she wasn't altogether sure it was her own. She narrowed her gaze on the man's eyes again.

"Enzo?"

"Yes," he muttered into the blonde woman's hair.

Buoyed by success, Charis continued. "Is yours the voice I've been hearing?"

The man seemed unable to answer, a frown creasing his forehead.

"Do you know Peyton?" she asked instead, and he raised his head, then nodded.

Charis pulled back into herself a bit, eager to observe as he seemed to want her to, rather than interrupt the scene.

"Come," he said to the woman, taking her hand and crossing to a ladder. Charis, in her ideal position, was able to look into their destination easily. A hayloft.

"What if someone comes?" the woman asked, a touch breathless and smiling.

Enzo look over his shoulder from halfway up. "I'm very much hoping we both do," he grinned, and there was mischief in his eyes.

The woman laughed, then started up the ladder, but before she could reach the top, Enzo leaned over from his hands-and-knees position, saying, "Wait!"

She looked up at him quickly, her smile fading. "What is

it?" She scanned the building quickly, her fear evident.

Enzo pointed. "Bring that."

Charis saw a rope looped around a hook opposite them at the same time the blonde woman did. She looked back up at him, her expression a bit dubious, but jumped down, nonetheless. When she begun to ascend again, she met his eyes. "You know it scared me last time," she said quietly.

Charis's stomach clenched.

Enzo reached for the rope. "It's for me this time, Stepmother."

The woman paused her progress up the ladder, her jaw dropping dramatically. "Really?"

Enzo nodded. "Why not?"

The blonde giggled and continued up the ladder, with speed in her steps, now.

Stepmother? Charis noted, but there was no time to ruminate. The two were already tearing at each other's clothes.

"You can't ever tell him," the woman muttered between hungry kisses.

Enzo buried his face in her chest until it was completely hidden between the woman's breasts.

She used both hands to lift his chin and he gazed up at her, a foolish grin on his face making her laugh again. "Did you hear me, child?"

"I'm not a child," he frowned.

The woman's expression turned serious. "That I know," she confirmed, then bent to take his lips as she reached toward his pants. She pulled away again, though, her hand flat on Enzo's chest. "But he mustn't ever know."

Enzo looked exasperated. "He doesn't give a shit about

what I do."

The blonde frowned at him again. "He most certainly does, and he *definitely* gives a shit about what *I* do!"

"You mean *who*," Enzo countered, grinning. He kissed her again, making her moan against his mouth.

"What's her name?" Charis asked, her voice low, almost unwilling to interrupt.

"Candace," he breathed, and the woman answered with another moan.

"Your father never wants me like you do," she said as he pulled her pants down, then pressed her to her back so he could remove them completely. Her hands went to her breasts. "I think I know how your mother felt."

Enzo froze.

The blonde sat up. "I'm sorry. I know her death is still painful for you -"

Enzo sat back a bit, looking deflated.

Charis felt the atmosphere change, somehow. Felt it charge as his face reddened.

He was angry.

"Especially considering – well, how she found out about me -" the woman went on.

Charis cringed. Either the woman wasn't very smart, or she was *trying* to wind him up.

"Shut up," Enzo said, his voice flat.

The woman nodded, and Charis decided on the former. There was fear in her eyes.

"Lie back," Enzo ordered, and she did, her chin trembling slightly. But then Enzo changed his mind. "No. Get up."

Candace frowned, but complied, seemingly eager to please him.

Enzo looped the rope around his neck, his face deepening in color slightly as he tightened it. He held the lengths out to the woman and she took them dreamily, her eyes on his face.

Then, Enzo laid back and Charis winced at the sight of his naked body, save the boxers and pants that were still bunched around his ankles. She couldn't help but notice, though, that he was no longer aroused.

"Suck it," he demanded, and Candace got to work, but soon he pulled her face up to look at his. "Pull," he said, taking her hands in his and yanking on the rope ends. He grunted as his head jerked forward, but his reaction didn't end there. His manhood was growing again.

Charis fought the discomfort that threatened to overwhelm her. To ease it, she resolved to change her viewpoint, and as soon as she thought it, she found herself behind Enzo in the hayloft, the blonde facing her but not seeing.

She looked like she was flirting with crying. "I – don't want to hurt you," she whined, her chin trembling.

"Now who's the child," he jeered, his voice a low growl.

Candace hardened her face, then straddled him, easing down on his hardness until her eyes rolled back in pleasure. Until Enzo grasped her hands again, demanding.

And she opened her eyes. "You want me to pull?"

He nodded. Charis could see his cheeks were nearly purple, and his breath was coming in rasps.

She tugged, hard, her face transformed with how it empowered her.

Enzo groaned in a mixture of pain and pleasure, grabbing her hips and thrusting upward.

She gasped, throwing her head back and unconsciously letting the rope go slack.

Enzo raised a hand to his neck suddenly, gasping as he tugged at the bindings.

The woman opened her eyes to half-mast, but they widened as soon as she did. "Oh!" she gasped, working to help him loosen the loops.

As soon as he could speak, he said, "That was so good. I nearly passed out."

Candace stopped moving.

"Don't stop," Enzo panted. But he reached behind himself with the lengths of the rope ends, and fastened them in tight knots around the post he reclined against

She started again, slowly, and building the rhythm as Enzo arched beneath her. Then he sat, the rope going taught as he strained against it

"You want to know why my father never wants you like I do?" he asked, grunting between groups of words, and Candace slowed a bit. "Don't stop!" he demanded.

Charis felt herself cringe back, but her eyes remained on the woman's face. *For Peyton,* she thought, and held on.

Candace nodded as she picked up the pace again.

"Because he doesn't want *you;* he wants little *boys!*" Enzo finished, then laughed, but it was choked and sad and not a little frightening.

Charis saw the woman's eyes widen, but thought there was more confirmation there than shock. She shook her head, even as Enzo grasped her hips and took over the motion of their thrusting, then flipped her to her back, the rope twisting as she let out a squeal.

"It's *me* he wants," he said, and there was rage behind his words. His face was an inch from hers, still a deep red, but more menacing, as though his father's crimes were her fault. "They *all* want me!" he bellowed, then thrust into her a final time, powerfully, and fell on her, crying as the rope slackened.

And she cried, too.

But then two things happened at once: the stable doors opened, and Charis felt a pull from behind her. Her shell, missing her.

She surged forward, fighting the pull. *Not yet!*

"Enzo?" The squat woman in the entrance called, and the couple beside Charis froze, their eyes widening as they looked at one another.

Enzo put a raised finger slowly to his lips and the woman nodded, then they inched their way apart, he trying to loosen his paraphilic noose and she reaching for her blouse.

The short woman stepped further inside, her eyes narrowing as she scanned the place.

Charis studied her stubby features, but her eyes stopped on her nose, then bounced to Enzo's. They were the same.

Another pull from behind, this one more forceful, escalating to intense nausea when she refused it. *I have to go back!* she thought desperately, but found herself in front of the woman with piggy features, instead. Panicked, she took in everything she could – her curls, the same tawny shade of Enzo's hair. Her eyes an unremarkable hazel-green.

A name, I just need her name! she begged inwardly, her eyes going to the hayloft, again, but Enzo and Candace were quiet, still.

But there was someone else.

She spotted a figure over the woman's shoulder and

snapped her gaze to it. A woman – it was difficult to gauge her age. Her face was smooth, and her dark hair carefully combed. And she stood awkwardly in the doorway, her puzzled eyes on Charis, only.

"Who are you?" Charis cried out, feeling her hold on this level of consciousness fade, seeing the woman's mouth move without sound as the woman directly in front of Charis turned her eyes to the hayloft.

She looks suspicious – she knows! was the thought Charis brought back to wakefulness with her, rocking forward forcefully as she came back to herself.

And then she vomited loudly over the side of her bed.

Chapter 15 – Peyton's Side

Peyton bolted upright in her bed, Charis's name still on her lips, and swooned as an intense wave of nausea rolled over her.

She clutched her stomach, the dregs of the dream still filtering through her mind like clothes on a clothesline in the breeze. Constance was there. She was sure it was how she found Enzo and the blonde – their stepmother, she now knew – together. Just before Enzo – but then there was Charis, as well. The psychic she'd found online and wrote to. She'd studied photos of her, then she'd drawn her. Her features were memorized, even though the psychic had refused her.

And there was the blonde woman, with Enzo, of course. No surprises there.

But the ghost that had led Constance to the barn had been.

She wondered if Charis had sensed her – the one that had pulled Constance out of bed, ever-whispering in her ear, and had stood at her shoulder, guiding her.

The ghost that could only have been Constance and Enzo's mother.

Chapter 16 – Calling Jane

Margot closed her eyes, taking a measured breath as the woman at the other end of the line cried.

"Ugh, I'm sorry," Jane muttered, then sniffled. "I just – I'm so grateful to both you and Charis for working on this for me. I feel like the police aren't getting anywhere."

Margot tried to temper her emotions for the moment, though the woman's desperation was painfully intense. She'd had to learn to separate herself from the emotions of others since her encounters with Wren when she was a teenager. She'd always been empathetic, but time and experience had taught her that sometimes, actions had to take precedence if anything was to be accomplished.

In other words, she liked to get shit done.

"That's because, if Charis is right, we're dealing with rare circumstances. One of the perpetrators is foreign. We suspect she's taken Peyton overseas – and the other person involved wouldn't be considered a likely suspect in *any* jurisdiction."

"Because he's dead?"

"Correct."

There was a pause. Margot could hear the woman wiping at her face (and consequently the phone) with something.

"You say the psychic – Charis – you say she dreamt about the circumstances of the ghost's death, right? Nothing about how Peyton was taken?"

"That's right; she doesn't have a lot of control over what

information the dead impart, and mostly their intentions relate to their own demise."

"Of course," the woman didn't sound surprised. It made sense, considering Peyton's experience with ghosts.

"But she did see a woman in the dream who knew her name. She suspects it was Peyton."

"But – oh, God. That doesn't mean she's -"

"No! I'm sorry; no, of course not. In fact, given Peyton's abilities, I think it suggests she's very much alive, still, and trying to make contact."

"You think she entered Charis's dream intentionally?"

Margot paused, thinking. "I don't know. But I think it would be OK to allow ourselves a modicum of comfort that she *seemed* to show up independently."

"And she knew Charis."

"Right. Charis has confirmed that Peyton has contacted her in the past, so that would make sense."

Jane sighed. "She was on an endless search for people like her."

"I remember."

"You're a good friend to her."

"I should've kept in touch," Margot said, and her eyes filled with tears of regret, despite her intent to stick to business.

"Don't blame yourself, Dr. Francis."

"Margot."

"Margot. Don't blame yourself. Peyton wasn't the easiest person to keep in contact with, even for her family."

Margot sighed, then shook herself, mindfully avoiding

the impending funk that hung like a pall over the conversation. "We need your help, Jane. Charis and I have mapped out some next steps, and I hope you can facilitate them."

"I'll do anything I can!"

"One of Peyton's students mentioned that Peyton tried to draw everyone she met?"

Jane laughed. "Yes! But she's had to narrow it down over the years. Now she draws people that 'interest' her."

Margot frowned. "And who interests her?"

"I wish I could give you a clear answer on that. She says she draws people she gets a feeling about – especially those who've affected her as a person, or *will* affect her." The woman made a sound of frustration. "I know that's not terribly helpful."

"No; it could be. At this point, *anything* could be. But Charis and I want to follow up on this. I'm thinking the woman she talked to after her last class – the one nobody recognized – could have fit into that criteria."

Jane gasped. "Why didn't I think of that? She may have drawn her before she was taken!"

"Don't get your hopes up too high. We still aren't sure exactly when she was taken – or from where. If she left the Center that night, intent on drawing the woman at home, she mightn't have had the chance."

"Oh, but she wouldn't have! She would have done it right away, so she still had the feeling – the *energy* – of the woman! That's what she called it!"

"OK; then we need to get into the Center."

"And – oh, I can't believe I forgot until now, but Clara – the Class Manager for the Community Arts Center? She called yesterday, asking me what I'd like done with Peyton's supplies!"

Margot smiled as her stomach did an excited roll. *Amazing how things work themselves out.* "What did you tell her?"

"I told her I'd come get them on the weekend. I can't get to Halifax before then, but if you and Charis want to go instead, I'll call her and let her know."

Margot paused, biting her lip.

"Dr. – Margot?"

"Yes, sorry. Charis mentioned Clara. She got the feeling the woman was less than eager to talk to her."

"Oh – I would hope she's not hiding something!"

"I don't think it's as sinister as that, but it might be best not to mention Charis to her."

"Right! I'll just tell her a friend of the family – you – will come pick her things up."

Margot nodded, grateful for the woman's willingness to prevent any glitches. "Perfect. Give her my name and number, if you like, and maybe Charis won't go in with me at first. We'll gauge things when we get there."

"When do you think you'll go?"

"Soon. I'll keep you updated. But there's something else. We'd really love to see *all* of her drawings. Do you think we could get into her apartment, too?"

"Of course. The police have already gone through it; they took her laptop. I was surprised they didn't take more. When I asked about it, they said they might need to later, depending on what they learn."

"Have they asked that her things not be disturbed?"

"Not really. They just asked that nothing was *taken*. And that I stay at the ready to let them back in, should they need."

"That's fine; we might snap some pictures, but we shouldn't need to take anything. But her place is in Halifax, right?"

"Yes; you could come get the key from me before you go."

"Thank you, Jane. I hope we turn up some clues."

"Thank *you*, Margot. I have the feeling you already have."

Chapter 17 – Recon, Take Two

Peyton was already awake when she heard the door unlock for the second time since Enzo had mastered it. She sat up in bed, her eyes going to the door, but it remained shut.

She peered into the darkness. She'd been pulling the shades over the windows since the first night she'd ventured out – she'd had a hard time sleeping since. And there were new noises since the Everleigh patriarch had returned. Different footsteps, a new voice, strange clanking in the walls as different water pipes were used, perhaps in the man's *en suite*. But Peyton's realization of his presence stopped there. She hadn't caught sight of him despite long hours sitting by the windows, her eyes on the trees as she thought of home.

Besides being a little more distracted during tea, Constance seemed her usual self. And Enzo – well, the difference in him was best measured in his absences. They were more frequent now, and when he did appear in Peyton's loft, he was often only a shadow. It was a stark change from his typical attention-seeking ways, and Peyton wasn't sure she preferred it.

It was as though the entire household was holding its breath, tiptoeing around until it could relax back into its routine, whatever that might be.

And then there had been the dream.

Peyton had recognized the twins' mother right away. Her energy would have been enough, probably, even without the familiarity of her visage. But thanks to the painting on the staircase wall, her tightly pulled-back hair and sharp features gave her away. The way Constance had woken to the woman's presence *was* shocking, though. She was completely unsurprised.

Did the woman whisper to Constance in life as well as in death? In all hours of the night? Did she lead her to reveal secrets she'd regretted taking to the grave? If so, why?

She'd come out of the dream with more questions than she'd ever thought to wonder about the former matriarch of the household. And something told her that the affair between Mr. Everleigh and Candace wasn't the only reason for the woman's suicide.

She startled when Enzo appeared at the end of her bed, a solid object in the dark. "Enzo?"

He placed a hand on the foot of the bedframe and leapt over it, landing heavily on the mattress.

Peyton squinted into the darkness, then turned and clicked the bedside lamp on when she continued to be unable to make him out. But when she looked back, she wished she hadn't.

Enzo was solid, but skewed, his physical features stretched and smeared as though someone had ran a hand through his paint, unhappy with their work.

"What's wrong?" she breathed, aware of the anxious hammering of her heart.

"I don't know why I'm here," he replied, but the odd, smeared mouth only pulsated while his hollow voice echoed around her.

Peyton took a steadying breath.

"I don't want to be here anymore," he went on, his words escalating in pitch and volume, and then he surprised her again by crying pitifully, the echoes reverberating off the walls in a way that made Peyton's arm hair stand on end.

"I'm so sorry, Enzo," she tried, terrified to say the wrong thing.

"Why should I stay?" he asked, but the question wasn't for her. Enzo's form raised its head up and back as he gestured at the ceiling. "And how can *he* live on? After – everything!" The shape crumpled into a ball, losing any semblance of human form, yet still emitting tortured sobs.

"What happened to you?" Peyton wondered aloud, wanting to do something to comfort him – to pat his shoulder or touch his hair – but unsure of how, given her own awkwardness. Not to mention the fact that Enzo was only a pulsating blob in that moment.

"He hurt me," his voice was quiet now, in her ears only. And then came a deafening roar that had the blob transforming to shadow and whizzing through the room, and had Peyton covering her ears.

"I *hate* it when he's here!" the ghost cried, ricocheting off the ceiling and then bouncing off the dining table in the corner. Peyton sucked in her breath as he careened wildly, finally smashing against a window, the shade clattering against the glass.

He rebounded clumsily, then disintegrated into nothing in midair with a howl.

The silence that ensued pounded in Peyton's ears. Her eyes widened as she got out of bed, her gaze on the window shade that was still moving in the darkness. She was positive she'd heard a crack, but before she could reach it to find out, there was a crash behind her and the light went out. She whirled, a yelp escaping her.

Silence.

"Enzo?" she called, her voice small. She could just make out the lump of fallen bedside lamp on the floor, the filament of the bulb still glowing orange.

The crying sounds were back, but the ghost sounded more than pitiful, now. He sounded... defeated.

"I'm going to turn the light on, OK?" Peyton said as she started toward the door, her hands held out in front of her, but something stopped her. He was suddenly there, and her hands were engulfed in the warm, vibrating presence of him. She let them drop, grimacing at the pins and needles feeling of him. "What?"

"You need to find her journal," he said.

She shook her head. "But, your father -"

"He's asleep."

"But if he -"

A blast of heat went through her. "Don't! He's *shit*, do you hear me? I don't care if he wakes up! I don't care if he finds us! Constance started a new journal today, and I don't know where she hides the old ones. You need to try and find it before she puts it away! Maybe she hasn't hidden it yet -" his voice trailed off.

She felt his presence fade, the air around her cooling instantly.

And then there was a crack of light as the door was opened, creaking a little on its hinges.

Peyton stepped quickly to it, saying, "Shh!" She grabbed the edge of it, stopping it midway and then freezing. Listening.

"I won't let him find you," came Enzo's voice again, but from the hallway, this time. Peyton leaned around the door and was surprised to find him on the other side, smiling a bit sheepishly. His feet were solidly on the ground, his hands in his pockets, his form very much the one he'd taken in life.

"I know you need me to find - something. The alarm

code, and, and whatever else I need to help you."

"To help us both," he corrected.

Peyton nodded absently. "But we need to be *careful,* Enzo! If he finds us – or *she* does – then something bad will happen to me, I'm sure of it. Which means your problem will remain unsolved."

Enzo's expression cleared as his eyes darkened. "You're right. I'm sorry. I just -" he looked at her beseechingly, his hands splayed out, "when he's around, I lose control."

Tears prickled in her eyes, partly for herself and partly for him. "No kidding!" She gestured back into the room. Then she sighed, letting her hand drop as she noticed the pained expression on the ghost's face. "Hey - I'm going to do everything I can to help you, OK?"

He bowed his head, his shoulders shaking.

"But if I don't survive this, neither of us will get what we need." She wasn't sure she'd gotten the sentiment right, but she forged ahead, regardless. "You need to trust me," she added, and he raised his head, nodding.

"You're right."

She smiled. *Thank God.* "Now, let's go find that journal."

He flickered out of view just as a grateful smile touched his lips. Peyton started down the hallway, padding as lightly as she could in her sock-covered feet. She became aware of the chill in the air and peered down at her legs. "Ugh," she groaned quietly. She'd neglected to put pants on in all the confusion. *This'd be a great way to get caught by Mr. Everleigh,* she thought, but shrugged as soon as the thought was complete. *I suppose it's only one small detail in the overall scheme of things though,* she figured. *I found out a stranger was living in my loft when I caught her prowling the hallways at night* would surely be as shocking as if the words, *in only her underwear, a Pixies t-shirt and socks* were tacked onto the end of it.

"Come on," Enzo's hushed words came up to her from the landing, and she pressed onward, the sound of her quickened pulse rushing in her ears.

She glanced at the painting of the Everleigh parents as she passed it, if only to confirm it was the woman she'd seen in her dream, but Enzo was beckoning her forward impatiently, the only visible parts of him an anguished face and the hand which motioned for her to speed up.

"OK, OK, sorry!" she uttered under her breath, and he was ahead of her again, a head and both arms floating as he glided into the right wing where tea was performed every day, and where Constance slept.

Or sits awake, waiting, Peyton's thoughts countered her own assumptions, but she shook them off. She had no time to indulge in catastrophizing, just then.

She glanced into the tearoom as they passed it. The silver, white and blue tones practically glowed in the dull light from the night sky. The effect was enchanting – the intricate scrollwork at the top of the walls, the empty chairs lined up, just so, and the curtains drawn to let in the light. A fantasy dollhouse setting, or fairy tea room – either option just as fanciful as the other.

But there was an eerie feeling to it, too. The table set with carefully-folded linen napkins, their silver patterns shining in the moonlight, the ornate tea set and tiered sandwich trays empty, but proudly at the ready. It was all too easy to imagine them full of steaming tea and petit-fours, but the image was haunting, juxtaposed as it was against the darkened room and lurking shadows in the corners.

It felt *expectant*, rather than inviting.

Peyton shivered involuntarily and tore her eyes from

the room. Enzo hovered by a door at the end of the hallway, looking back at her impatiently.

"Sorry!" she whispered again, though her own ears were the only ones close enough to perceive it.

"Come," he beckoned her forward again, then went straight through the door, making Peyton stop in her tracks, just for a second. Silvery wisps of him lingered on her side, as though the door had filtered his form and left the dregs behind.

His head suddenly appeared through the door and Peyton had to clasp her hands over her mouth to keep from screaming. He frowned at her, shaking his disembodied head, then looked toward the door handle, his eyes tilting unnaturally to the diagonal. Then he was gone again.

Peyton let her hands drop slowly, panting. But she only gave herself a second, lest her lack of action trigger another appearance through the door.

The door was unlocked. It surprised her, but only because her own door had been such a solid barrier to her – until Enzo had learned to unlock it, of course. But even then, it did not represent freedom. The dangers of her passing through it loomed as menacingly as if she stayed put, passively awaiting the determination of her future.

Enzo was bent low over Constance's sleeping form. Peyton held her breath, noting the soft snores that came from the woman's throat. Wondering at the conflicting emotions flitting over Enzo's face. There was sorrow there, certainly, but anger, too.

He turned his gaze to Peyton, though he remained bent at the waist. It was an odd effect. He pointed to the bedside table.

Peyton tiptoed to it, her eyes on Constance again. Her

busy brain tried to calculate the risk of her actions, but she halted the visions of what *could* happen before they were fully conjured. She couldn't turn back, now.

She spied a journal right away and flicked her gaze to Enzo's. He shook his head, his lips pressed together, then pointed to the drawer.

Peyton paused. How could he be sure this wasn't the journal they needed? Before contemplating it further, she picked it up and flipped through the pages. Enzo's rage was palpable – a prickling heat – and she raised her eyes to his again just as she realized the book was mostly empty.

Of course he knew this was the new one. He had to have been watching her to know she started it.

Sorry, she mouthed at the frowning ghost, then replaced the journal as quietly as she could manage.

Constance rolled in bed, muttering unintelligibly as she faced the wall. Both Peyton and Enzo froze, watching her with wide eyes. Finally, Enzo stood upright and pointed to the drawer again.

Peyton nodded, then crouched, studying the handle before pulling it. Entreating it to be silent. It complied, but there was nothing to be done about the sound of wood against wood when she pulled the drawer toward her. She halted when it was only partially open, her eyes going first to Constance's figure, and then to Enzo's eyes. He looked exasperated. She wondered what he was like in life – whether he suffered the trials of others' failures to meet his expectations as frequently. She thought maybe he did.

The ghost studied the partially-opened door, then raised a finger, meeting her eyes again. She sat back, frowning, but didn't wonder long. Enzo flickered, then transformed, his presence shrinking to a ball of light that would fit in Peyton's palm, should it need to. She felt her jaw drop. Enzo was proving himself to be a versatile spirit. She'd witnessed similar transformations, but none as varied and surprising as Enzo's bag of tricks was becoming.

Suddenly, he whizzed into the drawer, the room darkening slightly, and then he reappeared beside her, back to himself. He shook his head.

It wasn't there.

Peyton scanned the room. A wardrobe filled much of the space on the wall opposite the bed. To its left, a heavily-curtained window, and to its right, what appeared to be an antique makeup table. There was a small drawer there, but Peyton had a hard time picturing an old journal inside, especially if Constance hadn't put it in the more obvious drawer of the bedside table, on top of which the new journal sat. She looked to the doorway, then to the open closet just behind her. Another bureau filled the corner between, the surface of which was more cluttered than the other furniture of the room.

Peyton stood. The closet seemed a plausible place to hide a collection of journals, but she was reluctant to start rummaging in there without a light source. She glanced at Enzo. His little ball of energy hadn't cast enough light to guarantee helpfulness, and she was much more likely to stumble over stored items in the darker room off the main one. She shook her head. Enzo watched her, unmoving. He seemed - distracted.

She walked instead to the bureau and was instantly glad she did. It looked more *used.* The objects on top included a charging phone and an open jewellery box, and to the delight of Peyton, a small stack of books. Enzo appeared at her shoulder. His energy felt strange.

She sent him a questioning look.

"He's awake" Enzo whispered, and Peyton froze, her ears pricking up for any sound.

"No, it's OK! He's still in bed – but not for long. Hurry!"

Peyton couldn't make herself move. "How do you know?"

He rolled his eyes. "I can feel him."

She nodded, then went back to the stack of books. Only one spine bore no title – no author's name or publishing-house masthead, either. She went for it, pausing when the sound of it sliding from between the other books raised a warning. She looked back at Constance. She hadn't moved.

"I don't know how she reads so much," Enzo murmured as Peyton went back to her work, slower, this time. "It's not like she's *learning* anything from what she reads," he finished, a distasteful note to his words.

Peyton flicked her gaze along the spines that sand-wiched the book she was easing from its spot. *Little Women* was there, with *The Princess Bride* and *Awaking the Giant Within* flanking it. A surprising combination, perhaps, but did nothing to convince Peyton of Enzo's observation.

After several more moments of painstakingly careful maneuvering, the book was finally freed of its place in the pile, and Peyton sent a happy grin to Enzo. He was already at the door, though, motioning her out.

No time for celebration, she thought, then paused again, thinking to open the book in her hands, just to make sure it was the retired journal.

"Peyton!"

She jerked her gaze to Enzo, her heart fluttering.

"That's *it*! Come on; you have to get back!" He gestured impatiently with his arms. "You have to trust me, too!"

She nodded, tiptoeing to the door and slipping through, closing it quietly behind her.

A surge of triumph shot through her as they traversed the hallway, but Enzo hurried on, oblivious. Peyton reminded herself to be careful, listening for sounds beyond her soft footfalls.

And there was something; she heard it as they reached the landing: a creaking from the wing opposite, and then footsteps. Peyton's eyes widened at Enzo, whose expression was panicked.

"*Go!*" he cried, motioning her to the stairs, and Peyton fled, the not-so-distant sound of a door opening in her ears.

She nearly tripped halfway up, and was only able to partially muffle the resulting high-pitched yelp that came from her throat. "Shit!" she gasped, then redoubled her efforts as the sound of footsteps grew louder.

She was using all three free limbs – the fourth carrying the journal – by the time she reached the hallway to the loft, and gasping for air in her terror.

"Quiet!" Enzo demanded, his voice in her ear, but his form nowhere to be found. "Don't move!"

Peyton sat against the wall, pulling her toes back from view of the landing below, and waited, hardly breathing, her lungs burning for air.

She felt Enzo beside her - a heavy presence, but invisible, still.

The footsteps reached the landing, then paused.

Peyton squeezed her eyes shut, but immediately reopened them, mindfully. She needed to see what fate was coming. And she did. She watched the back of the man's head as he crossed to the wing opposite, from which Peyton had fled only moments earlier.

She leaned forward slightly, wanting to memorize him before he was out of view, but she caught only snippets of detail. Pinstripe silk pyjamas, slippers, and a head of grey hair. The man was slim but broad-shouldered. And there was none of the menacing presence she'd expected. His painted visage was more threatening.

Still, her discovery, especially by the man himself, would surely spell disaster. As soon as he was out of view, Peyton started crawling toward the loft door.

The man's voice caused her to freeze, his words wafting up the stairs. "Was that you, Constance?"

Peyton gasped. He'd heard her cry out on the stairs.

Enzo's voice was in her ears again, his presence pushing on her back. "Go, Peyton! Now!"

She went.

She reached the loft doorway and crawled through it, then stood, closing the door carefully, a pained expression stretching her face.

She backed away from it, becoming aware of the sallow early-morning light that brightened the sides of the window coverings.

The lock clicked, and Peyton nearly wet her pants, but then Enzo was there, his back against the door and his eyes on her. "It's locked," he gasped. He tilted his head to the bed and muttered, "Go!"

The footsteps became louder as she pulled the covers up to her neck.

"Oh, no!" she whimpered.

"Shh!" Enzo was beside her suddenly, hissing into her ear and clamping a ghostly hand over her mouth.

Peyton writhed, pushed beyond her fragile comfort zone, but then froze again.

There was a voice.

"Enzo?"

Enzo froze, too.

The man's voice was at the door of the loft. Tentative, but clear.

"Son, I'm so sorry," it said, and Enzo's rage sizzled.

Peyton thrashed again, the heat of his hand on her face nearly unbearable.

"I know you won't forgive me, but I needed to say it," the voice came again, and after a few agonizing seconds, the footsteps started up again – this time, fading down the hallway.

Enzo released her and Peyton bolted upright, gasping and crying, her face in her hands.

Enzo threw the covers back frantically, his hands on the mattress, first patting, then feeling in long swipes for something. Peyton let her hands fall to her lap, watching him, bewildered. Finally, he brandished the journal with a glow of triumph in his eyes. Peyton couldn't remember bringing it to the bed with her, but she must have. She eyed it suspiciously, half terrified it would prove to be the wrong book, half uncaring.

She was drained and well-past shaken.

But Enzo opened it, hissing a barely-contained, "Yes!" when the well-used pages came into view. He raised his eyes to Peyton's, pure joy transforming his features. But his smile faltered immediately. "Oh," was all he said, his gaze fixed on the lower half of her face.

"What?" Peyton demanded, her fingers going to her mouth and chin and feeling a roughness there. And the skin was hypersensitive; even her light touch made her grimace. "What did you do?" she demanded accusingly, her voice low, before stepping lightly to the bathroom and flicking the light on.

She gasped as she focused on her reflection in the mirror, her fingers going to her cheeks, this time. A defined handprint marred the lower-half of her face, making red and rough the skin, as though she'd been badly sunburned. Or branded. The imprint of Enzo's thumb reached along her hairline to the edge of her cheekbone. She looked ridiculous.

Her mind raced – how would she explain this to Constance?

Enzo appeared behind her, but she was unsurprised. She watched him study her reflection in the mirror, his eyes widening. But his expression changed quickly, his impish humour taking over. "Cool!" he exclaimed.

Peyton rolled her eyes and slunk past him, falling heavily into bed when she reached it, intent of sleeping as much of the day away as she could.

Chapter 18 – Fred

"How are the kids?" Fred asked.

Charis pinched the top of her nose, letting her eyes close. "They're really good. Thanks." She inhaled deeply. She'd mentally prepared to call her ex-fiancé – well, she'd tried to – but hadn't counted on being so affected by the sound of his voice.

"That's good. I – I think of them a lot. Of all of you."

Charis straightened, placing a palm on the cool marble of her kitchen counter and focusing her eyes out the window and on the barn where the goats were kept. Spring was definitely transforming the landscape. If she bent forward a bit, she could even make out the remains of Maggie's garden from the year before, bent and withered, but dark, having shed their snowy blankets.

"Char?"

She shook her head. "Sorry. Thanks – uh – for saying that."

He cleared his throat. "I still don't feel good about how I handled things."

"It's fine, Fred."

"No. I keep thinking of calling you. I'd love sitting down for a talk if you've got time."

"Haven't we done that already? More than once?" She sighed. He begun to reply, but she ploughed on, "I'm calling for another reason, anyway."

"Oh," he cleared his throat again, easily slipping into

cop-mode. "What can I do for you?"

She clenched her fists. Always the mask of professionalism. Fred was an expert. But today, she'd use it to her advantage. "An acquaintance of mine is missing – we believe she's been taken against her will."

Fred was silent.

"Anyway, I've been asked to help."

"You're very kind to agree."

"I'm hoping you can fill in some blanks."

"Ah," he sighed. "You know I'm bound to the rules here, Charis. Just because I have access to the file, doesn't mean I can just give out the information."

"The missing woman's mother called yesterday to put a note on the file, giving the officer in charge of the case permission to share information with me. Oh, and a friend; Dr. Margot Francis."

"Oh. In that case, I can take a look."

A surge of relief shot through her as she gave Fred names and dates. When he put her on hold, she exhaled.

"What doin', Mommy?" came Demi's little voice from behind her.

Charis turned and knelt, smiling into her boy's eyes. "I'm working, sweetheart." She touched the paper in his hands, bringing it up for a look. "What are you doing?" She smiled as she took in the drawing – stick figures and flowers, with trees in the background.

"I drawed us. And Daddy, too," he pointed at the tallest of the stick figures.

Charis smiled and kissed his forehead. "It's beautiful, Demi."

"Can I put it on the fridge? Wif the magnets?"

He loved the magnets. "Yep. Where's your brother?"

Demi shrugged, then turned to the fridge.

"Charis?"

She started at the voice in her ear, then wondered when Fred had come back on.

"Was that Dmitry?"

She prickled at his passive interest, but refused to let anger over the past color her purpose for the call. "It was. He's quite the little artist." She stood, smiling at the boy while he pointed proudly to his newly fridge-mounted drawing.

"He's special," Fred said.

She could hear the regret in his voice. Thought fleetingly about the conversation she'd had with a friend recently, about Fred having been seen with a young woman in a restaurant. It was fine that he'd moved on. *Good*, even. "Anyway," she said, her voice over-bright, "did you find the file?"

She heard papers shuffling in the background. Imagined him scowling at the contents.

"Yes. It's Henry's file, the note of permission is on top, plain as day."

"Cool. Can I have a copy, or..."

Fred laughed. "Sorry, Charis. Ongoing files can't be given out, not to anyone. If you want to look at it, you'll have to come in."

Charis rubbed her forehead, her eyes closing again.

"Or, you could ask what you need to know and I can give you the answer."

She perked up. "Oh! In that case, have you guys made any progress on the timeline? When Peyton is most likely to have disappeared?"

More shuffling of papers. "February 28th. Says here she taught her art class and then stuck around at the – says here, 'Community Arts Center, Halifax' - for a bit after, then went home."

Charis frowned. "You're sure she went home?"

"Says here the woman who runs the Center confirmed that she left on time, and that she saw her getting on a city bus."

"*That's* news," Charis muttered.

"Looks like the assumption is that she was taken from her apartment shortly after."

"How can they say that – couldn't she have been taken from her parking lot? Or even the next morning?"

Fred paused, then cleared his throat again. "Nope. Apparently there's some evidence that she'd packed some things – essentials. But all her electronic devices – phone, tablet, laptop, even her fitness tracker – were piled on the kitchen table as if to prove she didn't have them on her when they left. We see that a lot with kidnapping victims."

Charis pursed her lips as a vision flickered in her mind – two women, one in tears and following the shorter one's instructions. Peyton. "Any theories or leads on suspects?"

Fred chuckled. "I would have told you that first."

"Right." She bit her lip.

"I see we have her laptop, but looks like the search through it hasn't been completed. These things can take a while."

"So, what's being done now?"

He sighed as the paper rustled again. "It's hard when

there are no suspects. Looks like the folks in her apartment building have already been canvassed, and her students from class that night were interviewed. A couple of them saw the victim talking to a woman -"

"I know," Charis interrupted, "so, nothing's being done *now*, then?"

"They're going through the laptop, Charis. And Henry would be able to answer your questions better than I can."

"OK. Thanks."

"That's it?"

"Yeah, unless I can talk to Henry now?"

"He's out on a call, apparently. I'll update him on your call and have him get in touch if anything new happens."

Charis nodded, her thoughts jumbled. The progress – or lack thereof – wasn't promising. *Margot was right - police process isn't going to cut it, this time.* A thought occurred to her and she perked up. "And the laptop!" she said. "I would appreciate an update once it's been searched."

"I don't see that being a problem, but Henry'll probably have you come in for that. I know you, but he doesn't. For all he knows, you could be the perp, if there is one."

"There is," Charis stated, annoyed.

"OK."

She sighed again.

"Charis -"

"I don't want to see you, Fred. I'm not being hard. Remember, it was you who ended things. Unless there's something new to say, meeting up isn't going to change anything."

"Might heal some old wounds, though."

"Well, I don't need that; not now. I'm busy."

He paused.

"'Bye, Fred." She hung up before he could respond, but she looked at the screen for a long time afterward. Her and Fred's relationship had been so – promising! So comfortable. His betrayal hurt that much more because she'd let herself depend on the strength of it. On him. She had plenty of support. Greyson was as much a father figure to *her* as he was to Demi, and her neighbors weren't just neighbors. They all helped each other out as though they were blood-related rather than just united by circumstance. But she was lonely.

Working with Margot was the closest she'd felt to being understood – being *seen* – in a long time.

She gave herself a little shake, then dialed Margot. It was time to plan a trip to Halifax. With what she knew now, there was no question they'd need to visit both the Center and Peyton's apartment. And they'd need to find a way to corner Clara, because Charis had been right; the woman had been holding back. Maybe now that they could inform her that they were privy to the police file, she'd be more motivated to spill whatever she knew.

Chapter 19 – Constance: A Look Inside

Peyton sipped her tea and gazed out the window. The bleakness of winter seemed left behind as shades of green took over, brave shoots of grass and bright new leaves uncurling on the trees that lined the perimeter of the property. The sky was wintry that day though. No sign of blue. Just dull whites and greys – which happened to fit her mood perfectly.

Peyton *had* slept the majority of the day away after the last venture out of the loft. Enzo had woken her just before tea, angry and impatient. But Peyton cared little. She'd been pushed too far the night before, and her face bore a tangible scar.

Constance had recoiled when she saw her, but her reaction was far less dramatic than Peyton had been counting on. She'd merely taken a moment to gather herself, then asked, "Enzo?"

She hadn't even waited for Peyton to reply.

But today she'd woken early. Constance had stricken a note of urgency in her at tea.

"Father's been acting strange," she'd stated, almost convincingly casual. But she eyed Peyton for a reaction. "He says he heard someone walking about last night."

Enzo had appeared beside his sister before Peyton could answer. He put a finger to his lips.

"That's strange," Peyton had frowned, clutching her napkin in her lap. Lying had never come easy to her. But Enzo was a good teacher. "Is there anyone else in the house besides the family?"

Constance narrowed her gaze.

"And me, of course," Peyton added, trying a smile.

Constance shook her head, her nose in the air. "Were you up at all?"

Peyton pretended to think about it, then perked up. She could use this to her advantage. "Actually, something did wake me. I don't even know what time it was; it was still really dark, but something banged into one of the windows. A bird, maybe?"

Constance frowned. "An owl flew into one of the first floor windows years ago. Remember that, Enzo?" she looked over her shoulder toward the ghost, making Peyton gasp and Enzo back up a few paces. Constance looked back at Peyton. "What?"

"How did you know -?"

Constance shrugged. "I feel him when he's close. He's warm."

Peyton sunk back in her chair. It was true.

"I miss him," Constance added, her eyes distant.

Peyton watched Enzo's expression, which was unreadable. It often was when he focused on his twin.

Constance had come into the loft when she'd returned Peyton, heading straight for the cracked window and clucking her tongue. "What shall we do about this?" the woman had asked, her voice barely audible. But then she'd turned and fixed her gaze on Peyton. "I think you should always leave the drapes open on this one. If the surface is darkened, it seems more solid. No continuance into the room to confuse an owl," she ended with a tight grin, looking smug.

Peyton nodded. "What if it breaks?"

"It *can't* break," Constance had replied, stepping closer to Peyton with each word.

Peyton shrunk back as Constance continued past her and out the door. "No walking about the loft tonight," she called. "Father leaves again next Wednesday, so we'll have the window replaced, then.". She peeked around the door. "We'll have to put you somewhere a little – less comfortable – for a few days." She disappeared into the hallways again and shut the door quietly. Then locked it.

The lock had never seemed so final. Peyton wondered where Constance would put her – imagined dark, small rooms with no windows. There'd be no bathroom attached, no kitchen, certainly. Getting used to any new place was always a trial for her, but being downgraded in an already undesirable situation seemed impossible. She needed to speed things up.

Peyton scanned the loft for Enzo for the hundredth time that morning. He'd been absent since she'd woken and made her breakfast. She'd been sure he'd appear when she picked up the journal and took it to the dining table with her tea, but he remained out of sight. No shadows, even.

She let her eyes wander to the cracked window again. Her heart took off at a gallop at the prospect of further change.

Fuelled with a sense of urgency, she opened the journal.

She'd skimmed through it just after waking up, acquainting herself with Constance's writing style. The woman wrote religiously, very rarely missing a day, which offered some hope that she and Enzo would find details they needed, but the vast amounts of space she used made Peyton worry, too. Perhaps the one day she needed to read about – that of Enzo's death – wasn't even in the full journal. Perhaps the pages they were looking for were already hidden away.

But she'd breathed a sigh of relief at the first entry date: November. According to Enzo, he'd died just before Christmas.

Peyton skimmed the first several entries. Reading Constance's daily thoughts proved challenging. Her every impression – every unique thought or imagined enlightenment – were recorded in self-reverent detail. There was so much fluff that Peyton found it difficult to distinguish between Constance's thoughts on actual reality and the version of reality she seemed to construct for herself.

But there was a common theme. There was always Enzo. Constance wondered what Enzo would think about – everything! Her pain in his absence was constant. Every captured thought echoed her loss. Which confused Peyton, for hadn't Enzo always indicated his sister to be at the heart of his death?

Frustrated at her lack of progress, Peyton thumbed the pages, then closed the book. She pushed it away from her and stared out at the trees. Nothing moved. She inwardly remarked at her own version of reality. It had never been fully comparable to the average person's, but lately it was even further-removed. She wondered for a short, but frightening few moments, if her own perceived reality was any closer to the truth than Constance's.

Enzo suddenly appeared beside her, making her jump.

"You're not done, are you?" he gestured toward the discarded journal.

Peyton sighed. "No. Just taking a minute."

"What's wrong?"

She shook her head. "It's – it's not easy reading."

"Focus on what you need to find, Pey."

She giggled. Only friends and family called her that.

"What *are* you trying to find?"

She frowned. "The day you died."

Now he shook his head. "No. That doesn't matter as much as her entries about other people. She solves everything in those entries, I'm sure of it."

Peyton gave him a look of disbelief. "Do you already know? Are we just doing this to find tangible evidence?"

He shook his head again. "I promise I'm not wasting your time. We need to find out exactly how it happened. Exactly why. *Who* did the pushing."

Flashes of the dream she'd had – the one with Charis – came to her. The dream had ended before anything had happened – and she'd only followed Constance to the stables for the majority of it. She wondered what Charis's perspective had allowed her to see?

"And there's something else you're looking for," Enzo snapped her out of her reverie.

"The alarm code," Peyton remembered.

He nodded. "Yep. And that part's simple. Just flip to the back."

Peyton reached for the journal and complied, her eyes widening on the series of numbers. "That seemed way too easy," she said, her eyes on Enzo again.

"It *is* the easy part. The hard part comes before you have to use it. Memorize it, Peyton."

Peyton nodded, then looked back at him, newly suspicious. "Why do I have to memorize it? Can't I just rip it out?"

"Constance won't be in the dark about her journal's absence for long. That stack of books on her dresser is only what she's been reading this week. She'll store them all on the weekend."

Peyton let her forehead fall to her forearms, which rested on the table. "We need to return it," she muttered, miserable at the thought.

"Yep, so get reading, girl. We need to get it back tonight."

Peyton jerked her head up. "*Tonight?*"

Enzo shrugged. "And don't write any of it down; Constance is shrewd." He looked around. "You don't know how - observed you are." He gave her a sobering look.

She stood, her eyes darting to every corner of the room.

"There aren't cameras," Enzo laughed, then whizzed about the room.

"Stop! Remember the window!" she cried, rushing to block the fragile pane with her body.

He halted in front of her. "You wouldn't want to be leaning against that if it broke."

She gasped, further convinced by the concern in his eyes. She sidestepped him, folding her arms and gripping her biceps; a quiet attempt at self-comfort. "If not cameras, then how does she see me?"

Rather than turning, Enzo's eyes migrated to the back of his head, bulging out beyond his light hair grotesquely.

Goosebumps rose on her arms. "Enzo!" she cried, "that's gross!"

His mouth appeared, then, but all it could do was sputter on his hair.

"Turn around!" Peyton demanded.

He turned, but his nose was his only remaining feature. Exasperated and not a little unnerved, Peyton went back to the table, prickling at his continued laughter.

"Sorry," he appeared beside her, making her jump again.

She glowered sideways at him. "I have a code to memorize." She hated being purposefully rude. Much of her other life had been devoted to learning what others considered rude and avoiding it. Upsetting people on purpose seemed counterintuitive when she seemed to upset them unconsciously, just by being herself.

"You have a photographic memory, Peyton."

It was true. She sighed, closing her eyes and letting her head drop. "I'm tired, Enzo."

"I don't mean to annoy you. I'm learning so much about this new level of existence, thanks to you. You've opened my eyes to possibilities I wouldn't even have considered without you!"

She peeked at him. "Most ghosts just want to solve an issue before they rest." At Enzo's blank look, she continued, "To move on, you know? *Leave?*"

"I like to play," he smiled.

She bit her cheeks to prevent her own answering smile.

"Besides, as much as Constance pisses me off, I'm her twin. It feels wrong to go *anywhere* without her."

Peyton straightened, frowning at him. "It's not permanent, you know. Your separation?"

He flickered, then raised a hand, his features hardening. "Don't start that shit with me. You know I'm not going anywhere until -" he faltered, his eyes going to the windows behind Peyton.

She glanced over her shoulder at the landscape. Nothing had changed. She looked back at Enzo. "What exactly *do* you need? I mean, every ghost I've ever encountered wants his or her death *known*...or solved, if need be. So, I just assumed that's what you want, too."

He looked at her. "It is. I'm not exactly sure how it happened. I need to know. I need to know whether it was all her or not, and if it was, *why*?"

"Her – Constance, right?"

He nodded.

They sat in silence for some time, each at the mercy of their own thoughts.

"Because she's as joined to you as you her. It's why she brought me here, after all. She was miserable without you."

He nodded again. "She can't see me or hear me, but she can feel me."

"So, why would she be involved in any way with your death?"

"Exactly." Enzo's face revealed honest puzzlement.

"I understand," Peyton couldn't think of a better way to empathize. "Maybe she was just jealous. You were spending more time with -"

He nodded, interrupting. "That's what I've been choosing to believe. But it's not – it doesn't…" he grimaced in confusion.

"It just doesn't sit right," Peyton finished, and he nodded.

"I would say it was impossible if it didn't seem like the only answer."

"So, you have to find the real answer."

"Right."

She opened the journal again, motivated anew.

"Thank you."

She smiled at him.

"And what I was saying before about Constance knowing what you do up here?"

Peyton perked up at the reminder.

"I don't think I'm the only ghost hanging around."

Peyton's eyes widened. "Your mother! She was in my dream!"

He pursed his lips.

"She'll know I've gotten out!" Peyton gasped. "What if – what if Constance sees her – *hears* her?"

He nodded. "She knows things sometimes. Things I haven't told anyone."

Peyton gazed down at the journal. "Why? How?"

Enzo was quiet.

"What if she learns I've been out?"

Enzo shrugged. "I thought of that after last time, after Father nearly caught you."

"*Us*," she corrected.

"No," he raised his eyebrows. "It's *you* taking the risk. You who has the most to lose. So, I'm going to do everything I can to prevent your being found out."

"I can't go out again!"

"You have to. Once tonight and a final time to leave, for good."

Peyton pondered his words, staring blankly at the journal, then turned to the first page. "It's hard to read word-for-word," she started. Enzo laughed. "But I have to. I will. And I'll go out tonight." She met Enzo's eyes, then looked toward the trees, her focus on the little space where the driveway ran through - to salvation, she allowed herself to assume. It had to. "This needs to end, somehow."

"Thank you, Peyton."

She nodded. "Leave me for a bit, or be very quiet, Enzo. I need to memorize everything, not just the code."

He nodded, looking every inch a chastised, but eager child. He flickered out of existence.

"That was easy," Peyton frowned.

And suddenly he dropped onto the bed, smiling at her as he folded his hands over his stomach. "Don't mind me," he sighed, closing his eyes.

Peyton couldn't help but grin. Maybe he wouldn't have been so bad in life.

Chapter 20 – Art Center, Revisited

Charis peered down at her phone as it buzzed.

Margot: Come in. I can't find Clara and I don't know which classroom is Peyton's.

She clicked her seatbelt off and got out immediately, her mind on making a beeline to the empty classroom before Clara sussed out their presence – or hers, at least.

Margot had filled her in on her conversation with Jane. The manager of the Center hadn't seemed to care *who* came to get Peyton's stuff, as long as *someone* did. She'd advised Jane that the Center would be open until nine that night, used only by a meeting in one of the conference rooms and the cleaning staff. It had seemed perfect.

But Charis frowned as she entered the quiet building. If they'd been the ones to pick the time, the way it worked out would have seemed serendipitous. But it had been Clara who'd picked the night, reasoning she wouldn't have time to help them on the busier nights. Charis wondered, though, if the fact that it would be easier for the woman to hide in an empty building was a more likely reason.

She stopped just inside the doors, opening herself up. She felt energy from the left at the same time as muffled voices reached her ears. *The meeting.* She closed her eyes, reaching out for connections. Margot's energy surged in like water loosed from a dam. Charis smiled, but reached past it. *Hello.* Clara's energy was undeniable. She looked to her right. A darkened hallway ran the length of the building. *Her office must be down there.*

"Hey!" Margot peeked around the corner that rounded the hall to Peyton's old classroom. "I felt you come in! How'd you do that?"

Charis smiled and walked to the woman. "Did you find the classroom?"

Margot nodded, eyes bright. "It's unlocked; I figure we should go in and get started, seeing as nobody was here to greet us!"

"How'd you find it?"

"It was obvious -" Margot stopped, frowning. "Huh. I walked right to it."

"*That's* how I connected to you when I came in. It's all about connection; doesn't matter if you do it consciously or not. You're gifted."

Something like frustration tilted Margot's features. "Maybe. I just have no idea how to use it."

Charis sighed. She'd known it for a while, but her tendency to simplify had held her back. But there was no stopping this, and even more, part of her looked forward to working with the gifted woman she'd brushed aside in the past. "When we find Peyton, we'll have to do some training."

Margot's eyes brightened as she smiled widely.

"If you want."

Margot bent to hug Charis, laughing. "You're amazing," she said, sending shivers down Charis's neck as her breath passed over her ear.

She pulled away. "Tell that to my exes," she muttered, and laughed sadly.

"Maybe you're not picky enough," Margot mused, her

face serious again.

Charis waved the subject away. "Come on, let's do this before someone comes along."

Margot paused. "OK, but if you ever want to talk about it, I'm here." She turned toward the classroom before Charis could answer. "I don't have a lot of relationship experience, but I'm an expert at being picky," she continued, looking back over her shoulder.

Charis laughed. "I guess you could teach me a thing or two, as well. But it'll be a skill I'm not in any hurry to use."

They went into the arts room and stood side-by-side, both scanning it quietly. Margot pointed. "I'll look through the desk."

Charis nodded, her eyes still roving about the room. They stopped on a file cabinet opposite them. "I'm starting there," she pointed, too.

The two rifled through drawers, mostly quiet.

Charis chuckled, finally. "She's – well, at first glance she seems completely disorganized, but if you open her files, you see she's got a reason for grouping things – here's a file labelled 'Sparkles', which seems completely random, right? But, open it up and there's a table of contents listing the works inside – all extraordinary – by the artist students who've donated them."

Margot straightened, her hands still in the top drawer of the desk. "She had her own method in school, too. Nobody knew how she did it. Her work was all mixed up. Science with math, art with business. I asked her once how she studied. Know what she said?"

Charis shook her head.

"All the *real* files are in here," Margot smiled, pointing to her temple.

"Huh," Charis frowned.

"She said it didn't matter how she organized things on the outside," Margot shook her head. "A psychologist had called it photographic memory, but in my opinion, she's got both photographic and eidetic, and I'm not sure what else." She shook her head. "Fascinating." She bent back to her task, now tossing Peyton's personal items into the backpack they'd brought.

"Oh yeah; we actually have to move this stuff," Charis groaned.

"Just her personal things. Jane said we should leave anything that would be considered part of the class. They want to store her files themselves – so, what you're looking through will most likely stay here."

Charis nodded and went back to it, shuffling through folders labelled "head", "heart", "brains" and, oddly, "insect". She laughed. "I'm starting to look forward to getting to know her."

"She's really very cool. Different, you know? But in a way that teaches you something. She was always surprising me."

"Hm," Charis acknowledged, closing the top drawer. She sighed and opened the second.

"I'm a bit confused about your failed relationships," Margot stated, surprising Charis.

Charis rolled her eyes. "I should be able to predict what's going to happen before getting in too deep, right?"

"You've heard that before."

She laughed. "Yeah, from myself!" She looked up at Margot. "Love fucks everything up."

Margot burst out laughing. "Maybe that's why I'm so

picky. I like my life, just how it is."

Charis went back to the files. Tried to recall if she'd read anything about the woman's sexual preference in her research. She was pretty sure boyfriends had been mentioned in there somewhere, but had to admit she was getting - different - signals from her. It wasn't something she'd felt before, so she remained mindful not to try and categorize it. In any case, it wasn't awkward – quite the opposite. She felt she'd known the woman forever. Frowning over her thoughts, she shuffled absently through the drawer, then whooped in triumph, pulling a stack of blue files out from between the brown ones.

"What?"

"Meetings," she replied, brandishing the files as she turned toward Margot.

It took a few seconds, but Margot's face cleared, her eyes twinkling. "The drawings?"

Charis nodded. "The label makes sense, I guess. I just wouldn't have expected it."

"See?" Margot gestured in mock frustration.

She put the stack on a circular table in the centre of the room. "There are lots."

Margot sped her actions, tossing items into the backpack with barely a glance.

Charis laughed. "Pretty sure that stapler belongs here."

Margot peered into the bag, then shrugged. "How am I to know? Nobody met us at the door!"

It was true. Charis spread the files in a fan. "Seven files, with who knows how many drawings in each," she mused, wondering how many they'd find at the apartment.

Margot jogged lightly to the table. The two women exchanged a look.

"Theoretically, her last drawing should be the one we're looking for," Margot said, quietly.

Charis nodded. "Shall we?"

Margot nodded in turn and looked at the top-most file. "You do it."

And there she was: the woman from Charis's dream, with her stubby features and fluffy curls, staring back at her from the stack of drawings. The name "Constance" was written in the lower left corner, and Peyton's was in the lower right. "Shit," Charis breathed, "this is her."

"The short woman," Margot said, her voice almost reverent. "And – holy shit, is that her *name?*"

Charis looked at her. "I think so." She ruffled through the pages, stopping at one she recognized, and pointing to the name in the lower left corner. "Jewel," she said, her eyes on Margot's again. "That's one of her students! I talked to her!"

Margot's raised her hands toward the ceiling. "Thank you, Peyton!" She looked back at Charis. "We need to get this to the police."

Charis pressed her lips together, nodding, but reluctant to stop, now. She continued rifling through the file, but recognized nothing more. "These files – they're not strictly class-related," she looked sideways at the taller woman.

Margot smiled. "Agreed. We're taking them." She went back to the desk for the backpack.

Charis opened the second file and started through the pages. She opened up, asking silently for help. She gasped when one of the pages slipped from her fingers and fell to the ground, landing face-up.

"What is it?" Margot asked, rushing back.

Charis held a hand out to halt her before she was on the

picture. Margot skidded slightly in her heels. "It's him. The guy from my dream," Charis said, squatting to pick up the page. Margot came to stand at her shoulder, looking at the young man whose entire body was drawn.

"Weird. She seemed to mostly stick to faces," she murmured.

Charis pointed to the shadow beneath the man's feet. "He's floating, Margot."

"You can call me Margie," she whispered.

Charis looked at her. "That's unusual."

"Margie-Mae," the woman smiled.

"OK. Thank you. Um - this man is the ghost."

Margot nodded. "I know."

Charis looked back at the drawing. "She's quite good."

"I know."

Charis ran her thumb over the name in the lower left corner. "Enzo."

Margot nodded. "Constance and Enzo."

"Let's pack these away and finish up. We need to get to her apartment and then the police," Charis said, hurriedly stacking the files after placing the drawing of Enzo behind that of Constance.

"How are they related, I wonder?" Margot mused, already walking about the room, open backpack in hand.

"That's just it," Charis said. "I think they *are* related. Their noses – they're identical."

Margot gasped, thinking about her brothers. "Siblings."

Charis nodded, but her eyes were clouded.

They finished their work in silence, then headed to the

door, nearly giddy with accomplishment, but an older woman stepped into the doorway before they reached it.

"Clara!" Charis exclaimed.

Chapter 21 – Constance

It mostly happened at night. Mother would waken her just like she had in life, and Constance had never been alarmed. She and her mother were a team, working together. Taking care of each other. Mother's death hadn't stopped it. In fact, Constance *hoped* to be woken. Every night, she wrote in her journal and then lay down, focusing on the face of her mother, like a prayer.

Please come to me. I miss you.

The only difference now was how she looked. She'd never been beautiful. Her looks hadn't been a priority for her. It was a fact evidenced by her hardened features, tightly pulled-back hair and simple way of dressing. Always tight, always flawless – and endlessly severe. But when her body died, her mother's spirit seemed to have lost some of her self-imposed restrictions. Her hair frizzed every which way, partially escaping its prison of a bun and appearing delighted with its freedom.

She wore the nightclothes she'd died in: silk pajamas – navy, with a boxy, masculine style, beneath her old, familiar bathrobe. Not different, not at all, except that she was alternately dry and soaking wet. And there was blood more often than not. Sometimes just a few droplets at the edges of her sleeves, and sometimes as much as the water that dripped from her. Neither the blood nor the water left a puddle, though, so while it was terrifying at first, Constance quickly grew accustomed to it.

Mother had reasoned that no amount of effort to fix herself up could resolve the effect of her blood-drained pallor, for though she could change her appearance, the physical state she'd been discovered in was the easiest to show Constance. It was what she remembered most, so it was the easiest to accept, pleasant or not.

Constance was nearly twenty when it had started. Suddenly Mother – live, warm, solid Mother - was looking at her. *Seeing* her. Constance figured she was feeling guilty about all the years of neglect. Even when Mother had paid them any attention, Constance was always in the shadow of her twin. Enzo was the favorite of both parents. And the staff. And eventually, of their stepmother. Even Constance preferred her brother to any of the other available company of the house.

It wasn't that Enzo was perfect, or even extraordinary. Constance could only reason that his charm was founded on his being better than herself, in some way. She'd come to believe it by the time Mother seemed to remember she existed. She was already untrusting, already sad. She was suspicious of everyone who wanted anything from her, but when Mother started changing, she'd pushed that pain aside and instantly trusted. It felt so good to be noticed.

Mother had started small, finding opportunities to get Constance alone. They'd bake a cake or do a puzzle. Constance had never felt so happy. For a while, she could even ignore the fact that even though Mother was finally talking to her, she was mostly talking about Father and Enzo – and of course, money. Constance had never been interested in the business. As long as she was able to benefit from it, she was pleased to leave it to her parents. But Mother kept going back to it, kept talking about the future with a warning behind her words.

She started coming to her at night, when the household was quiet. She would shake her shoulder, whispering, "Wake up, Constance," and the two would roam the house. Mother would talk about her worries, saying Constance was her only friend.

"But Enzo -" Constance had replied, frowning.

Mother had shaken her head. "Enzo doesn't even know he is a threat to us!"

Constance remembered the first time Mother had revealed the secret of her ongoing angst. She'd leaned close, so close Constance could smell her skin, and some distant memory from her childhood tried to surface. She used to know her mother's smell well. But now, she'd almost forgotten.

"Your father will leave the business to your brother," Mother had whispered, fear behind her eyes. "Do you really want Enzo deciding your future? *Our* future?"

Constance had been confused. "Won't the business go to you?"

Mother had shaken her head, sadly, then muttered something about Father tricking her; cutting her off.

"But, why?"

Mother's eyes had flashed in anger. "It is the business of his family, Constance. You know that. And under certain – circumstances, your father and his *relatives*," (she said the word as though it tasted bad in her mouth) "are legally able to ensure that it continues to benefit the family."

Constance hesitated. She hated that look Mother got when she asked questions. That *are you stupid?* look. But she had to ask, "What circumstances?"

Mother had clenched her jaw, her dark eyes on her daughter's. "All you need to know is that he will make sure I don't get anything if we should – if things change."

"But, why?" Constance had felt the tears well in her eyes and fought to hold them at bay.

"He's no longer interested in holding this family together," was Mother's answer, and it shot fear into her heart.

Constance had never had a reason to question the stability of her lifestyle, much less the family itself.

So, she was recruited to her mother's mission of finding out what Father was planning. It went on for years, and even when Mother's motives seemed weak, Constance followed her, glad for the attention. Fearful of the change her mother kept reminding her was right around the corner.

She heard her parents arguing, sometimes. Mostly muffled, but loud, Father spewing words like, "insane" and "get help". It made Constance wonder if Mother had been mistaken all those years. Was it just fear, or was it real?

And then, things changed. Mother turned scatter-brained and scared, refusing to open up to Constance. She started focusing on Enzo again, asking question after question about her boy, who was a man, now, and working at headquarters. It was strange for Constance to feel that he'd outgrown her, his own twin, becoming an adult while she seemed stuck in her childish ways.

Maybe it made sense that Mother asked questions about *his* future. About *his* happiness. She began to cry. A lot.

And when Constance sought comfort in her twin, as she had when they were younger, he was distracted. He started talking about change, too – about *his* life, rather than theirs – and suddenly, the persistent itch of worry that had been eating at her slowly grew new teeth.

With Mother and Enzo – the only two allies she'd ever had – on their own paths, Constance was adrift and alone.

She panicked.

Going to Father would never have seemed like a viable option if Mother had kept her in the loop. Or if Enzo was available to her at all. But somehow, after a lifetime of distance, Father seemed the closest bit of land in an ocean of loneliness.

It hadn't gone well.

She'd approached him in his first-floor home office, trembling slightly with a mixture of uncertainty and hope.

Father had been interested to learn that Mother was worried. He'd asked lots of questions, called her paranoid, then got a faraway look in his eyes, and Constance realized her error with a sick roll of her stomach.

She'd betrayed her mother.

And then she made another mistake. Instead of retreating, she tried to change the subject. Tried to talk about Enzo - but Father went cold. He clammed up, then he waved her away. It had been so easy for him, like brushing away a fly.

And two weeks later, her mother was dead.

But the waking of Constance didn't change.

Only their mission had.

Now, it was up to Constance to learn the crimes of her father and expose them, so she and Enzo would be safe and taken care of...but Enzo had committed crimes, too.

Mother said it was his crimes which led to his death, not Constance's. Not *her*, either. She spent a great deal of time after his death convincing Constance that neither of them was at fault. First, she said it was Enzo, then she blamed Candace, the despised replacement of her, young and beautiful and with claws that sank deep into the man of the house – the *men*, it was revealed later. But over time, Mother had blamed Father. More and more, she turned Constance's focus to the patriarch, hell-bent on revenge.

Regardless of who was at fault, though, now she was really alone, with only ghosts to keep her company. And Mother was frightening and confusing, alternately loving and guilty, crying often, but refusing to tell Constance the details of what held her here. And it turned out that ghosts could cry *indefinitely*, never tiring. It made for stressful times.

And, frustratingly, Constance was unable to *see* her brother. Even as Mother kept at her, refusing to go even when Constance was frustrated and tired, Enzo hid in the shadows. She knew he was there – they were uniquely connected, after all. She'd *always* been able to rely on his presence. Until Candace, that was. Until everything that had seemed good and sacred in her life had twisted beyond recognition.

What she would give to be able to go back – to make different decisions.

But it was too late, now, and though she still had Mother, the pain of her absent twin (at least in body) was overwhelming. Which was why she'd committed *her* crime. And for a while, Peyton had seemed like the answer. But now, Enzo had befriended her – he never really talked to Constance anymore, not even through the strange woman in the loft. And mother hid from the woman, resolving only to appear to Constance. She'd felt it as a compliment, at first, but came to question it as time wore on. Why not appear to Peyton, the seer of all ghosts? Why not watch her for Constance? Help *her*, for once?

And why not Enzo? Shouldn't the two exist on the same plane?

How was it that she was the only one who saw Mother?

And thus, a seed of doubt was planted. And it was easy for it to take root. She'd spent years believing herself inferior, after all. Maybe she *was* stupid. Maybe even *crazy*, like Father had said about Mother. She didn't know anymore.

But it was clear that nothing was working out. Mother had been saying it for weeks, and now Constance considered her options. She'd made a mess.

The only option seemed to be to clean it up. Only one

question remained: whether would trust the ghost of her mother to guide her actions, or seek out the advice of the living family she had left. Or maybe she would do something just for her, for once. Something that revealed all of the secrets and punished all of the crimes.

She'd never been overly concerned with doing the "right" thing. It hadn't been required of her as both a privileged and neglected child. She wasn't even sure she knew what was "right."

But maybe, after everything, and considering the future, it was time to figure it out.

Chapter 22 – Skype
With Spencer

"There!" Margot straightened from her squat, having plugged the laptop in behind the desk. "I use it a lot on campus, and forgot the charger today, so now we can be sure it won't die on us while we talk to Spencer."

Charis smiled from mid-pace in Margot's living room. "Good." She started back up, chewing on a thumbnail as she walked back and forth.

"I thought you liked the carpet," Margot folded her arms across her chest.

Charis stopped again, looking up. "Huh?"

Margot laughed. "You're wearing a hole in it!" Charis looked down at her feet. "What's *wrong*?"

She shook her head, her curls bouncing. "I don't know. Ever since we were in Peyton's apartment, I feel antsy, but I can't put my finger on why, exactly."

"Could it be that we found nothing of interest except a drawing of you, from years ago?"

Charis nodded. "Yeah. Could also be that the police seemed to think very little of the drawings of Constance and Enzo, and certainly aren't going anywhere to find them."

Margot pursed her lips. "I know. But at least they have first names, and they're doing a search here at home. If nothing else, it'll eliminate the possibility that she's been held close-by."

Charis gave her a dark look. "You're smarter than that,

Margie."

Margot's face fell. "OK, so it'll only eliminated the possibility that Constance and Enzo are locals, but that's *something*, Charis! We have to focus on any progress."

Charis started pacing again. "I feel like time's running out."

Margot raised her hands up from her sides and let them fall, looking frustrated. "What about what Clara told us? That she'd actually spoken to the woman – and she *confirmed* it was Constance, from Peyton's drawing! – twice that night? And that she'd called a week earlier, asking about Peyton's class?"

Charis let herself flop onto the couch and put her face in her hands. "That's something," she muttered into her palms. "And it's something that she came to talk to the police with us, too." She let her hands fall into her lap and looked up at Margot. "I keep going over it, you know? I felt she was holding back, but I think a part of me hoped she was holding something more earth-shattering back. Something that could lead us straight to the answer."

Margot crossed and sat beside Charis. "It still might. It's a puzzle with many pieces, my friend. Each one of them's important, even if a lot of them look like nothing."

Charis looked sideways at Margot. "I'm sorry. I think I'm just tired. Demi's done school in two months, and has zero interest in daycares – I'm still at my job part-time, but I know I can't keep doing everything by myself -" she felt regretful tears prick at her eyelids and put her face in her hands again. "And I'm worried for Peyton. I keep seeing her face, everywhere I go." She sobbed. "I'm sorry to come and cry on your couch," she said, her words again muffled by her hands.

Margot grasped her wrists gently, pulling her hands away from her face. Her look of concern was sincere. "You don't have to apologize for that. You're going through a rough

CONSTANCE & ENZO'S TEA TIME WITH PEYTON

time, and you opened up to me about it. Thank you."

Charis nodded, a tear falling onto Margot's hand, which still held her wrists, but gently.

"Clara told us a lot. She said the call she got from Constance was indeed long-distance, confirming your suspicion that she's not from around here."

Charis sniffed.

"And we knew the woman was talking with Peyton after class, but *now* we know it was Clara who directed the woman to her. And that after Peyton left that night – after drawing the biggest clue we've hand, mind you – the woman came back, and bribed Peyton's address from her!"

Charis wiped her nose on the back of her hand. Margot's dropped to her lap.

"Don't you see? The police know so much more, now!"

"Doesn't matter if we don't find her."

Margot sighed and let herself rest back against the cushions.

Charis laughed. "I'm sorry. You're right! It's just getting to me."

Margot sat up again. "Me too! But we *will* find her. Don't you know that?"

Charis frowned, thinking. Her eyes cleared. "I do."

"Good!" Margot was up and walking back to the laptop. "We'd better call him; your little breakdown's made us late," she grinned impishly over her shoulder.

Charis gasped, then laughed. "I like you, Margie-Mae."

Margot paused at the laptop. "I should hope so. I don't think I've ever had a friend I feel as comfortable with, and *excited* by! You actually teach me things!"

Charis laughed again. "That doesn't happen very often with you, does it?"

Margot rolled her eyes. "I'm not bragging. My brothers teach me, and so does my Mom, still. My Dad did -" she stared through the arched doorway off the living room, then shook her head. "Do you want tea?"

Charis said she didn't.

"I find I almost always love the people who make me realize how small I am in this world. How *lucky*."

"Like Wren?" Charis asked, a bit hesitant, but terribly curious to know the story of the ghost-boy from Margot's past.

Margot only nodded, though. "And Chris – he used to live just at the bottom of your hill in Greenwood Square," she smiled.

Charis made a face. "Amazing how everything comes together, isn't it?"

Margot smiled, nodding, too.

"When it comes right down to it, I only came to live there because of ghosts," Charis mused quietly.

"Tell me," Margot said, sitting in one of the chairs she'd set up in front of the laptop.

Charis jumped, realizing they'd gotten distracted again. "I think we have lots of stories to tell each other," she said as she got up to join Margot. "It's weird," she frowned at the dark-haired woman as she sat, "I don't feel like you're an old friend. I feel like we're catching up."

"Me too."

"Dial, before we go off-course again!"

Margot startled, then moved her mouse around, waking

up the screen.

He answered on the first ring, his face filling the screen and looking anxious. "Is everything OK?" was the first thing he said.

The women apologized quickly and thanked him for talking to them.

He exhaled, sitting back in his own chair and placing a hand over his heart. "It's crazy. It takes nothing to freak me out since Peyton's disappearance."

Charis connected to him instantly. Kindness was the first trait that came across, then a charming boyishness that only complimented his extraordinary mind. "We can relate," she smiled. She held back from asking what he was studying, resolving to find out more about him, later. He felt – interesting.

Margot spoke next. "Peyton told me so much about you while we were in University. You're the same age as my brothers," she smiled. Then she giggled.

Charis eyed the woman quietly, fighting a grin. Apparently, Spencer interested Margot, too, but differently, perhaps.

"She told me about you, too. I've always wanted to meet you, you know. Thank you for being a friend to my sister during that time. It was often dark, for her."

Margot nodded. "I tried. I'm afraid I couldn't help her as much as I would've liked to, but I listened, you know?"

He nodded. "Sometimes, that's enough."

The two smiled at each other from differing ends of the world, connected by modern technology. And by something else, too; something palpable. Charis knew in that moment that they'd be together. She could see it. And she could see herself in their lives.

She was suddenly clear about the signals she'd been getting from the extraordinary woman beside her. She was open, she was kind, and she was exceptionally generous with the people in her life she felt connected to. And Charis suddenly felt grateful for falling into that category.

She leaned forward, suddenly determined to get things moving. "Let's talk about what we're going to do to find your sister."

Spencer's smile faded, but Charis liked the commitment she could see in his handsome features. "Tell me everything you know."

"First, tell us where you are, exactly," Margot countered, and Charis nodded.

"I'm in a teeny-tiny, but functional flat in London," he gestured around himself with a grin, "living a minimalistic lifestyle is required, but worth it for the location. I'm doing my final Doctorate year here, working on my thesis."

The revelation only heightened Charis's curiosity and she could push it aside no longer. "What's your thesis topic?"

"Religion as a construct for order versus alternative faiths and practices."

"Including science?" Margot's voice was high and her eyes wide.

"Yes, of course!" Spencer smiled.

"That's – interesting." Charis frowned in mock confusion at Margot. "Aren't you tackling a similar topic, from the scientific viewpoint?"

Margot stared at her, baffled, then rolled her eyes as she elbowed her friend. She looked back at the screen. "Do you know what I do?"

Spencer frowned. "You're a scientist, right? I've read a

lot of your brothers' work."

The woman was practically vibrating with excitement. "We need to talk."

Charis laughed. "But for now, let's stay on track."

Margot blushed, and Charis thought Spencer echoed her embarrassment. It was difficult to see it on-screen, though. She stifled a giggle.

Margot elbowed her again. "What did you have in mind, Charis?"

Charis leaned forward, getting serious. "We need you to search, Spencer, and I *think* you're in just the right place to do it."

He nodded. "Research has been my life for months. I don't know why you'd think I was in the right place, though?"

"Because the woman we believe took your sister had a British accent."

"We think she's closer to you than to us," Margot interjected, her tone newly somber.

Spencer looked shocked. "What can I do? What am I searching for?"

"A family," said Charis. "A very prominent one, I think. I see wine. And we have the first names of two of the family members: Constance and Enzo."

"Siblings, we think," Margot added.

"And we think one of them is dead. Enzo."

"How do you know all this?" Spencer asked, his face openly puzzled.

Charis faltered.

"She's a psychic medium and I – I'm smart and have better-than average intuition," Margot said quickly, then glanced at Charis, eyes widening. "Oh! Not to say Charis isn't smart; she's really smart." She looked back at the screen, flustered. "And I've seen a ghost, too!" She gestured aimlessly with her hands before resting her forehead in them, completely discombobulated.

Both of her companions laughed. Charis looked for Spencer's reaction, hopeful he'd be on-board and not turned off.

She was not disappointed.

"Cool," he said when his laughter had quieted.

Margot peeked over her hands.

Spencer seemed distracted. "Wow," he said, absently.

"What?" both women chorused.

"I should have Googled your names before. I would've been better prepared if I had," he grinned, looking into the camera.

"Don't believe everything you read, though," Charis cautioned, her mind on the newspaper article that had been published shortly after Demi had been born – an only partially accurate rendition of the events that had occurred on the Maplestone property, with Charis portrayed as the quirky psychic.

Spencer shook his head, holding a hand up. "Nothing shocking here. Really impressive, actually," his eyes moved back and forth as he read.

"Try Googling Constance and Enzo," Margot said.

Charis could feel everything slow, her heartbeat the only reminder of time passing as it pounded in her chest.

Spencer's features turned focused.

"You're not studying to – preach – are you?" Margot's

words seemed entirely out of place, but Charis lacked the presence to poke her.

Spencer looked into the camera. "No; I'm interested in how we've crafted our versions of God, not ministering under any one organization."

Margot nodded, obviously relieved. Charis spotted the woman's clenched fists, her knuckles white.

"What do you see?" Charis demanded, suddenly overwhelmed with impatience.

"A million articles," he shook his head, "but no obvious clues. I'm going to have to go through them carefully for connections." He levelled his gaze at the camera. "And, if your suspicions are accurate, I'm even more likely to find something relevant at local libraries and archives."

"When can you do that?" Margot asked.

"I'll work online tonight and go into the archives after class, tomorrow," he smiled. "If I find anything interesting, anything at all, I'll contact you. Margot, I have your number, but maybe I should have yours too, Charis?"

Charis nodded and recited her number while Spencer added her to his phone.

They sat in silence, all three feeling as though they were on the precipice of discovery, but unable to vocalize it.

"Thanks, both of you," Spencer finally said, and they echoed his sentiment.

When they signed off, Charis turned to Margot with a smile at her lips. "You love him!" she teased, still high on the possibility of progress in Peyton's case.

Margot blushed deeply. "He was so good-looking, don't you think?"

"And smart," Charis nodded, knowing that appealed to

her new friend.

Margot smiled. "There's no way he's single."

Charis shrugged, pulling a buzzing phone from her back pocket. She read the text then looked up at Margot. "He's just making sure he has the details right before he continues." She fiddled, focused on her phone, then muttering, "I need to add him to my contacts, now."

"Ah," Margot looked vaguely disappointed.

The phone buzzed again, and this time a look at the screen had Charis laughing.

Margot frowned. "What?"

Charis turned the phone to face Margot, her eyes bright.

Margot's eyes widened at the last text from their new contact:

Spencer: This is probably wildly inappropriate, but I have to ask (I blame my sense of distance for making me brave/stupid) – is Margot married? Betrothed? Surely, she's not single – but she's fascinating. And beautiful! So, I'll regret it if I don't ask. I'm going to push send now, before I come to my senses, but rest assured I can be solely professional, if required.

Chapter 23 – Pre-Recon

It felt wrong.

She was so doubtful about returning the journal that night that she lay awake, on edge, until Enzo came to get her.

She'd read and reread the journal and now passages of Constance's writing mingled unhappily with Peyton's own thoughts. Her head felt full and heavy, and not in that wonderful way it had when she'd learned something new or when she was analysing something from every angle possible.

Regardless, she'd completed her task, though her new understanding of Constance's perspective did little to answer the questions around Enzo's death. Or their mother's, for that matter.

Constance wrote about Enzo as though he were a part of herself, just separate from her physically. It was the way a parent might write about a child, or vice versa. In the absence (even in the presence) of their father, and the strange actions (or inaction) of their mother, the two had spent much of their lives floundering, with only each other to hold onto. But Constance talked about Enzo from their mother's perspective, too, repeating, it seemed, things that her mother had confided to her.

In the end, Peyton had a new perspective on Enzo, or at least how he was perceived by his sister. She still wasn't sure she had any sort of accurate ideas about who their mother *was*, but she did have a feeling for what the woman *wanted*.

It was without hesitancy that Constance wrote about her mother's deep and abiding interest in the business. It seemed that, over the years, Mr. Everleigh's interests had wandered often, veering from the cornerstones of the Everleigh product line -- wine being the largest investment and most dependable source of profit – to various flights of fancy. The hotels and the restaurants seemed to have had a mixed effect on income, but ventures into trending produce like soybeans and kale, often undertaken at the expense of the wine, were openly opposed by members of the board. Which was, as far as Peyton could make out, largely made up of family members, Mrs. Everleigh included.

Poor planning combined with clouded foresight were the accepted culprits of the Everleigh patriarch's questionable decision-making, but there were undertones in Constance's writing that suggested other contributors. She used words like "creative" and "trailblazer", but without conviction. What rang true were the occasional comments around her father's disinterest; how remarkable she found it that her father's negligence affected all areas of his life rather than being limited to his wife and children.

He was like some glorified figurehead whose true self was a mystery, even to those who should have been the closest to him.

And her mother was scared that his disinterest would mean her demise, for though she was the partner that kept things running, she would have no rights to any of it, should her marriage collapse. A solid pre-nup had seen to that, as it had for the spouses of Everleigh heirs throughout the history of the apparent patriarchy.

At the suggestion of her mother, Constance had begun to doubt her father and fear the distance she could feel growing between she and her brother, the heir-apparent to the Everleigh enterprise. She puzzled over priorities, wondering what her father's interests truly were, until Enzo died. After that, her focus was on her brother. She still wrote about her mother and father – the business, too, but she cared for those far less.

What Peyton would have given to have had access to earlier journals. What had happened before their mother died? Had she been sick, as Constance said, or was her death self-inflicted? Constance knew she'd been very anxious about the business; that much was clear.

But it was the things that were *unclear* that gave Peyton pause.

There was a hint that their mother had figured out where Mr. Everleigh's interests truly lay before she died, but no details were explored – at least not in writing.

And Peyton knew the twins' mother had been dead for some time. They talked about her like she'd left them years ago, yet Constance spoke of her mother in the present tense, always. "Mother says," and "Mother wants." Anyone without knowledge of the family would expect the woman to be very much alive after reading her daughter's account of her. But that was another thing. Constance only wrote about her mother's direct interactions with her, as though that was the only time she existed.

Peyton considered Enzo's suspicions that another ghost roamed the halls, and had no doubt it was true. But then, why didn't Peyton see her? And stranger, still – *why didn't Enzo?*

And if Constance could see her mother, why did she need Peyton to see Enzo?

Enzo had theorized that Constance was a lot like their mother, which to him meant she wasn't right in the head. Was Constance "sick" too?

Peyton knew that a person's perception of a ghost wasn't solely dependent on the person. The ghost had something to do with it, too. But the questions that arose as she read the journal had brought all of those wonderings back into the forefront of her mind. As pestered as she had felt by some of the ghosts in her life, it was all too easy for her to slip into the assumption that she was seeing *all* the souls that lingered beyond death.

She'd been reminded more than once that her assumption, though comfortable, was incorrect.

Peyton had probed for information or explanations as far as Enzo would allow, but he disliked the conversation, revealing snippets of thought or opinion and then closing back up. Peyton thought it must be like mining for gemstones: the flash of hope when something glittered in the dirt, and subsequent frustration when the hole filled up again before the gem was in her grasp.

She reviewed the things she'd managed to glean.

Enzo had said their mother got pregnant late, that in-vitro was her only option because she was older.

He said the pregnancy wasn't the result of a desire for children, but a means both to produce an Everleigh heir (apparently the business was passed down like the crown was in the royal family, with the men taking precedence over the women as per the old ideas written in old strategic documents for the Everleigh empire), and to protect herself.

If her marriage failed, her children would take care of her.

"Too bad she didn't consider her treatment of us an important factor," Enzo had commented as he idly spun a spoon on the dining room table. Practicing his interactions with the living world, always.

The entries around Enzo's death were chaotic and grief-filled, but they were angry, too. Constance hadn't described the event in detail; she only raged about it, or lamented it - sometimes both in quick succession, like a rapidly-cycling bipolar off her meds. But, no. She'd lost her twin, and in effect had lost herself, too.

Several weeks after it happened, though, she seemed to have come to a number of conclusions about all that had happened. Firstly, she was as much a victim in her brother's death as he was.

And second, the sins committed against her (whether directly or not) constituted her right to commit an act, or acts, that may be considered sins by those who were unaware of the reasons behind them. Committed in order to set things right again.

And while she remained bereft of solutions to appease her mother (as they'd involve the business and her father – two arenas she was less than eager to involve herself in), she knew without a doubt that *she* wanted one thing above all else. She wanted Enzo back.

Peyton shook her head, her hair rubbing against the pillow in a way that was surely tangling it. Her mother used to say that the more tousled Peyton's hair was in the morning, the more thinking she'd been doing before she went to sleep, and it made sense.

I miss her.

So, Peyton became the new goal. The new obsession of the grieving sister. Get Peyton, and in some way, she'd get Enzo, too.

It had been all too easy for Constance to find her; Peyton hadn't hidden her gifts away. Quite the opposite! In her search for others like her, she'd splashed her own truths like a swath across the internet. All it took were the right search words to find her – *medium, ghost, talking to the dead* – it was too easy. And that made Peyton grimace with regret, for her loved ones had warned her – Mom, Spencer – even Dad had tried to lecture her on paying attention to her own safety, but her Dad's words barely touched her anymore. He'd given up on her – on the whole family – ages ago, as though her brother's Asperger's diagnosis was the final straw. Why should she listen to him?

Enzo popped into existence, startling her out of her thoughts so suddenly she nearly screamed. He sat on the edge of the bed, watching her reaction with a mischievous grin.

Peyton had sat herself up and pressed herself against the headboard when he appeared, and she remained frozen against it even as she growled, exasperated.

Enzo laughed.

She let her muscles relax and turned the lamp on. "I'm glad to be your constant entertainment," she frowned, folding her arms against the chill air on her newly-exposed flesh.

"I thought you'd be asleep. I always pop in like this, unless you wake while I unlock the door." He raised his eyebrows defensively, still smiling.

She threw a pillow at him and was impressed when it merely bounced back at her. "Wow; you're all the way here, aren't you?" She leaned toward him and gave his bicep a poke.

He nodded, "It means I'll be tired later, but I wanted to do this *with* you."

She sighed. "I have a bad feeling."

He nodded. "I know, but we have no choice."

She hesitated, thinking, then inhaled sharply as an idea took shape. "If I can touch you, you can probably hold the journal -"

He shook his head before she could finish. His form was levitating lazily away from the surface of the bed. "I could never make it all the way there! It's hard enough being solid!"

"But you could try!"

Enzo looked at the bed, a good six inches below him, now, and rolled his eyes. Clearly frustrated, he dissolved into a wisp and flitted about the room. His voice came from everywhere. "It's not easy, Peyton! I'll drop it and she'll know. It'll ruin everything!"

Peyton watched him anxiously, thinking about the window. "Come back!"

He flickered out of existence, then popped back into solidity beside her, his back against the headboard.

"I'm sorry," she muttered, sitting up to face him.

He stuck his nose in the air dramatically, then peeked at her from the corner of his eye.

"This is fun for you," she accused, trying not to smile.

He peered sideways at her. "Very little is, these days."

Her smile faded. "You're right. If you don't make it all the way into her room, journal in-hand, the gig is up."

"Isn't it, 'jig'?"

She frowned, then laughed. "I've never really known."

Their eyes met. "I'm worried about tonight, too. I feel like we've come a long way, and we could erase all our progress with one wrong move," Enzo said, a look of genuine angst on his face.

Peyton thought about tea that evening. Constance had been very quiet, but that wasn't the only thing that threw Peyton for a loop. She'd caught the woman studying her several times, her eyes narrowed as though she were trying to make a decision.

And she didn't ask about Enzo; not even once.

"Let's just get it done," she said quietly, and Enzo nodded.

And they did very well, at first. Better than either could have expected.

Until, high on their success, Peyton pushed their luck just a little too far.

Chapter 24 – Caught

They were back at the landing when she stopped. On their return, Enzo had given up on being solid; he accompanied her in varying displays of wisp and shadow now, with any effort at consistency producing only remnants of his physical self. It wasn't disconcerting. He was too excited to focus on how he appeared, and Peyton was too relieved to care.

When she stopped, though, he materialized from the waist up, looking back at her from halfway up the staircase.

"What's up?" he hissed, concern darkening his smile just a bit.

Peyton regarded him, thoughtful. "It's so quiet."

"So?"

She let her eyes wander to where the stairs continued down, presumably to the first floor. Presumably to freedom, blocked only by an alarm system whose code was etched into her memory.

"What are you doing? We're almost there!" Enzo whispered, but he was beside her, now. She could feel anxiety sparking in him.

"Why not now?" she looked at him sideways. "I have the code; the journal is returned. I could get away!"

He shook his head, instantly blocking the stairs by positioning himself between she and her idea of freedom. "We still haven't found all the answers!"

"Your father's adultery alone is enough to -"

Enzo's semi-transparent eyes widened. He jerked his

head to look toward his father's room, then back at Peyton. "Are you crazy?" he accused, his face only millimeters from hers and the rest of him floating upward.

In a moment of impulse – something she'd worked excruciatingly hard to recognize and then gain control over, she ducked under the ghost and started down the staircase.

Her heart raced in her chest as the reality of the risk she was taking crashed down on her. She gasped, raising her arms against the weight, then realized it wasn't just reality pressing down on her; it was Enzo – or a semblance of him, but dark. Heavy.

Peyton waved her arms about her head, but they only flailed through him, frustrating her beyond measure. "How can you put so much weight on me when I – can't!" she grunted between each word, "Even! Touch! You?"

"Shut *up,* stupid!" he hissed in her ear and she froze, her words still hanging in the air.

There was a sound on the second floor. Enzo disappeared so quickly he made a whistling sound in the air. Peyton stood stock-still, eyes wide and ears on alert.

This is not good.

Flirting with panic, she forced herself to scan her surroundings and formulate options.

Up: back to the loft until Constance stores me somewhere else – somewhere less comfortable - for who knows how long.

Down: the door out. Freedom.

It was all she thought in that moment. She didn't recall the presence of Mr. Everleigh, didn't consider Enzo's need for answers. Nor did she figure in the chance she'd get caught, or lost in the woods that lined the estate, much less the fact that she had no idea where she'd go if she managed to make it though them and into civilization. She just wanted, more than anything, to go home.

She was hurrying down the remainder of the stairs and sprinting toward a heavy-looking wooden door before she'd realized she'd made a decision. There was a shuffling sound behind her – Enzo, maybe, but maybe someone else, too. Maybe someone on the stairs.

She'd assumed Enzo had disappeared to find out who was making noise, but maybe he'd gone to alert someone, instead.

She choked back a cry as she skidded to a stop in front of an intricately-carved wooden panel on the wall beside the door. "I don't blame you, Enzo!" she muttered in a high voice as her fingers fumbled around the edges of the panel, desperate to open it.

She glanced around. No Enzo. But she could hear it; *someone* was on the stairs.

"Oh!" she cried, tears springing to her eyes. She'd messed up, and it was too late to turn back.

"You idiot!" Enzo hissed into her ear.

"I'm sorry!" she cried, the panic in her voice intensifying her trembling. "Who is it?" she looked around again, but the stairs were still empty. Enzo, on the other hand, was in quite a state, his attempt at appearing whilst losing his shit altogether having jumbled his parts into an impossible tangle in midair. It made Peyton's head hurt. She cocked her head, momentarily distracted by the sight. "How – how are you -?" She couldn't finish her question. Slippered feet appeared on the stairs behind the disarranged ghost. Instead, she shrieked, but managed to pull the sound back before it reached full volume.

The slippers sped up.

"*Shit!*" Peyton cried, going back to the task of opening the panel.

There was a frustrated groan in her ear, and then a heaviness that stopped her movements altogether.

What is he doing?

"You really aren't very bright, are you?" Enzo muttered, seemingly from inside her head. Peyton could only widen her eyes in surprise as her hands moved to the panel on their own. As if controlled by – *Oh, my God,* she realized. *He's possessed me!*

Completely unable to intervene, she merely watched as her own hands found a little lever on each side of the panel and pulled, causing the wooden cover to flop down loudly.

"Ugh!" Enzo grunted as he wrenched himself out of her, then tumbled to the ground in a soundless heap.

Peyton stared at him with wide eyes. "Don't you *ever* -"

He gazed up at her, but his grasp on this level was fading, evidenced by the fact that Peyton could see the patterned carpet through him. "The *code,* you idiot!"

She jumped and focused on the keypad in front of her.

"You horrible, stupid, unappreciative, ungrateful little *wench!*" Constance accused as she reached the landing, then went silent, save her rasping breath. No footfalls, though.

Peyton pressed the first three numbers. "Four, three, nine," she panted, then snuck a glance back toward the stairs, where Constance stood, bent at the waist and panting.

"Get *over* here if you ever want to make it out of here *alive!*" the woman hissed, but her words only pushed Peyton to go faster. To succeed.

She turned back to the keypad, but made a mental note to recall the list of names she'd been called by her captors in the space of the last two minutes. *The names* hissed *at me,* she thought absently, the analytical part of her trying to piece together the ways that the twins were alike when angry.

But Enzo helped, she thought as she pressed the five, then the one, then tried to press the three...

But Constance was there, finally, diving at Peyton, who collapsed under the considerable weight of the woman who'd stolen her away from everything she cared about.

She was instantly overwhelmed, her instant reaction to being touched aggressively taking over. She wanted to fight, but found her body disobeying her again, curling into itself as every cell attempted to recoil from her attacker, just so she could be free of that feeling – that rough disturbance to her person.

"Fucking Asperger's!" she grunted as she fought herself, and failed, finally collapsing into the fetal position and sobbing.

Constance stood, hands going to her hips as she planted her feet. Her eyes bulged from the deep red of her cheeks. "You *bitch!*"

She felt her brain add the insult to the list.

"What do you think you're doing?"

Peyton strained to look up at the woman while her brain motored on, considering the disappointment of losing control over oneself in a new light, having just been overtaken by a ghost. Being unable to control her own body because of who she herself was, she discovered, was much worse than having a separate entity entirely cause the affliction.

Constance regarded the open panel, her forehead bunching as she scrutinized the numbers Peyton had been able to enter. "What the..." she looked accusingly down at Peyton. "Where did you find that code?" she demanded.

A tear dropped from Peyton's eye to the carpet, and she found she was able to wipe it away. "Oh, thank you," she muttered, bringing both palms to her face and letting her legs relax. Discovering, as she did, that her pants were wet. "Oh, no," she cried into her hands.

"What?" Constance walked around her, then giggled. "Aw! Does baby need a new diaper?" she snorted into laughter, then leaned over Peyton. "Oh, you've *really* lost it, haven't you?"

Images of Peyton's youth bubbled up to further torment her. Being bullied on the playground, being so different than nearly everyone that she believed for a while she was an alien, being hounded by the dead and rejected by the living. And the worst blow of all, being ignored completely. She'd worked so hard. Tried everything the experts suggested.

She thought she'd come a long way.

But now, she only felt failure.

"You have to get up," came a gentle whisper in her ear, and she gasped, then froze again.

"Enzo?"

Constance froze, too. "What is he saying? Did he have something to do with this?"

"You have to cooperate," the ghost said, gently again, into her ear.

She nodded.

"WHAT'S HE SAYING?" Constance bellowed, but then her eyes went to the stairs as her hands flew to her mouth.

Peyton remembered Mr. Everleigh, too. It would not be good for anyone if he woke to find this scene.

"I'll come with you," Peyton spat, finally in control of herself, thanks to Enzo's encouragement.

Constance jerked her gaze to Peyton as she sat up. "What?"

"I'm sorry; I messed up! I'll come with you, quietly, back to the loft."

Bald relief passed over the woman's piggy features. "Get up," she whispered, gesturing sharply with her arms.

Peyton got up, grimacing at the quickly-cooling wetness between her legs. She hated the feeling of damp clothing on her skin.

"Ugh, you *stink*," Constance scowled, plugging her nose with one hand and taking hold of Peyton's forearm with the other. She squeezed tightly.

Peyton fought the urge to throw the woman off her.

"Good," Enzo said in her ear, but she shook her head, a new film of tears blurring her vision. "Yes, Peyton, you're doing well. Everything is going to be alright."

"I'm sorry," she wailed, and Constance slapped her.

"Be *quiet*, stupid girl!"

The oddness of Constance, who was surely fifteen years younger than Peyton, calling her 'girl' was not lost on Peyton. Nor Enzo, it seemed.

"Girl," he giggled.

They made it to the second floor with no hitches; it seemed Mr. Everleigh was sleeping deeply that night.

"Thank God," Peyton muttered as they rounded toward the second set of stairs.

But Constance led her right past them and into the West wing, instead. "Don't thank 'im yet," she muttered, a smug smile at her lips.

Peyton begun to tremble again, and reached out to connect with Enzo. It was a surprising relief to realize he was still with them – just a warm presence, following.

Constance led her past the tea room and down the hall, finally stopping at the door across from her own room. "This will have to do." She gave Peyton a smile that left her eyes blank, striking a new note of panic in her prisoner.

"No," Enzo said, then popped out of existence. But of course, Constance didn't hear him.

But then maybe she did, because she cocked her head and said, "I *have* to. Don't worry!" Then she seemed to catch herself and gasped, meeting Peyton's eyes with the look of a child who'd been caught doing something naughty.

"Did you – can you hear him, now?"

Relief washed over the woman's face. Her cheeks remained bright red, though. "Uh – hear who?"

Peyton frowned as Constance opened the door and flicked the light on.

Enzo was solid again, and sitting on the bed. He looked miserable. Peyton glanced at Constance, who showed no evidence of perceiving him.

"It's not me she's listening to," Enzo said.

And there was defeat in his voice.

"This was Mother's room," Constance said, finally releasing Peyton's arm.

And then there was someone else, standing beside the bed, just behind Enzo. Looking drenched and wrung out, with blood oozing from her wrists and all over her bathrobe.

Peyton very nearly screamed.

"I don't want you here," the woman said, and with a deafening shriek, disappeared.

Chapter 25 – News

Margot stopped chopping carrots and looked toward the dining room. She'd thought she heard a noise, but the house was silent. She shrugged, going back to prepping her vegetables. She had a craving for a big stir-fry and intended to satisfy it. The week had been so draining, what with finals approaching and deadlines looming, not to mention the increasing urgency she faced where finding Peyton was concerned. Tonight was just for her.

She knew she'd need to travel, but couldn't bear to ruminate on it until there was no other option. The prospect of fitting in a trip to the UK during finals was nothing short of intimidating.

But the reality of it loomed in the background always, pushing her to prepare in whatever ways she could. Consequently, she'd worked minor miracles all week, finalizing exams for her classes and taking care of lingering paperwork to get the students' marks up-to-date. She'd organized supervision for the exams and scheduled marking workshops with her Teacher's Assistants. She'd even given a heads-up about the likely need for her to travel to the Dean of Science and the Admin staff.

She frowned. She was still feeling a little uncomfortable with using the old, "family issues" excuse. Otherwise, she allowed herself to feel she'd accomplished much despite her anxieties – or because of them.

She paused again. This time, a muffled hum disturbed the silence of the old house. It had its share of creaks and groans at nearly a century old, but that hum wasn't the house.

She grabbed a dishtowel and jogged to the dining room, where her scarf was lighting up in a bright rectangle as her phone buzzed beneath it. She went to grab it and fumbled, sending scarf and phone over the edge of the dining table. She sighed, more exasperated than surprised by her enduring clumsiness.

She found the phone, which had gone silent, beside her leather satchel, which had been discarded on the floor when she'd come in. On hands and knees, she looked at the screen.

Three texts from Spencer Hale.

She sat against the wooden table-leg and scrolled to her new texts, her stomach suddenly uneasy.

Spencer: Can you talk?

Spencer: Just tried to get you on Skype.

Spencer: Sorry; had to try Charis as I couldn't get you. I don't know what your plans are tonight, but she's on her way! She's not one to let things sit, is she?

Headlights lit the living room window, then the dining room as a car pulled in. Margot scrambled up off the floor and to the window, thinking *how the hell did all of this happen in the time it took to cut up some carrots and celery?*

She recognized Charis's car and shook her head. *The woman lives forty minutes away. Is she magic, too?*

But it was her, climbing out of the driver's side and heading for the door without pause.

Well, something's up. She could be sure of that, at least.

She opened the door just as Charis reached the top stair.

"Spencer got you?" she asked, out of breath.

Margot stepped aside so the she could come in. "What is going *on?*"

Charis frowned, but continued to remove her jacket and

boots. "Oh – you didn't talk to him?"

"No; I took a few minutes to chop vegetables and apparently missed something important. I just got his texts."

Charis opened her mouth to speak, but Margot held up a hand.

"Nope! First: spill it. How did you get here so fast? And don't tell me it was magic, psychic lady, because my limitations are already -"

Charis laughed. "No! The kids and I are at the Wolfville cottage for the weekend! It's only a few minutes outside of town."

Margot folded her arms, feeling mildly ridiculous. "Oh. You did tell me about that place."

The petit woman eyed the arched doorway to the kitchen. "I did leave just as Ashleigh was serving dinner, though. What were you making?" She passed Margot without waiting for an answer, headed for the kitchen.

"Why do I always feel like you're two steps ahead of me?" Margot called after her.

"Ooh! Carrots!" Charis took a handful of the raw sticks and met Margot at the archway, already crunching her stolen treats. "Where's your laptop?"

"What?" Margot frowned. "Slow down, already!"

Charis spotted Margot's satchel on the floor and went for it, talking non-stop as Margot watched her find her laptop, position it on the table, and turn it on. "Sorry. I'm used to tackling things quickly because I always have so fucking much to *do*." She laughed, then looked up at Margot, "and I feel that way with you, too. You're insanely smart." She fumbled with the touchpad, making a sound of frustration.

Margot burst out laughing. "Here, let me help you with

my stuff," she exclaimed, fishing through her bag to retrieve her mouse.

"Oh, good," Charis took it and plugged it in.

Margot sat, defeated.

"So, Spencer did a bunch of research – he's really smart too, by the way, and I'm *dying* to see the two of you together. I know it's meant to be. You guys are gonna make super-genius babies. Did you know he's on the spectrum, by the way? Asperger's, like Peyton, but obviously very high-functioning. He says he wouldn't have been diagnosed, probably, if it weren't for his parents being on the alert because of Peyton. Makes you wonder about that particular diagnosis though, doesn't it? Where is Skype?" the woman frowned at the screen.

Margot hadn't even moved to point to the icon before Charis was back up and running.

"Found it!" she clicked then straightened, bending back in a stretch, her eyes on Margot. "Where was I?"

Margot took a deep breath. "Dude, you just said so much that I need to process…"

"Oh! Anyway, he said it was surprisingly hard to find anything with just the names we gave him. Apparently the Everleighs keep their personal lives very private, despite how well-known the brand is." Charis sat, her eyes on the screen.

"It'll take a minute to fully boot before it'll open Skype," Margot said, as calmly as she could. Hoping it would catch on.

Charis looked at her. "But then he searched for 'death' along with 'Constance and Enzo', and *boom!* There it was."

"Are you talking Everleigh, like Everleigh wine and spirits, Everleigh?" Margot asked, having taken the opportunity while she was assaulted by facts to narrow down her questions.

Charis nodded. "Yep. I'm talking the London Everleighs, whose *twins* are named Constance and Enzo."

"Holy shit!" Margot struggled to maintain her Zen.

"Right? And the latter passed away in December."

That was it. Margot stood. "This is *huge!* Has Spencer contacted the police?"

Switching roles, Charis turned to watch Margot pace. "He says he went there right away! He's going to tell us everything tonight."

"That's it?" Margot stopped in her tracks.

Charis looked thoughtful for a moment. "Uh, no! He said it'll likely be Monday or Tuesday before they'd do anything, whatever that means."

"What the hell?" She started pacing again.

"I guess because it's Friday and they need to talk to the police here – I don't know; that's why we need to talk to him!"

Margot plopped herself into the chair beside Charis, her eyes on the "loading" icon. She looked at Charis in the sudden quiet. "Hi," she smiled.

Charis laughed. "Hi. Sorry."

Margot waved the apology away. "It's exciting stuff. Did you leave the kids with – the older kids?"

Charis shook her head. "Greyson and Ashleigh are here for the weekend."

"Right. Wanna hang out tomorrow? Since you're here?"

Charis looked at her like she was nuts, then giggled. "Sure. What should we do?"

Margot shrugged. "Take in a movie? I'm not fussy, and I've got tons of down-time right now."

"Me too. Ladies of leisure," Charis smiled, then jumped as Skype appeared on the screen. "Oh!"

Margot straightened in her seat and scrolled down to Spencer in her contacts, then pushed the video call button.

"Ah, if only, hm?" Charis muttered.

"I have a feeling we'll both be thankful to have someone to call when things do settle down," Margot said, smiling sideways at her friend.

Charis looked doubtful. "Settle down? You don't know me very well yet, do you?"

Margot laughed.

"So, do you like him?" Charis jerked her head at the screen as the program sounded its connecting tone.

Margot rolled her eyes. "Duh."

"And the Asperger's thing doesn't worry you?"

Margot made a face. "It's just a label, Char."

"There you are! Oh, thank God!" Spencer's face appeared onscreen. His hair was messed up and he had significantly more stubble than he had last time.

Margot felt a part of herself melt at his frazzled appearance. It made her think of Wren, somehow. Awkward and a bit strange, but so handsome and intriguing.

Charis was staring at her expectantly.

"What?" she shook her head.

Charis laughed.

"I was asking how soon you could come," Spencer said, a bit of a dopey grin on his face.

"Is it time?" Margot asked, caught off-guard. She'd known it was coming, sure, but suddenly it seemed too soon.

"The authorities here are going to request the file from your contact there. Once they've reviewed everything, they'll decide on next steps."

"Why so complicated?" Charis exclaimed, her voice high. "Can't they just go over there and get her?"

Margot shook her head in tandem with Spencer. "It's obvious to *us*, but think about what they know."

Spencer nodded again. "Even when they have the file, the only evidence they'll see is Peyton's drawings of the twins and my research. Nothing to connect them, really, unless Peyton's drawings are very accurate."

Margot smiled. "You know as well as I do how talented she is."

He nodded, smiling, too. "I know. Hopefully, it'll be enough for at least an informal visit, you know? Enough to get some information."

"Like whether the sister – Constance – travelled to Canada recently."

"Exactly."

Charis bounced in her seat. "This is crazy! We know where she is!"

"Which is why I asked when the two of you can get here." Spencer's expression turned serious. "I'm not sure what the three of us can do while we wait for the process with the police, but I'm thinking we could at least do some more research on the family, maybe even ask around."

Margot sucked in a breath as Charis bounced again, then placed her hand on the woman's shoulder in an effort to calm her. "Is there anything stopping *us* from going to their home?"

Charis stilled immediately. "Yeah!" she added.

Spencer pressed his lips together. "They've urged me to

stay away. Even if Peyton *is* there, any sort of visit from us could tip them off, you know?"

The women sat back in their chairs at the same time.

"But the Estate isn't just their home," Spencer added, a twinkle in his eyes.

"What do you mean?"

"There's the home and private stables, sure, but the Everleigh property extends past that, to property that's open to the public."

Margot frowned. "How so?"

"They own acres and acres of land across the UK, but a significant portion of their acreage – for grapes, mostly – is in or around London. Ten of them right beside their home, separated only by an acre or two of woods."

"And the – the grapes – they're public, somehow?" Charis frowned.

Margot smiled. She was adorable.

"The outbuildings on the property are," Spencer grinned. "During business hours, anyway! There's a museum of sorts - you can tour the grounds, learn about the various types of grapes and how they're processed, see the cellars, have a tasting. There's even a gift shop."

"Oh!" Charis looked at Margot with wide eyes.

"OK, so we can visit the property *next* to their home without raising suspicion, but where will that get us?" Margot asked.

Charis's expression fell as she looked back at the screen.

"The business side of that particular property was taken over by one Candace Snelling after Mrs. Everleigh killed herself," Spencer said, and then he sat back in his chair, smiling.

"Whoa," Margot said.

He raised a finger, obviously enjoying sharing what he'd found out. "And oh yeah, it's not 'Snelling' anymore. It's 'Everleigh'. She married the CEO and figurehead of the Everleigh empire shortly after his wife died."

"What? Wait. What?" Charis bumbled.

"That's fascinating," Margot said, always logical, "but I still can't imagine what good it would do to speak to the new Mrs. Everleigh."

The three sat quietly for a few moments.

"I haven't seen the dead wife," Charis said, quietly. "I haven't seen her at all." She looked at Peyton, "Sometimes they hide. Could the circumstances around her death have anything to do with her son's?"

"Or with Peyton's disappearance?" Spencer asked, and both women regarded him soberly through the monitor.

"If any of it is connected, this Candace woman might know about it, but she might not, too. Do you know anything else about her?" Margot asked.

Spencer smiled again. "I know she doesn't actually live on the family estate. The police didn't mind gossiping a bit about the family."

"She could be estranged – maybe the relationship is on the outs!" Charis perked up, leaning toward the screen.

Spencer nodded.

"And maybe she wouldn't mind gossiping a bit, either, especially if there's been no indication that the police are interested in the family," Margot reasoned.

"You got it," Spencer pointed at the screen.

"But how do we approach her?" Margot couldn't ignore the doubt that poked at her.

"I'll do some more reading – maybe we're a group of investors looking to talk with someone close to Mr. Everleigh. Or maybe we've heard about the stables at the estate and wonder if we could see those?" Spencer frowned as he theorized, his forehead lined with concentration.

"Or we could be old friends of the twins?" Margot suggested.

Spencer shook his head. "They're too young for that. Constance is only in her late twenties, now. But we could know them from somewhere else. I'll look into their interests. Oh! And I read that Enzo had just started leading the research and development team at Everleigh Headquarters. I'll look more into that. We could say he was in early talks with us about modernizing processes or something!"

The women nodded.

Charis eyed Margot. "I can go this weekend. Can you be persuaded?"

Margot looked at Charis and then Spencer, then inhaled deeply. "I don't know if I could convince a curious onlooker – or even my parents, for that matter, but I know my brothers would be pushing me forward right now. And while the reasoning is a bit weak, I have to admit I have an overwhelming feeling that we need to go." She nodded, decision made. "Let's do this."

Charis and Spencer nodded, smiling. "Woo!" Spencer cheered, but the celebration was a reserved one. All of them knew what was at stake.

"Your brothers are twins too, aren't they?" Spencer looked thoughtful.

Margot rolled her eyes and nodded. "Twin pains in my

ass."

Charis laughed.

"And they're what – ten-ish years younger than you?"

"How'd you know that?"

"I may have researched you two a little, as well," Spencer pushed his glasses up on his nose, looking embarrassed.

Margot laughed. "Well, you're right. Wait, that would make them very close to the Everleigh twins' age!"

"I wonder if the Everleigh twins ever did anything like conventions or research. You know, things twins do?" he asked, eyebrows raised.

"It's another good possibility, even if they didn't. If nothing else, we could say we learned of them while reading up on twins that – work together, or something like that," Charis added, looking hopeful.

"I have the feeling the way to approach this will become clear," Spencer said. "It has to. Peyton's important."

Margot felt the heaviness of reality roil in her stomach.

"We're going to find her," Charis said, and there was conviction in her words.

Margot nodded, then looked at Spencer. "We'll get our itinerary to you ASAP."

"I'll pick you up at the airport."

The prospect of meeting the man who'd been popping into her thoughts way too much since they'd first met had Margot's stomach feeling uneasy again. But in an excited way, this time.

"Uh, guys?" Charis waved a hand between Margot and the screen.

Margot came out of her thoughts, blushing, and giggled

as she realized Spencer was doing the same thing.

"See you soon," he smiled, cheeks red, and signed off.

Charis jumped up. "I gotta go. There's a lot to work out before I can fly to London," she talked as she put her jacket on, then looked at Margot. "Should I come back tomorrow? We can book our flights?"

"What about the movie?" Margot whined, mock-disappointed.

Charis grinned. "See you tomorrow, Margie-Mae."

Chapter 26 – Sins Of
The Everleigh Family

Peyton stared up at the ceiling.

Virginia was the woman's name who'd occupied this room before Peyton. She was mostly absent, which was good, but on the rare occasions she'd appeared, it had startled Peyton considerably. She figured the ghosts who aren't interested in you in particular were the ones that both founded and fired the stereotypes – the mid-night appearances at the foot of the bed, the tendency to look just as they had in the moment of their demise, the odd noises, the eerie sense of being watched.

It wasn't that she hadn't experienced it all before. It was that she was already on edge, and the fact that Enzo had no desire to interact with his mother on this plane or any other meant that he was mostly absent, too. So, she was feeling lost.

She was a master of keeping herself company - her mind provided a rich landscape for much-needed distraction. But the room itself was dim, always, and musty. Peyton's sinuses filled up and clogged during sleep, such that she wondered whether the bedclothes had been laundered at all since the death of Virginia Everleigh.

Happily, though, there was a bathroom. She hadn't expected such luxury, but in hindsight, couldn't imagine Constance having to take care of any sort of bedpan or bucket situation. She herself would have been in dire psychological straits had the conveniences and comforts of a bathroom been withheld.

The kitchen was a sore loss, though. And Constance

seemed to think Peyton could be sustained on air, pieces of fruit and the odd leftover sandwich or treat from tea. The irony of eating delicate cream cheese and chive pinwheels and French macarons to fill a sorely empty stomach was almost amusing. At least she could drink water from the bathroom tap.

So, she missed the loft immensely. There, on the good days, she'd sometimes had to remind herself that she was being held against her will. Just the freedom to sit by the windows and read for hours on end had healed so much of the insult of her circumstances. And the one small, second-storey window in the bedroom hardly did justice to the view she'd enjoyed just one floor up. Her cravings for paints and canvas, at least, had lost their sharp teeth. Without tangible inspiration, she felt stunted. Which was a strange relief, now, when her creativity had been purposefully diminished.

Her wakeful hours were passed largely on the bed as she was now, her hands behind her head and her eyes staring blankly upward as she combed the vast libraries of her mind. There was no darkness there. Only towering bookshelves, gilded ceilings of artwork and sunbeams that streamed through massive windows, illuminating dust motes and pixie glitter. Here, she not only fantasized and contemplated. She analysed. Strategized. Rather than being lost in despair over what her future might hold, she comforted herself by imagining every possible outcome and devising plans of action for each one.

She spent hours at it and came to the same conclusion every time: the best she could hope for was escape for herself – which promised to be messy, regardless of the method – with enough knowledge to fuel an investigation into Enzo's death.

At least, she thought that was what he wanted. He only ever said he wanted to *know*, but what if the knowing affected people still alive, too? Still with the family business in their hands, or still bereft of a mother or a friend?

She'd spent far too long philosophising over the outcome for Enzo – or Constance, or Virginia, or for the elusive Mr. Everleigh, for that matter. But she had to admit it; she needed Enzo's help for that part of the equation.

She sat up, scanning the room again, hoping to fine a hint of him in the shadows. "Enzo?"

She couldn't even feel him.

Sighing, she fell back atop her pillows and picked a different book out of the mountainous stash of her internal library. She'd looked at Constance's journal from every angle she could imagine, yet was still left with many questions. She'd given up trying to find the answers there, though. The act of journaling wasn't an effort at recording history for Constance, she'd finally realized. It was only a record of her feelings about it - or her perceptions. So, while events were not described in any sort of dependable way (at least not in the journal Peyton had read), the way Constance viewed it was on display in all its glory.

Peyton had never been one to be disappointed. Instead of failing, she looked for ways to learn, at least. And looking at the journal with that goal in mind did prove interesting.

She did find, for example, that Constance was smarter than she let on. She'd accepted the role of "The Bossy Princess," but only because Enzo's never-ending drive had earned him the title of "The Ambitious One." *Funny how often children strive to be what people tell them rather than who they are.* Peyton thought of that one summer at Gran and Grandad's where she tried – and failed - to be "normal," convinced it would please her family.

She wondered if Constance had ever had that epiphany where you find yourself willing only to be your true self, the rest be damned? *It would have to have been very recent if her last journal was any indication,* she thought, then flipped back in her mind to a page of the journal that had taught her something new upon closer inspection.

It was a list, titled, "Sins of the Family," and it took up an entire page with scribbled notes and eraser marks, and additions, too. And while it raised more questions than it answered, Peyton thought that at least she had some of the *right* questions, now. At least for Enzo.

At the top of Constance's list was the name, "Father," whose list of sins had the most obvious additions, interestingly. Enzo's came in second for additions, while Constance's list was the longest and had only one obvious addition, having been written in the margin with an arrow pointing to her name. It seemed she'd tried to stick with the seven sins of the Christian theology at first, but veered off when she came back to modify the list – and she'd done that more than once, as evidenced by the difference in writing utensils used. Peyton wished, for the hundredth time, that she herself had a pen and paper, then closed her eyes, willing herself to build the list anew in her mind. A cleaner version, you could say, according to her own understanding.

SINS OF THE EVERLEIGH FAMILY

Stewart Johnson Everleigh – husband to Virginia and father to Constance and Enzo.
Sins: Pride, Greed, Gluttony, Sloth, Wrath. Added later (here, Peyton decided to include everything, regardless of the added "sins" overlapping. It was significant that Constance added each of them, she thought): Envy, Lust, Negligence, Deception, Sexual Abuse, Psychological Abuse, Selfishness, Betrayal, Adultery, INCEST (the last was written in all-caps and with such force that the page had been torn).

Virginia Calliope Everleigh (nee Meridon) – wife to Stewart, mother to Constance and Enzo.
Sins: Greed. Added: Negligence, Suicide.

Enzo Stewart Johnson Everleigh – son to Stewart and Virginia, brother to Constance.
Sins: Pride. Added: Lust, Greed, Gluttony, Bribery, Keeping Secrets, and Desertion (Peyton found the last particularly sad, and strange, given Enzo's enduring belief that Constance was involved in his death).

Constance Meridon Everleigh – daughter to Stewart and Virginia, sister to Enzo.
Sins: Pride, Sloth, Greed, Wrath, Gluttony, Selfishness, Kidnapping, Keeping Secrets, Failure to save Mother and Enzo, Fear, Hate. Added: Indecision.

Peyton reviewed her version of the list and, satisfied, puzzled over the questions it raised. Who had Mr. Everleigh committed incest with? Was it the same act which had prompted the addition of "Sexual Abuse?"

Both Enzo and Constance had been pegged with "Keeping Secrets." What secrets? How had they learned them? Were they the same? Were Mr. and/or Mrs. Everleigh's sins (the former the more serious, if true) committed against them? Or one of them, hence their knowledge? And Mrs. Everleigh's list was the shortest, even though she'd committed suicide. Surely, she'd had her own secrets, and they had gone with her, including the reason she'd killed herself.

Peyton had asked after a suicide note, even if it was told to her in a Cole's Notes version, but Enzo had only shaken his head.

Regardless, she knew something else: the woman wasn't hanging around to solve her own death, or else Peyton's help would be attractive. There was something else.

And then there was the absence of the stepmother. Candace, Enzo had said. Enzo had also said that Constance was jealous of the woman, having taken Father's attention and favour after Mother's death before the twins could even try for it, and then for taking Enzo's, too. So, Peyton knew Enzo and Candace were involved. But Enzo was tight-lipped about it, explaining away his reluctance to talk about it by refuting its importance.

But Peyton couldn't imagine an affair with one's step-mother being of no consequence. Quite the opposite – and hadn't Enzo and Candace been together in the stables loft in that dream she'd had? The one with the psychic, Charis? She made a mental note to confront Enzo when she saw him next. *If* he came again.

She sat up again, her eyes going to the window. It was getting dark. With Spring in bloom, the darkness was coming closer to six-thirty, these days. She frowned. Had they missed tea?

She stood and crossed to the locked door, putting her ear to it. Constance almost always spent some time in her bedroom before collecting Peyton for tea, but she could hear nothing, now.

She looked about the room again, then flicked the light on, trying to extinguish the growing panic that rose in her. Constance had missed tea once that week, already. She'd explained it away the next night, with stories of a visit to the Everleigh office headquarters in the city. Peyton had come to attention; Constance had never shown an interest in the business before. But that night, she was different.

"I need to start paying attention and contributing," she'd said, her nose in the air. "After all, I should be a part of it - as much as Enzo was!"

"But of course, you'll inherit everything, won't you?" Peyton had broached, too anxious to gain information to remember her manners.

"It doesn't work that way with Everleigh Enterprises," she'd replied, then anger flashed in her eyes. "It's none of your business anyway! After your *failed* escape attempt, you're lucky I have anything to do with you at all!"

That comment echoed in Peyton's head, now.

What if Constance *was* done with her?

A hand on her heart, she raced to the bathroom and turned on the light. She splashed water on her face, but stopped when her hair became stringy, hanging down in soaking clumps on either side of her face. She looked in the mirror and saw someone drenched and frightened, and thought of Virginia's ghost. She glanced at the bathtub, wondering if it was here that the act was carried out with a stab of discomfort. Then she left the bathroom, but with the light on to help chase away the shadows in the bedroom. It only partially worked.

She sat on the bed, fiddling listlessly with sash tied at the waist of her dress. She was always ready for tea early since changing rooms. It was easy with the loss of her distractions – the windows, her books – she stifled a whimper as the potential loss of tea time, too, bubbled to the surface. Even spent with Constance, it was her only bit of freedom each day.

Her whimper gained strength and sound, though, when Enzo popped onto the bed beside her. She jumped as she cried out, landing hard on the floor as Enzo reached out too late to help her. He stood over her, hands over his mouth, but his eyes giving away his smile.

She put a hand out. "Help me up!"

Enzo complied, his face reddening at the effort to fully solidify and then to help Peyton stand.

They stood facing each other for a moment, both with much to say, but neither knowing where to start.

"She's not coming," Enzo said, finally, and despite his mischievous ways, his eyes were sad, so Peyton knew it was no trick.

She bit her lip as tears filled her eyes.

"Don't cry," he muttered, reaching out to wipe away her tears but failing, only making Peyton's cheek tingle a bit instead of touching her. He let his hand drop. "Sorry. I'm out of practice."

"This is really bad!"

"She's missed tea before."

"Only once! And it was three days ago!"

He frowned.

"Even on the day your father returned she had tea with us! She was late, but it happened!"

"I don't think she wants to try and talk to me anymore," he said, his eyes on the carpet.

"What? Of course, she does!" Peyton's heart galloped uncomfortably. "That's the whole reason I'm *here!*"

"I know," he said, meeting her eyes again.

Peyton sat back on the bed, digesting. "Oh, my God," she said, feeling dizzy.

Enzo got down on his knees, facing her. This time, his hands were warm on her knees when he placed them there, but only for a moment. "We'll figure it out!"

"How?" Peyton cried. "You're barely here anymore, and when you are, you're, well -" she waved a hand through his chest, "you're barely here!"

He observed her hand as she dragged it through him once more. "That feels weird."

"Sorry." She let her hand drop.

"I'm working on a way out. You have to trust me! I'm

coming up with a plan!"

"When will it be ready?" Peyton cried. "Because your mother doesn't like me here, and your father has no idea I'm here! And if what you say is true, my only reason for being here is gone now, too! Which means Constance doesn't need me anymore, either!" she finished with a muffled sob, burying her face in her hands.

"I've been busy, but I still need you," came Enzo's voice, but it was from behind her, now.

Peyton looked at him over her shoulder. "Doing what?" She sniffled, absently wiping her nose on the back of her hand.

"Just doing some detective work," he smiled.

Peyton frowned.

He patted the bed beside him. "Come here."

She scrambled up the bed and lay on her side, facing him, as they'd done so many times before.

"Would it make you feel better if I told you a story?"

"Only if it's true. Only if it will help us figure this out."

He paused, his eyes darkening slightly. "OK."

"What's it about?"

"It's about me. Me and my father."

Chapter 27 – Sins
Of The Father

"Everleigh Enterprises," Enzo sighed as he started. "Ask anyone in London – in all of England, really, and further! – about the country's most prominent families, and the Everleigh name will be on their lips, right up there with the royals." He looked at Peyton. "Certainly, most would think Constance and I are -" he paused to look down at himself and shook his head, "- well, I think past-tense is more appropriate for me, given that I can see the duvet right through my stomach, but I'm sure most would say Constance *is* in an enviable position. What most don't know, though, is that Constance isn't the heir-apparent, even though I've gone. Most don't even know that even while we both lived, it was only I that would inherit the entire Estate."

Peyton frowned. "Is it just an old-fashioned way of doing things, or is there some other purpose to operating like that?"

Enzo looked thoughtful as he fixed his gaze on the ceiling. "A bit of both, actually. It was all written down during a time when the male was the head of the household, and the head of business, too. But as the business has grown and time has rolled on, the importance of maintaining the practice has taken on new meaning. You see, the Everleigh business benefits *all* of the Everleigh family, but just how much it benefits each one is up to the head – the CEO. Board members and family-born staff alike are ensured financial success for themselves and their families. It's as much about associating the family name with luxury as it is about greed." He looked at her again. "We must appear rich – privileged – so that our brand is associated with those values, and therefore prized highly enough to justify premium prices."

Peyton nodded, though talk of business strategy had always made her feel as though her head was overfull with information she hadn't a clue what to do with.

"The risks, therefore, of allowing Everleigh women to inherit the lead role, revolve around the name itself. The impact that a woman heir would want to change her name when married, or even hyphenate it, could be catastrophic."

Peyton scoffed. "Can't that just be written into the – processes for heirs transitioning into the role, or something? You know, make it a – condition!" she suggested, proud that she'd been able to remember the term.

"It's been considered – repeatedly. But then someone always brings up the potential for a female heir who is *not* of Everleigh blood – such as a spouse, or an adopted child – to move into the apparent heir position."

Peyton shook her head, "Seems silly, still. I understand the importance of the name, and of the perception of consistency and tradition, but that shouldn't preclude the business being run by any of its female members! After all, it's about perception, right? Not the actual org chart!"

Enzo chuckled. "I thought you hated this stuff?"

"I do. But it's not because I'm dumb. It's only because I'd be a terrible businessperson. It all feels – conniving to me, somehow. I would have no idea how to convince people to buy my products..." she trailed off, scrunching up her nose as if the idea offended her.

"Well, you're right, and you put it into the same terms that the women of the Everleigh family have over the years. Somehow, though, they've all been placated by the idea of the heir as the figurehead only. That they'll profit just as much as if their names were on the doors on the top floor – or nearly as much, anyway."

"So, why is it an issue at all, then?"

"Because it keeps coming around, doesn't it? Look at my situation, for example. My father is as shit at running the business as he was at being a father. Or a husband, for that matter. When I was very young, I thought he was distant because he was so busy, but it wasn't true. He was distant because he wanted to be. He had no interest in Mother, or Constance and I. The family was for appearances, full-stop. And by the time he did start paying attention to me, I knew it was because he wanted something from me that no parent should ask of their child." He pressed his lips together, going quiet.

Peyton could feel his energy buzzing and held her breath. "Don't go," she said, her voice small, after watching him for a few long moments.

He let out a breath, prompting her to do the same, and folded his hands over his chest as if to hold himself down. "I've never talked about this. Not even with Constance, and talking to her was like talking to myself, much of the time."

"Maybe it's important that you do," Peyton wondered aloud, but bit her tongue before finishing her thought, because she knew how upset he got whenever the idea of him moving on was broached.

Luckily, he nodded. "I know it is."

"He did something to you, didn't he?"

He let out a burst of sardonic laughter, then wiped at his eyes. Peyton watched in fascination as ghostly tears dampened the duvet cover, little dime-sized imprints of suffering that probably defied everything that was known about physics.

"I'm so sorry, Enzo," she said, still quiet despite his outburst, and fighting tears, herself. It was unfair. Unfair hurt the worst.

"I don't know if he ever would have looked at me if I hadn't found a stack of pictures in his safe," he continued, but his voice was robotic, now. "I was always watching the safe, peeking in to his office a dozen times a day, hoping against hope that he'd forget to close it. I knew we had money, but in a child's mind, riches are made up of found treasure – sparkling gemstones in all colours and piles of glittering gold coins."

"Like pirate stories," she smiled.

He grinned, just a little. Nodded his head. Then, his expression darkened. "But the things my father treasured and hid away didn't sparkle." He looked up at the ceiling as he swiped at his tears. "They were pictures, stacked behind the money and bonds as if all that wealth could protect him from his sick perversion. And I guess it has!"

Peyton swallowed a sob, unwilling to distract him, but desperate in the same moment to comfort him.

"And do you know what's funny?" he asked, his eyes still on the ceiling. "At first, I saw those boys – those naked *children* – and was hurt! How could my father ignore me entirely in favour of these boys that were my age and put together in just the same way!"

"Oh, Enzo," Peyton's voice wavered.

"I was jealous of them, Peyton!"

"You must have been so confused."

He met her eyes. "I was seven years old. The only thing I knew about adults and their interests in children was that we were mostly just annoyances! Even the Nannies we had were stiff and uncaring!" He laughed. "Mother probably chose them that way on purpose, just to keep us from knowing that we *should* expect our parents' interest. Our parents' *love* and *devotion!*" He gestured toward the ceiling. "Instead, the first time I knew I had something of value was when my father found me with those pictures and said I could atone for the atrocious sin of going through his safe by being his real boy doll." He looked at her again. "I thought I'd won what I always wanted. I thought he wanted to *play* with me, Peyton. Like a friend." With that, he released a sob and faded into nothing.

Peyton could still feel him, though. She reached out with splayed fingers. "Hold my hand," she whispered, letting the tears roll down her own cheeks, too.

And to her surprise, he did. It was the only part of him that materialized, but she grabbed onto it, weaving her fingers through his and bringing them to her mouth, where she pressed them against her lips until it almost hurt.

It was a long while before he spoke again, but when he did, his face appeared independently of the rest of him, somehow, floating above her. His hand was still nestled comfortably in her own.

She tried desperately not to be afraid, but it was hard. "That's a little scary," she confessed, then had to giggle when he looked around, seemingly perplexed at the achievement, himself.

"Is it OK though?"

She nodded and squeezed his hand.

He frowned at their intertwined fingers again. "That *is* a bit strange."

Peyton shrugged, willing him to go on.

"I don't know what he was thinking that day. He didn't consider the consequences of what he was asking me to do, for sure. And he didn't think about how he would handle my questions as I grew and lost some of my naiveté. In short, he didn't think about the fact that someday, I would know that what he'd done to me was wrong, and that I would make him pay."

"How?"

"By revealing the truth. It was all I had to do, and while my father is made to look the strong, upstanding leader the public expects him to be, he's really very weak. His predilections, coupled with the strangling noose the family kept on his movements, made him so. I don't know when it happened, and I don't know who he was meant to be, but the man who hides away from everything is nothing but the creation of his circumstances. He doesn't even *do* anything for the business, except for travelling and attending the meetings, but even then, he's accompanied."

"So, how does that amount to making him pay?"

Enzo's face blipped out of existence and then he flopped next to her, the rest of himself back to where it belonged, attached to the hand she held. "Thank you for this," he said, wiggling their joined fingers.

"Can we – don't let go, OK?"

"Is this scaring you?"

"Of course."

He laughed. "How is it this that scares the girl who's seen ghosts as much as live people all of her life?"

"Human monsters are worse than anything a ghost has shown me," she said. "The living ones, I mean, because of the damage they're still capable of."

"Haven't you met ghosts who were monsters in life?"

She nodded. "Yes, but I get rid of them quick."

"How?"

"The same way you chase a living person away: by ignoring them."

He nodded. "I'm sorry for the hard time I've given you."

"I think you've been through a lot," she replied, and that seemed like enough to give Enzo some relief.

"Should I go on?"

She nodded.

"He tried for the last time when I was fourteen. I kept thinking it was done every time it happened, especially as I matured. He made such a face when he saw I had pubic hair – yelled at me to cover myself, then looked at me with a new sort of recognition in his eyes. But instead of stopping, it just changed. Instead of touching me, he made me touch him. Just - closed his eyes and gave me instructions. And I followed them, because..." he paused, looking about the room and then squeezing his eyes against a renewed supply of tears.

"You don't have to tell me," Peyton offered, but he shook his head.

"I do, I think."

So, she waited. Breathing in, and out. Focusing.

"I think I kept doing what he wanted because at least that way, I was *something* to him, and if I stopped, I'd become invisible again!" he finished, anger and confusion lacing his words.

"I don't think you knew you had a choice," Peyton said, hoping to comfort him.

He grimaced. "But then, I caught him, and I knew it wasn't just me he was using. We were *all* just means to his ends!" He took his hand away and wiped his face, breathing heavily. "Constance and I were only solutions to his requirement to appear as a family man, for the business. 'Normal.' Mother, much the same, but she brought a much more valuable set of traits. She was a business genius, and handled everything for him! And then I was an outlet – a release, and I was the cleverest one, because I was his son, therefore blind enough to believe that even though it hurt, he *loved* me!" Enzo clenched his fists as he fought his rage, but it overtook him.

Peyton shrank back as he let out a roar, then blinked into shadow that ballooned and filled the room with an oppressive weight. Her chest ached from it, but she closed her eyes and counted, holding on as best she could so she could still be there for him when he regained himself.

When he did, it was to reappear back on the bed, curled up beside her, head in hands.

"You didn't deserve any of it, Enzo." She tried to place a hand on his shoulder, but he was mist.

It was some time before he was able to start again. He looked up at her, a hint of mischief in his eyes. "Almost done. You still with me?"

"Can you hold my hand again?"

"I think so," he reached out and they were connected again. "OK?"

"OK."

"I caught him and another woman together," he shook his head. "I still wonder about it – wonder whether he had any clue what he actually wanted, or if he just took, took, took whatever he could, and the riskier it was, the better. I don't know about him, but for me, learning about his affair was the nail that closed the coffin on my willingness to do anything he said anymore."

"Thank God," Peyton whispered.

"But I waited for him to try again. I wanted him to feel it when I rejected him, be terrified at my ultimatum. And it was worth the wait at the time. Now, it doesn't seem to have mattered, the waiting," he frowned. "Things are different after you've left your physical self."

"What happened?"

"I told him to fuck off."

Peyton whooped, relief freeing her of the need to be careful with her reactions.

A smile echoed hers on Enzo's face. "And then, I told him that I'd be taking over the CEO position on my eighteenth birthday."

"Oh!" she gasped, but her smile didn't falter.

"He agreed to it immediately. All he could see was the freedom it would give him, I'm sure of it. But I had other conditions, too."

"Conditions? For keeping his secret safe?"

"Yes." He rolled his eyes. "If only I could go back in time. I'd tell myself nothing is as important as – as validation! That being reassured that it wasn't my fault would have done more than a position in a Fortune 500 company, even if that position was at the very top! I would have talked to Constance. We could have run the business together – but, oh God…"

"What?" Peyton leaned into him, perplexed at his self-flagellation.

"But maybe I'm just like him, Peyton! Maybe I could only see what I could gain! So, I did everything wrong."

"Enzo, you were fourteen."

"I was on that first day, but then years went by, and I got worse. And he did it again! He used me! As my eighteenth birthday approached, he convinced me it would be suspicious if I took over while he was still so young. I didn't see it then, but he was being manipulated by others, too. The family, Mother, and others. And I figured it out. I figured it out when I caught him, *again!* The fool was stupid enough to cheat again!"

Peyton's eyes widened. "Candace?"

He nodded. "But that time, instead of confronting him with threats, I decided to get my revenge another way."

Peyton inhaled sharply. "The affair!"

He nodded. "I think I was sick. I know I was. In *here*," he finished, tapping on his head. "I couldn't talk to Constance anymore; I couldn't let her know what had been going on for so long – and Mother only seemed suspicious of me, looking at me with narrow eyes when she passed me in the hallway or saw me at a meeting."

"Do you think she knew any of it?"

"No!"

The reply hadn't come from Enzo. The two both jumped, then Enzo flickered out completely as Peyton bolted upright.

"Don't go!" The ghost at the end of the bed cried. And then Virginia Everleigh howled.

Chapter 28 – Plane

Charis bolted awake with a gasp, startling Margot in the seat beside her and several other passengers.

Margot put a hand on her forearm as she tried to get her breath. "You OK?"

Charis nodded, then squinted as she raised the shade of their little window. They were way above the clouds, flying in clear blue sky. Her heart slowed a bit as she breathed it in.

"What happened? Did you have a bad dream?"

Charis settled back into her seat and looked at her friend, who was visibly shaken. Had been, actually, since they'd entered the airport. Dr. Francis disliked flying, it turned out. "Yeah, yeah," she tried to smile, patting Margot's hand, "I'm OK, everything's OK. I just -" she paused, recalling bits and pieces of her dream. "Wow, that was a dream and a half."

Margot relaxed back into her seat. "It's terrifying flying with a psychic, especially when she acts like the sky – and everything in it – is falling!"

Charis laughed. "I hadn't thought of it like that. I'm sorry!"

Margot waved it away. "What was the dream?"

Charis frowned. "It was Peyton again, but this time there was a woman ghost with her – the mother, I think," her eyes widened. "She was telling Constance she only found out about Enzo – whatever that means – the night she died."

Margot said nothing, but Charis could sense her wheels turning.

"And at the end, the other ghost – the brother – appeared out of nowhere. I was so fixated on Peyton and the woman that he shocked me."

"Did he say anything?"

Charis shook her head. "I woke up."

"Huh," Margot seemed perplexed.

"There was something else. They were in a dark room. Peyton looked a bit panicked." She rubbed her eyes, trying to formulate her thoughts into words less shocking than the scene had been. "I felt…"

"What?"

"Like we don't have a lot of time," Charis finished, opting for honest. "She didn't just look scared; she looked thinner - sick. Something's changed."

Margot pursed her lips. "I'm glad we flew out today."

Charis eyed the clouds far below them. "I just hope it's enough."

Chapter 29 – Constance

The days had changed drastically for Constance since she'd started working at headquarters in the city. It had only made sense to take the entry-level position that had been open for her always, if ever she deigned to take it. And with the increasing instability at home, she'd finally stepped up to claim it.

She'd seen no other option.

Since she'd caught Peyton attempting an escape (thanks to Mother, who'd woken her, shrieking about the girl, *The girl! She's getting away!* Constance had woken in a panic, but the visage of her dead mother floating above her, ribbons of blood appearing to tether the ghost by her wrists to the bed on either side of her daughter, sent Constance into shock. She'd lain frozen, eyes bulging at the face above her screaming words she couldn't comprehend. Her first coherent thought was to wonder whether she, herself, had died and was paying for her sins much as she had in life: via the alternating wrath or negligence of her mother. And in that moment, she knew she preferred the negligence.

When she finally grasped the situation her mother was screeching about, she'd bolted from the bed, then just as quickly swooned as she blacked out. She'd been holding her breath as her heart raced, her oxygen racing through her body at top speed and then depleting without replenishment. She stumbled against her bureau, blinded for a moment and gasping.

"What is *wrong* with you?" her mother screamed, jabbing her in the back. "If she gets away, your future won't just suffer the loss of privilege we expect unless we can get that stupid clause changed. You'll be rotting in *jail!*"

Constance shook her head hard and her eyes filled with bursts of white light, then hints of her surroundings as she regained herself. "Where is she?"

"At the *door,* you stupid girl. Go!"

She shuddered to think how close Peyton had come to ruining everything. Her driver glanced back at her, but said nothing. She gazed at the darkening landscape as they kept on for home, and she let her thoughts take her.

Perhaps the worst realization that night was that she had felt Enzo there, but got the distinct notion he was there to help Peyton rather than his own sister.

It had enraged her at first. But now, it only scared her.

Preventing Peyton from escaping that night hadn't solved the dilemma of what to do with her. Even worse, Constance had precious little time to tend to her, now. Work had seen to that. She regretted ever hunting her down. Enzo had never cooperated with her plan, anyway.

And Mother had been different, too. Absent, in fact. Constance knew why. She loathed the fact that Constance had gone to Father for anything, even if it was just to notify him that she was going to take her position. She *had* to do that if she wanted to work, but mother couldn't understand why she wanted to.

She can't understand what it's like to live anymore, Constance told herself.

Work proved to be a wonderful distraction. Even more surprising, she felt she had a natural affinity for it. She felt the level of work was far beneath her, but knew it was temporary. So, while she was only doing administrative tasks for the sales team to start, she worked to prove the business-sense that had surely been passed down to her. All the Everleighs – save her father – had been natural businessmen and women. Despite some dark looks and obvious jealousy around the office, she felt it was going well. She was already spotting opportunities for improvement and bringing them to her uncle, Bertie.

Bertie didn't seem surprised by her progress, though. He seemed – irritated by it. Constance knew he and her father only pretended to get along for appearances. Bertie despised his older brother for being born first and then pissing the privilege of his position away. For causing worry and work and relying on his late wife for everything business-related. Since she'd died – by a method he was openly understanding of within the confines of his office, incidentally – the entire board had been forced to spread her work amongst themselves, with no word of apology - or thanks - from their CEO.

If Mother had been loyal to Constance, if she'd come even *sometimes*, Constance could have told her all that she'd learned. Surely it would be useful in the eventual downfall of her father! But she'd been abandoned all over again.

And the thing was, she knew she couldn't affect the kind of changes she and her mother had dreamed and devised. Not on her own. If she was going to bring her father down *and* have it benefit her, she had to force a change to company policy. And she was no pioneer; it had been tried before by many an Everleigh lady, yet remained unchanged. It had been acceptable, though, as long as they all profited.

But would they, all? If Father continued to plummet into the crash and burn he'd been unwittingly orchestrating for decades, with the law of heirs still firmly in place, Constance knew she'd be lucky to hold on to her job. Bertie made no secret of his intentions to step into the position of CEO at his first opportunity, and since Enzo's death, he was right to expect just that.

She stewed on her options as the driver pulled up to the

door, then drove off. It was an uncomfortable sort of stewing, because it felt rather like the time she went to Father about Mother, and that had backfired spectacularly. If she was going to go to him, it would be with demands, this time, rather than requests. But she was missing the most important part – the gem of a bribe that Mother had hinted at, but refused to tell, saying she needed to be sure, first. Saying they needed to be careful, lest the changing of the Everleigh way result in Candace winning the spot at the top of the hierarchy, rather than Constance.

Constance had been patient, trusting that the knowledge would come when it was time. But what now, when Mother was quiet?

It was enough to overwhelm her.

She headed for the stairs, her ears perking up at the sound of a one-sided argument coming from her father's office. Father was most likely on the phone with her uncle again. She threw a dark look at his office door as she passed it, then carried on upward, Peyton filtering into her thoughts as she did.

She reasoned internally that her current state of overwhelm was sufficient to justify her negligence of the girl she'd stolen. Something would have to be done with her, for certain, but it seemed too much until she figured all this mess out. Best just to leave her be until she could figure things out.

She paused at the end of the hallway, standing between the two rooms – hers, and what used to be her mother's - and listening. Peyton had tried calling out to her in the first few days after she'd been moved from the loft, and then knocking lightly after Constance had scolded her. But it had been several days since she'd tried either.

She shrugged and opened her own bedroom door, a memory surfacing. She recalled a childhood pet, a mouse brought in from the stables by her brother. Constance had become obsessed with having a real, live creature to love and be loved by, but if their parents heard her plea, they did not acknowledge it. Enzo and the staff took the brunt of her obsessive begging, but there was little they could do, except listen.

But Enzo had done something. Just the notion of it had been like a miracle to Constance, a loving gift from the one person who saw her. Who cared. It hadn't mattered that it was a filthy mouse – not much, anyway. It hadn't mattered, either, that Enzo had smirked at her as he handed the little box over, saying "Here. Now shut up about having a pet."

She remembered how she'd giggled, making Enzo's expression soften a little before he turned away. And she remembered the first few days, the excitement as she trained the mouse to take little offerings of cheese and leftover bits of deli meat from her hand. It didn't take long for her to win its trust, and it took only slightly longer for Constance to grow bored, then apathetic. She found him gone from the box several times over the next few weeks, the little thing proving clever enough to gnaw its way out to find food, no doubt. It wasn't like she was starving it. She tossed crumbs at it after her own meals or snacks. Maybe not *every* time, but certainly every day. Mostly. She sighed each time she found him in her closet or under the bed, or when she'd first find the box empty, turning it to rest on the side with the hole, so the top of her bureau was the only bit of the outside that showed through. But then he figured out how to lift the box, using his nose to expose a space where the hole came away from the smooth wood, and bolting through it like lightning. She'd watched him do it once, just to figure out his method.

And then one day she didn't find him. He'd chewed a new hole, this time in a corner, so no turns of the box could mend it. She remembered feeling partly irritated and partly relieved. The mouse had become more trouble than he was worth to her, and Enzo's constant wonderings about it were beyond tolerable.

When it didn't appear over the following few days, she resolved to assume her pet had found its way back to the outside, maybe even back to the stables, to return to its former way of life. Enzo had been angry, but he forgot about the little mouse soon after, just like Constance had.

It was only when she was storing one of her journals that she learned how wrong she'd been.

It wasn't just her journals she stored in her closet. She hoarded favorite snacks, her stuffed animal collection, and other little objects of significance that brought her comfort. A monogrammed pen of her father's, a pair of Mother's pantyhose, Enzo's first lost baby tooth. Little things magicked away in secret – little things that meant something. That told her who she was.

The little mouse hadn't found his way back home. Instead he comforted himself in Constance's closet, too, feeding on her secret snacks and making a cushy nest in her dirty laundry. She'd been nearly impressed when she found him peering up at her with dark, reflective eyes from his makeshift new home.

But upon further examination, she saw the nest was lined with bits of paper, her own handwriting looping and swirling haphazardly. She'd gasped, her eyes going to her journals on the little bookshelf installed in the back corner of the closet, mostly covered by hanging clothes.

She flipped on the light of her closet now, recalling with some distaste how she'd felt when she saw the chewed, torn pages.

How she'd used the damaged journal in her hands to flatten the little beast that had defaced it before she'd even considered her actions.

Little asshole, she thought, even now.

She spotted her bookshelf and smiled. Then perked up, remembering the journal that was ready to store, along with her latest reading. She frowned as she extracted her journal from the stack, then placed it on top of the pile. She'd had very little time for reading in the past week. She still wrote in her journal, of course, but she hadn't added to her reading stack in many days.

She knelt with the pile of books, then lined the reading on the lower shelf before pushing her hanging clothes to the left so she could place her journal in its spot on the second-highest shelf. She paused, her eyes roving with pride over the neat lines of them. She'd counted; there were thirty-three. "Thirty-four," she whispered, sliding the latest one into its spot.

But she stopped halfway.

Mother had been encouraging her to be ready, reminding her often that her journals would no doubt be valuable assets when they went to the authorities about Father. If they couldn't convince him to effect a change in the rules about the hierarchy, that was.

She gasped, seeing the lines of books, her handwriting filling each one, with new eyes. She hadn't written with any audience in mind, much less the police. And yes, there was surely damning evidence against her father in them – but there was so much more, too. And without Mother to make light of the possibilities, they crashed down on her quite suddenly.

What about Enzo?

A hand flew to her mouth. *And Peyton!*

She stood so quickly she got a headrush, just as she had on the night Mother had woken her because Peyton was trying to escape.

It wasn't just her father who'd be destroyed by those journals; it was their author, too. And Enzo. Her dead brother's reputation would suffer greatly if the wrong eyes saw what she'd written, not to mention his pride. Even in death, Enzo's pride meant something.

I have to destroy them.

She was racing to Enzo's old room in the West wing, intent on retrieving a duffel bag to throw them into before thoughts of Mother entered the equation.

If I do this, what other evidence will we have? She slowed as she reached Enzo's door. *Maybe I could just destroy the ones that would hurt me – or Enzo.*

She entered the room, the familiar pang of loss hitting her in the chest, but failing to stop her. His room was bigger than hers, with better light. It was cheerful, decorated with football banners and riding trophies from when they were children. But she headed straight for his closet. It was the only part of the room that paled in comparison to Constance's. Her closet would no doubt be a satisfactory tiny home for the less discerning, while Enzo's was shallow and chaotic, the pile of dirty laundry at the bottom so tall it touched the shirts he actually made an effort to hang. They hadn't had the staff do their laundry or cleaning for years before Mother had died, yet neither had been taught to do it themselves.

She rifled through sweaters on the upper shelf with some difficulty. It was something Enzo would joke about, if he were here. Her height had meant lifelong teasing material, especially in moments such as these. She cursed as a sweater fell, covering her face just as her fingers touched something smooth and flat. Frowning, she wrenched the sweater from her head and went back to the mystery object, then exclaimed in disgust as she pulled it out, then another. She'd discovered his porn stash. "Ugh," she muttered, flipping through one of them. His taste certainly fit his predilections: curvy bimbos ready to pay for a shot at comfort and wealth with their bodies. She dropped the magazines with another sound of distaste, then shuddered, waving her hands as if to rid herself of the filth.

She looked down at the glossy magazines with a frown, imagining the reaction of whomever would be lucky enough to clean out Enzo's room in the future. Sighing, she bent to retrieve the tossed glossies, and felt a surge of triumph. Enzo's duffel was just beneath them.

She shoved the magazines beneath the pile of sweaters and grabbed the bag, then ran back to her room, only pausing once to close Enzo's door, gently (Father's office was directly beneath that area of the wing), and then again at the landing, tiptoeing past the stairs and then breaking into a jog again.

She was gasping by the time she was back in her closet, but she made quick work of kneeling in front of the bookshelf and opening the bag. Only then did she pause. Breathing heavily and noting an uncomfortable patch of dampness at her lower back, she considered first the rows of journals, then the empty, subtly mildew-scented bag. And for one anxious moment, she felt desperate for guidance.

"Mother?" she shrunk at the sound of her own voice. She heard it – what Enzo had always said. She was whiny. Snivelling.

She reached back to touch the damp spot of sweat through her blouse.

Disgusting.

Even an insult from her brother would be welcome, now. Something. *Anything.*

"Enzo?"

She pursed her lips at the continued silence. *There's nobody to take care of you now, Constance. You'd best make sure you take care of yourself.*

Nodding, she cleared the shelves of journals in seconds, then zipped the bag with a sense of satisfaction.

And if Mother isn't going to help you confront Father, you're going to have to do it on your own.

She breathed, a welcome sense of calm rolling over her. She felt clearer than she had in months. Her internal voice switched to first-person. *I need a plan.*

She left the duffel in the closet and was sitting on her bed, current journal in hand, in seconds. *I need to sort things fast,* she thought. She started a list:

1)   Research – reread company policy.

She perked up, then added, "pre-nup details?" beside it.

2)   Go to Father with everything, ~~ask~~ demand that he change company policy re: inheritance.

She sat back. She knew that if she went to her father today, she'd have nothing but weak accusations. Her father had neglected his business commitments for years, yes, and had neglected his family duties, too, the most damning act in that category being adultery. It would likely be enough to knock him off his throne, but Constance couldn't see him being motivated to change the policy before he scampered off with his tail between his legs.

And Uncle Bertie would step in before Constance could raise her hand.

She sighed, tears welling in her eyes. *And here I am again. Lost.*

She gazed at her tiny list through the tears, feeling helpless. She squeezed her eyes shut. *Maybe the pre-nup, the pol-*

icy itself - maybe I'll find something there. She shook her head. Others had tried and failed, and *they* had been familiar with both documents before combing through them. Even Mother hadn't found a way.

Constance jerked her head to the door, thinking of the room just across the hallway. Thinking she needed Mother's advice. She needed to know what Mother knew!

Thinking of Peyton.

She added the final item to her list while making a mental note to add the current journal to the bag before she got rid of them all. Noting, too, that it had to be soon.

   3)   Make Peyton fulfill her purpose.

Chapter 30 – Spencer

Spencer glanced at his watch and, seeing it was precisely one minute later than it had been the last time he checked, rolled his eyes at himself.

It wasn't so much *meeting* new people. He and Peyton were similar in that way. It was what followed the introductions that put his nerves on edge. Especially today. He'd admired the Francis twins and their wacky ways of bringing advanced science to the masses. He hadn't known much about the sister until Peyton connected the dots for him one day as he extolled their virtues.

"They're Margot's brothers," she'd said, her head turning slightly toward him, but her eyes stuck on whatever she'd been painting that day.

He remembered wondering absently who Margot was before continuing to describe the latest YouTube video by the twins. He didn't truly make the connection until he was at his desk that night, his mind running on auto while he pounded out an essay on the laptop. His fingers had frozen when he put the Francis twins' surname with "Margot," then opened Google for a quick familiarization with the more feminine, perhaps less celebrated sibling of the Francis family.

He'd been impressed. He remembered that much, but then he'd gone back to his work, having satisfied the itch that'd had his subconscious whirring since Peyton's comment.

He jokingly compared his mind to a sieve. His strength was in discovery, not memory. It was one of the many ways he was different from his sister, his inability to interact with the dead being the more obvious.

But Dr. Margot Francis would be in front of him in moments, and though he'd better familiarized himself with whatever the internet had to offer, the fact that he couldn't stop thinking about her – hadn't even been able to focus on his thesis since their first conversations, if he was honest – had thrown all of his progress with socialization out the window, he feared. In short, he was quite sure he was going to blow his chances, modest as they were, being comprised only of a short text from Margot's psychic friend, which said, "She is single, actually. And I would gather you are, too. How convenient."

It wasn't much, but it wasn't negative, either. And he thought he'd seen something when they chatted over Skype. Margot was intimidating, but there were moments of silliness that had charmed him time and again, his desire for more overlapping into something quite a bit more solid than his confidence regarding her feelings.

He shook his head, feeling foolish. He couldn't expect *anything* from her. Feelings shouldn't even be a consideration, especially now, when his sister remained in the clutches of one of the richest (and most mysterious, once one dared to look behind the shiny reputation they'd carefully cultivated), families in the UK!

He clenched his jaw. *Focus, Spence.*

He'd always been a devoted brother, but it had been easy. Despite their many differences, he and his sister were connected in more fundamental ways. He'd naturally looked out for her, somehow always knew where she was and if she needed help. And now, he knew she was close, and that she was failing. But he knew with one-hundred percent confidence that she was alive, too.

He saw Charis first; a petite woman whose bouncing curls and youthful grace could trick a less observant person into thinking she was unremarkable, save her wild hair and pixie-like stature. But her eyes told the real truth, her gaze careful and intelligent. And something else – there was a *knowing* about her. When she found him and smiled, he felt she was staring straight into him. But his eyes moved, finding the tall, bored-looking woman beside her immediately.

Margot was scanning the place, leaning slightly to say something into the psychic's ear, making her laugh. But then she was straightening up and smiling, her eyes firmly on him. He felt himself smile back automatically, a warmth spreading over him.

This was *not* like him. He felt a heat in his cheeks and imagined himself as the skunk in those childhood cartoons, floating helplessly behind a very disinterested cat. Poor guy hadn't even known he'd fallen for an unwitting enchantress of a different species altogether. *Probably wouldn't have cared if he had known,* Spencer thought. He was grateful as the women approached for the advantages he had over the misdirected skunk. Margot Francis, despite her exquisite mind and a beauty that seemed apparent to everyone but her, was human. He wondered absently if any other creature on earth was capable of blushing so prettily.

He reached out to shake her hand, "Dr. Francis," he said, his voice cracking and his cheeks reaching a new temperature of embarrassment.

"I'm glad to meet you, Spencer Hale," she smiled back.

They stood like that for a moment, nearly eye-to-eye and beaming happiness out at each other, before Charis waved her hand in a rather pathetic wave. "Hi. I'm Charis," she said, then bent to insert her head between the two. She smiled up at Spencer, who dropped Margot's hand with a flustered, "Oh!"

Charis straightened, her lips tight against what Spencer could only assume was the urge to laugh. But at least she'd be laughing at both he and Margot, and that was a very, very nice realization.

"We only have the carry-ons," Margot said, gesturing to their rolling luggage.

"Great!" Spencer startled himself into motion, first reaching for Charis's hand and meeting her properly. "Pleased to meet you, Charis."

"Likewise."

He clapped his hands together. "Well, then! Unless either of you has an idea of what to do first, I suggest we swing by Police headquarters to keep them on their toes, then back to my flat. I'd like to show you both what I've managed to gather about the Everleigh family."

Charis shook her head, which he'd anticipated. The woman was understandably impatient. If she was as skilled at using her gift as he'd read, she was two steps ahead of them all.

He held his hands up in defense, but added a smile. "Nobody wants to rush in there and find my sister more than I do," he said, his smile fading. "But I don't want her kidnapper to panic, either." He let his hands drop. "I don't want her hurt."

Margot touched his arm compassionately, then looked at Charis. "I can't imagine what it must be like to know something and be unable to act on it."

Charis let out a cynical laugh. "You'd think I'd be better at it by now. Come on," she motioned them onward, "let's go. Your ideas for next steps are good, Spencer, but as long as we're taking our time, I'm going to need a drive-through of some sort."

Margot laughed. "You're the hungriest pixie I know!"

Charis shot her friend a look, and Spencer laughed.

"Have you two known each other long?"

"Not in this lifetime," Charis said over her shoulder, then sped up a bit. "Come on, I'm starving!"

Margot hung back to fall into step with Spencer. He could feel her warmth, though their skin never touched. "The first time we met was weird," she said, her voice low as she gestured toward Charis. "It was like meeting someone who was already your best friend, for the first time." She frowned.

Spencer's stomach did a somersault. "Funny how you can meet some people and it'll be years before you realize their role in your life, and then there are those rare ones, you know? The ones you already know, somehow, even at first sight, or the sound of their name." He shook his head, chuckling. "Peyton always said we all have a bunch of soul mates we travel through our lives with. Over the years, I've come to realize what she meant." He looked at Margot sideways, suddenly aware of the connotations of his words.

But she was beaming. "She says that, too," she jerked a thumb toward Charis.

Spencer fought the urge to clam up. "Let me take that," he said, reaching for Margot's luggage.

"Oh!" Margot stopped, looking down at her rolling suitcase as though she'd just realized it was there, then handing the handle over. "Thank you!"

They started walking again.

"It's been a long time since someone's wanted to help with…" she laughed, adorably flustered, "stuff," she finished.

They filed through the door to the parking lot, which Charis was holding open for them. Spencer was surprised she wasn't tapping her foot impatiently. "Thanks," he offered, then pointed. "My car's the Jeep."

Margot clapped her hands. "Oh, I've always thought Jeeps must be so fun. I love the colour!" she bounced off, surprising Spencer with a flash of childlike abandon.

"Is she always so -" he made a face, unable to find the word.

"Yep," Charis answered. "And by the way," she looked up at him, "it's not just the knowing before others do. It's the *seeing.*"

He frowned at her.

"I can *see* Peyton. Images of her come to me all the time, and I'm worried about her. That's why I'm impatient."

Spencer had stopped in his tracks, his heart galloping. "Shit," he said, his mind racing and his instincts telling him to change his plans. To *go.*

Charis walked back to him. He could see Margot behind her, looking back at them curiously. "Don't worry. When it's time to forget process and procedure, no amount of reasoning will keep me from going straight to her. OK?"

Her face was sincere. He nodded dumbly. "I'm sorry."

She shook her head. "No need to be; I'm used to folks not getting it when I'm overeager. I just wanted you to know."

They got the luggage in the Jeep and strapped in, Margot calling dibs on shotgun with no argument from Charis.

"Let's go talk to the police," Spencer said, a new sense of urgency and determination behind his words.

"Hang on to your seat, Margot," Charis muttered from the back seat as Margot made a show of standing, her upper half breeching the roll bars, "shit just got real."

Chapter 31 – A Sad Decline

Peyton lay in bed beneath the covers. It was the first day she'd found herself too weak to do anything beyond taking herself to the toilet when the urge was upon her. And it wasn't often. She'd been drinking water, but it had been two days since she'd seen Constance, and therefore since she'd seen any sort of meal.

While the hunger had been painful at first, it seemed now that her body was too weak even to make an effort at hurting. She just felt tired.

Enzo had been trying so hard. The lock mechanism in his late mother's door was different than that for the loft, and the proximity to Constance's room meant he'd been caught trying to figure it out more than once. All it had meant was Constance bursting from her room then standing in the hallway, her eyes suspiciously on the door for several moments before trying the handle. Unfailingly, she'd turn back to her room once she was satisfied the door was held solidly closed, without a knock, even, to see if Peyton was still alive.

Thus, the only food Enzo had been able to smuggle in had to fit under the door, and precious little did. They'd celebrated the discovery that an entire crepe could pass through, but it had been short-lived. Breakfast had been of the grab and go sort since Constance had been going in to the office. Besides, just carrying the thing from the kitchen to her second-floor doorway had been a monumental effort for the ghost. He'd disappeared until tea time after delivering it. The state of it had been deplorable, but Peyton had gobbled it even as she'd imagined it dropping to the floor several times when Enzo lost his focus.

And there'd been no tea for days. Peyton had lost count, but she thought it had been five days since the last actual tea, with dresses and the tea room and stiff, uncomfortable conversation with Constance.

What she would give for tea today, though even imagining the effort it would take to eat frightened her.

She'd never been good at feeling ill. When she was very young and living in her own little world, it had terrified her to feel differently within herself. She was the only person she could count on, after all. Nobody else could see what she saw – could feel what she felt! As a result, she took great solace in the fact that despite everything, she felt good. Sickness, therefore, was devastating. As she grew, she changed, but she'd never figured out how to handle being unwell. By the time she was a teenager, she'd learned not to fight it, at least, and was able to rest and let it run its course for the most part. But when she reached adulthood, even that took a strange turn, wherein Peyton seemed to give up completely whenever she was sick. Her mother said it was disturbing to watch her let go as she did, wholeheartedly. As though she was making peace with her fate.

And maybe her mother was right. It felt - calmer - to accept the possibility of the worst rather than having to convince herself everything would be OK.

So. there she lay, even her usually busy mind a blank slate, ready for what came. It was with some humour that she recalled her actions just the day before, when she'd crouched at the door, her ear to the wood, listening to the commotion outside it. She couldn't imagine what Constance had been doing. She certainly hadn't ever moved as much as she heard her move that day. There were sounds of sliding and banging, of objects toppling and zippers zipping. Peyton wondered if the woman was cleaning. She hadn't heard any staff in the wing at all since Constance had locked her in her dead mother's room. And she certainly was making enough noise to be cleaning. Arranging furniture, even! She'd even run off down the hall, returning several minutes later at a barely diminished speed.

Peyton hadn't even realized the woman could move that fast.

But in the end, the chaos had faded with no answer as to why it had happened in the first place, and Peyton found herself once again without entertainment. Enzo had brought her crumbs at tea time, when Constance failed to retrieve her again. He'd tried to encourage her to have hope. He was still working on the lock, after all, and with Constance away on weekdays now, they'd have plenty of time to attempt an escape!

Peyton had been tired, though. She'd asked him to let her lay close to him to keep warm and he'd looked at her in dismay, a rare show of concern on his face. But it was hard to keep warm when you weren't eating, and your flesh was fading slowly into bone. So many of her ghosts had looked this way, ravaged by illness or neglect.

She thought to turn onto her side, but her limbs were too heavy, so she just turned her head, her cheek on the musty pillowcase. She was fading into sleep when the lock clicked, but she wasn't alarmed. She thought *Enzo must be at it again.*

But it was Constance.

She stepped into the room purposefully, the sound of her pantyhose shushing between her thighs. "What is the meaning of this?" she demanded, her tone shrill. Peyton was surprised to feel some comfort at the sound of it.

She opened her eyes. "Constance?"

The woman hesitated.

Peyton took a deep breath and pressed herself to sitting,

then swooned as her vision went dark.

"What's wrong?" Constance pressed, her voice hard. "Are you sick?"

Peyton's eyes fluttered. "I'm just - hungry, I think."

Constance smoothed her blouse over her stomach, looking smug. "Strange, I would've thought you'd be dressed and ready for tea, if you were hungry!"

Peyton gasped, relief washing over her and nearly overwhelming her senses. She had to catch herself as she listed dangerously toward the edge of the bed.

"Oh!" Constance reached without thinking, her palms meeting Peyton's shoulder and pushing her upright. She jerked her hands back as soon as Peyton was stable, even shook them a bit, as if to get the germs off.

"Sorry," Peyton whispered, unable to push any strength into the word.

"If you're sick, I'll leave you to rest."

The words would seem fine on paper, but Peyton heard the threat in them.

"No! I'm not sick! I'll be -" she paused as her dizziness intensified, thinking of the cool water in the bathroom sink. "Ugh," she raised a hand to her head, but was quickly dismayed at how ineffective it was to try and steady herself with part of her unsteady self. "I just need some food, I think," she finished quickly, her words slurring slightly.

"Good heavens!" Constance looked put-out. She started back out of the room, but paused, rummaging in a skirt pocket and then thrusting something toward Peyton. "Eat this. I'll be back to take you to tea in a few minutes. But *do* get up. If you're still in bed when I return, I won't try again."

Peyton's heart fluttered. *That* threat was clear in every

way. She reached for what Constance was offering, muttering her thanks, then tore it open when she saw it was a granola bar.

Constance made a disapproving noise, then went out.

Peyton devoured the bar, her mouth rejoicing at the sweetness, then closed her eyes, letting herself feel something in her stomach that wasn't water, or crumbs.

It felt good.

For a minute, anyway. By the time she'd gotten herself out of bed and staggered to the bathroom, she was quite sure it was going to come right back up. "Oh, no you don't!" she whispered, leaning over and turning the cold water on. She envisioned each gulp as a plug, shoving the much-needed food down so it could stay. So it could do her some good.

She stopped after three gulps and stood, entirely uncertain if she'd done more harm than good. She stared at her reflection as she waited for her stomach to decide. She was instantly mesmerized, any thoughts about the need to vomit vanishing. Her eyes pricked with tears for, staring into eyes that yearned for freedom and at a face that told a story of deprivation, she recognized herself. Her reflection had been eerily unfamiliar to her all her life, but now, at her worst, she saw herself.

Chapter 32 – The Evolution Of A Plan

By the time Constance returned, Peyton was sitting on the edge of the bed, hands folded neatly in her lap, and feeling the positive effects of the granola bar.

Constance looked almost disappointed, but resolutely stuck her nose in the air. "There! That's better. Up!" she motioned for Peyton to stand, and she did, but slowly, distrustful of her strength.

They looked at each other warily.

"Well?" Constance motioned her toward the door.

Peyton frowned. "What about the blindfold? And the -"

"Pfft!" Constance waved the notion away. "You know the tea room is just down the hall as well as I do."

Peyton remained frozen to the spot.

"What? Don't trust me?" the woman's expression was unreadable.

Peyton, unable to help herself, shook her head solemnly.

Constance laughed. It was such a strange sound that Peyton recoiled.

"Good Lord," the woman rolled her eyes. "I don't know what's gotten into you, but let's get a move on, shall we?" She raised her eyebrows.

"Aren't you afraid I'll run?"

Constance looked her up and down. "Not at all, actually. But if you do, there's always this," she patted a lump at her waist, beneath a fold of her blouse. Her eyes sent a challenge to Peyton.

A gun?

Peyton nodded, shocked on some distant level but ultimately too stretched to care. "I see."

She was terribly self-conscious as they traversed the hallway, Constance behind her. She cringed against the sound of the woman's thighs rubbing together, and wondered if her own frailty was still as easy to spot. She was walking, yes, but she could feel herself weaving, just slightly.

Constance snickered. "You look drunk," she said, answering Peyton's unspoken question.

She stopped at the tea room door, her hand going reflexively to her nose at the wall of stench she'd hit. In the twilight of the evening, remnants of a tea unattended were displayed quite beautifully – the tiered platters stacked with familiar sandwiches and treats and the teapot and cups proudly ready and waiting. But the smell gave the setting's age away. Peyton wondered how Constance hadn't realized the state of the place.

Constance flicked on the light and gasped. "Oh, this won't do," she muttered. Peyton peeked sideways at her. Her face was scarlet. Constance pursed her lips, then flicked the light back off. "Come on," she said, taking Peyton roughly by the upper arm and leading her further down the hallway. "I forgot I'd fired Cook," she lamented angrily, then giggled. "I wondered what that smell was..." she trailed off.

Peyton stumbled as Constance led her, unprepared for the speed they were carrying even with the granola bar fuelling her. But her speed benefitted from the lifting of her spirits as Constance turned them toward the stairs to the third floor.

"Are we going to the loft?"

Constance made a face. "It's the only thing up here," she answered.

Peyton bit her lip. She was afraid to smile, lest Constance change her mind for spite.

"The window's been fixed for a couple days, but I was too busy to bring you up. The kitchen's stocked too, I think, though it won't be again until I find some new staff, so don't rush through it."

Constance unlocked the door, then pocketed the keys. She looked up at Peyton. "We can have our tea here – I trust you can make us something simple?"

Peyton could barely contain herself. She held back tears of relief, but barely. She wanted to run, to open the fridge and lay out on the floor in front of it, just admiring its contents before diving into it. Instead she nodded toward Constance, wanting to thank her. Wanting to *hug* her, but grateful for her difficulties in situations such as these, because she knew on all logical levels that hugging Constance would be something she'd never forgive herself for, no matter how overwhelmed she was in that moment.

"Good!" She waved Peyton in. "Tea and sandwiches will be fine. I have something to talk to you about."

Peyton bit back the questions that bubbled up at her captor's words. "Tea and sandwiches," she repeated, almost to herself, and got to work, moving comfortably, if not more carefully, given her diminished energy and strength, around the kitchen. It was easy enough to get through the preparations. She simply reminded herself over and over that if she passed out, she wouldn't get to eat.

It was only as she carried Constance's plate and teacup to the corner table that she wondered what Constance had to talk to her about. "There. I hope ham, cheese and sweet pickles on rye is alright?"

"You would've done better to wonder that before you made it, but as luck would have it, I *do* happen to like them," Constance said, her face tight.

Peyton smiled, and was about to turn to retrieve her own meal when Constance went on.

"Sit down," she motioned to the bench diagonal to her.

Peyton nearly broke into tears. "Can I -" she stopped, having seen the disapproval on Constance's face. She sat, her chest heavy with disappointment.

"You can eat once we've chatted."

Peyton folded her hands in her lap. She was quite sure she'd never felt as compelled to invite the Universe to claim her as she did in that moment.

"I know things haven't been as I promised, or intended," the woman started, but she didn't meet Peyton's eyes. "I thought having you here would allow my brother and I to have some sort of life together, as unusual as it would've been. But then, I suppose my brother has always done things his own way," she tittered. "That said, I have, too!"

Peyton made herself smile politely.

"In any case, things have changed, and I find myself eager to start a new path, but there are a couple of things in my way."

Peyton gulped involuntarily. "I guess I'm one of those things?"

"You are," Constance said, and she did look at her, now. "But I don't want things to get...messy. I want to work things out so that we can both have a new start."

Peyton didn't move, nor breathe, for fear the positivity in the words she'd just heard would fade away.

"I need to make sure the family business comes to me, and you need to get back to – whatever life you had before," she said, a touch distastefully.

Peyton couldn't help it; she leaned toward Constance in her eagerness to hear what would surely come next: a plan.

"Calm down! I haven't worked everything out yet," Constance said, then took a large bite of her sandwich.

Peyton's stomach growled uncomfortably.

"Ugh," Constance muttered in response. "Anyway, my mother used to help me figure out plans of action, even after she died. She's gone now, just like Enzo. But I know a girl that can talk to ghosts."

Peyton sat straight up, her mind whirling. "You – you know I've seen your mother?"

Constance smiled. "I do, now."

Peyton deflated. "Oh." She hadn't known whether Constance was still talking to her mother. Virginia hadn't appeared to Peyton again since the night Enzo had confessed everything. Besides that one time, when she thought she saw regret in the woman's pale features as she looked at her son, Virginia Everleigh was very much a mystery to Peyton, still.

"And I don't care if she's told you not to talk to me or tell me anything. The truth of the matter is, I'm the only one here who can help you get back to your life."

Peyton was having trouble sorting her thoughts. Her hunger bit at her even as the granola bar churned in her confused stomach, and she was still so tired. "She hasn't said anything to me, really," she managed, her eyes darting to her plate on the counter. "What do you need from her?"

Constance put her sandwich corner down and sipped her tea delicately. "From *them*," she said as she replaced the cup on its saucer. "Ugh; needs sugar."

Peyton stood to retrieve it out of habit, but Constance motioned her back down.

"Oh, no you don't. I don't want you sneaking anything while you're in the kitchen."

Peyton sat hard in her seat, bouncing a bit. Constance raised her eyebrows. "Sorry," Peyton muttered.

"I want you to ask them what, *exactly*, I need to confront Father with in order to get him to change the heir policy." She said it casually, as though the task would be simple, her eyes on her tea again. Peyton supposed she was debating whether to drink it, sweet or not.

Something stirred in Peyton. *She* knew what Stewart Everleigh had done that would destroy everything he owned, if revealed. She could tell Constance now and be done with it.

She scanned the loft, her heart happy for the familiarity even if it had been her prison. *It's all relative*, she thought. Then, she thought of Enzo. She couldn't betray him, even if it meant her freedom. She looked back at Constance, ready to tell her just that.

But Enzo was suddenly beside his twin, his eyes darkly on her expression.

Peyton struggled to hide her surprise.

"What?" Constance asked, her hand stopping in midair so that her teacup froze halfway to her mouth.

"What is she playing at?" Enzo puzzled over his sister's intentions aloud. He looked at Peyton. "Hello, darling."

Peyton giggled

"Enzo?" Constance looked around frantically.

"I've always wondered why she can't see you," Peyton asked.

Enzo shrugged.

"She can see your mother, though." It was something that continued to puzzle her, despite her many theories.

Constance had stopped looking around and was still, her eyes on Peyton.

She wants to know, too.

But he ignored the question, addressing Constance's request instead. "Tell her I haven't decided whether she should know just yet," Enzo said, his eyes narrowing.

Peyton opened her mouth to talk, but Virginia Everleigh appeared, effectively shutting her up. The woman hovered at the outside edge of the table, her slippered feet a foot above the floor, and she looked – terrible.

"*What now?*" Constance's voice had gone up an octave.

Peyton looked between the wet, pale woman in pyjamas and Constance.

"I was going to tell her," the woman said, her eyes only on her son, "but only to ruin Stewart." She begun to cry. "I hate how selfish I've been!"

Enzo flickered, his expression revealing his discomfort.

"What?" Constance wailed, clearly oblivious to both ghosts.

Peyton put a hand up. "Wait."

Constance folded her arms and sat back, like a three-year-old giving in.

"Oh, Enzo! I won't ask you to forgive me, because I can't even forgive myself! But I want you to know that I'm so sorry – for being so blind all those years, for not making you and your sister my priority – for so much! But above all, I'm so sorry that you lost your life. It's my fault! None of it would have happened if it weren't for me!" The woman sobbed, putting her face in her hands. Blood begun to stream from her wrists and Peyton recoiled again, but she put a silencing finger up before Constance could say anything. Her eyes were on Enzo.

The boy she'd known to be impulsive and unpredictable, mischievous and selfish – and incredibly temperamental – had changed in the past several weeks. And now, Peyton saw something entirely new.

Enzo was completely and utterly stumped. He looked like a child who'd been singled out in class with no answer to offer, nor any jokes to fill the silence. "I – I always felt that *your* death was *my* fault!"

His mother's eyes appeared over slightly lowered hands. "Of course it wasn't! It was *my* fault and nobody else's. I only wish I had made different decisions."

"But that night, when you came to ask me about the affair, I should have talked to you rather than rage about Father. I'm sorry, too," Enzo said.

"Enzo?" Peyton reached across the table as he looked at her. "Maybe telling Constance could help the real villain pay for what he did to you – to both of you." She looked to Virginia.

She held her breath. It had been a risky move, and one she hadn't considered enough, perhaps. But she couldn't help it; the sandwich on the counter felt like salvation, and she needed it. Soon.

Enzo looked back at his mother. "I – I don't think it was your fault, either."

Virginia let her streaming arms fall to her sides. Peyton cringed as blood splashed onto the table and streaked across the floor.

"What is *happening*?" Constance cried, tears rolling over rounded cheeks.

"What do you mean? You sound unsure - surely you know the circumstances of your own death?" Virginia was frowning. Peyton thought she glimpsed the no-nonsense businesswoman she was in life.

Enzo shook his head. "I don't remember."

Virginia looked at Enzo for a long time, and then at Constance. Finally, she looked at Peyton. "I couldn't stay that day. As soon as Constance was in the stables, I was gone." She cast her eyes on her son again. "I wanted her to know about your affair, so she could use that against her father, too," she shook her head. "It was wrong. I knew it was as soon as I'd accomplished it."

"I think it would be fair to put some of the blame on Father," Enzo grinned. "He made us all crazy, apparently."

Virginia looked unsure. She looked at Constance, then at Peyton. "I don't know how to make her see me anymore. I feel like my strength here is fading."

Peyton sat up. "I can help."

"What are you doing?" Enzo asked.

Virginia looked at her son. "It's time for secrets to be unearthed. All of them."

Enzo paused, then nodded, and Virginia looked at Peyton again.

"Tell my daughter that we'll give her what she needs to go to her father with *if* she describes her brother's death."

Enzo's eyes brightened.

"In detail," Virginia finished, then smiled at her son.

Peyton took a breath, but Enzo interrupted her. "But tell her no deal if you can't stay here tonight!"

"What?" Peyton frowned at the ghost that had become

her friend.

"You're sick, Pey. You need to eat and rest before you bolt. I'm worried about you."

Virginia put a ghostly hand on her son's forearm. Peyton noticed the arm that reached across the table to complete the task had stopped streaming blood. "She's not alone. There are helpers coming."

Peyton's eyes bulged. "What?"

Virginia met her eyes. "Don't let Constance know. You have friends coming."

Peyton swallowed, hard. There was a sudden lump in her throat, and a surge of determination roared through her. She couldn't even imagine her hopeless state of only an hour earlier. For now, she knew she would live. She turned to Constance, who appeared frantic in her efforts to wait quietly.

"Your mother and Enzo are both here. They want to make a deal."

Constance narrowed her eyes, clearly dubious. "What *kind* of deal?"

"They will tell you the information you need to confront your father with, but only if you tell them exactly how Enzo died."

Constance's eyes widened, but only for a moment. She nodded. "It's time to set that record straight, too."

Enzo gestured, urging Peyton on.

"And they – Enzo, actually – wants me to stay in the loft tonight, so I can eat and rest."

"Ah-ha!" Constance pointed triumphantly, her finger inches from Peyton's face. "You think you have all the power, don't you? Being the only one who can see them? But I'm not stupid, Peyton Hale. I know when someone's looking out for number one!"

"She should," Enzo said.

Virginia looked between her children, her expression pained. "She learned from me," she cried, and Enzo looked regretful now, too.

Constance stood, edging out from the padded bench straight through Enzo, who exclaimed, "Aaaah!" and grimaced in protest as she did. She stood, her full five-foot-zero inches trembling with emotion, and pointed again.

"I will *not* be manipulated by you, or anyone! If Enzo is so concerned about you, he has to know *I'm* in control of what happens to you, here! Not him!"

"Bitch!" Enzo grunted, his face red. Virginia floated backward, somehow knowing as her son pulled an arm back straight, then swept it mightily across the table, Constance's tea and what remained of her sandwich flying dramatically into the air as her brother's ghost roared in fury.

Constance screamed, backing away so fast she stumbled and fell, yelping like a puppy when she landed on the hardwood.

Peyton stood, her entire body shaking in horror and fear. But when she saw Constance, dripping with milky tea and the last bits of her ham sandwich in various pieces on her lap, a little bit of joy mixed in there, too.

Constance looked at her, then reached upward. "Help me!"

Peyton went around the table, but Virginia calmly blocked the way, hovering above her such that Peyton had to crane her neck.

"She has to start taking care of herself," she said, her voice quiet.

Peyton glanced at Constance. Nodded.

"Well?"

Peyton shook her head. "Your mother says it's time for you to take care of yourself."

Constance's face cleared, her mouth hanging open slightly as she seemed to consider the words. She looked back up at Peyton. "OK."

"OK," Peyton repeated, backing up again. Enzo was suddenly at her side, still angry, but his energy felt hopeful too.

Constance got herself up, but made quite a show of it, slipping twice on the wet floor. Peyton knew she'd laugh about it someday, but just then she wanted nothing more than to race to the counter and shove half her sandwich into her mouth.

Constance sat again, this time on the outside edge of the bench. She took a moment to straighten herself up as much as possible. She looked at Peyton. "Tell me."

Peyton looked at the ghosts in turn. Both nodded.

She sat and made herself meet Constance's eyes. "Your father abused Enzo." Constance stared at her, her face blank. "Sexually," she added.

Constance frowned. "What? He didn't even *talk* to Enzo – or me, for that matter."

Enzo, who was still on the bench, but between them, now, spoke, his eyes on his sister. "Tell her he found me when I got into the safe, looking at pictures."

Peyton repeated Enzo's words and Constance reacted immediately. "The ones he told me about? The ones of – naked children?"

Virginia was crying again.

Peyton nodded.

"But Enzo made a joke of it." She shook her head, but tears welled in her eyes. "He never said anything else…"

"He paid dearly for learning your father was a pedophile. There are pictures on his computer, too," Peyton said, fuelled by the words of the ghost between them. "All you have to do is tell the police and they'll find them, and your father will be charged with – well, enough to be stripped of his title and any rights to Everleigh Enterprises."

"Wait!" Virginia screamed, startling Peyton and Enzo, both. "She must have him change the policy first, or the business will go to Bertie!"

Peyton frowned. "Is that really the priority?" She looked at Enzo, then back at his mother. "Don't you think it's more important to get this out? For Enzo?"

Virginia wrung her hands. "Of course! But – I feel I must take care of my living child, too, seeing as how terrible I was to them both in life!"

Enzo scoffed. "Why? Constance will never be a pauper, Mother. The family would avoid such a scandal. But she saw me die. She never told anyone that, though. She let Candace take the brunt of suspicion! She just wanted people to come to their own conclusions – and they did, didn't they?"

Virginia couldn't help but grin. "That Candace is lucky to still have a position in the family at all!"

"All Constance wanted was to have something I needed. Something she knew I'd stick around for, when what I really need is to move on."

Peyton gasped.

"Just like you," he finished.

Peyton looked at Virginia. She *had* to see it, now. But she was fraught, her tears still streaming as she wrung her hands.

She could stand it no more. "Plus, she's a *kidnapper!*" Peyton cried, instantly sucking her breath in as though she could pull the words back with it.

"Hey!" Constance tried, but it was weak. "What's happening?" she asked, instead of pursuing any anger at Peyton.

"Tell her to do it fast," Enzo said.

"Yes, tell her. And what happens, happens," Virginia agreed.

Peyton looked at Constance. "They say you need to confront him soon. As soon as you explain about Enzo's death!" she added quickly, making Enzo smile gratefully.

Constance pursed her lips, then stood again. "Right. Then I'll leave you to eat and rest, shall I?"

The ghosts stirred, obviously upset. Peyton realized they hadn't gotten a commitment from Constance.

"When are you going to -?"

"Tomorrow," she cut Peyton off. "I'll take you to the stables, where it happened, and then you'll be free to go, as long as you promise that this will be behind us," she said, studying Peyton. "Meaning you go home, you apologize for disappearing, but take full responsibility. You can use your – condition – as an explanation. And the truth stays a secret. Forever."

Peyton looked at the ghosts. They were both nodding. "Remember, you have friends," Virginia whispered. "Once you get away, you owe nothing to her."

Enzo looked questioningly at his mother.

She smiled. "I should have taught you both about consequences. I see now it's a dangerous lesson not to learn."

Peyton looked at Constance. "Deal," she replied.

"Good. Then I will see you tomorrow, and if any funny business happens before then, the deal is off."

Peyton nodded, though she was puzzled over what Constance could do to her now, if she did escape. She eyed Enzo and remembered her role in his getting some peace over his death. *Right. There's that.*

Constance patted the butt of her gun before turning to go.

That, too.

Chapter 33 – A Path Develops

The Jeep was quiet as the three pulled out of the police headquarters parking lot. Spencer had put the top up as the sky clouded over with angry, pendulous shades of dark grey. He missed the sound of rushing through the air in those moments, when everybody was introspective and nobody filled the silence.

"It wasn't a complete failure," Margot said, finally, from the back seat.

Charis turned to smile at her friend, but quickly went back to her own thoughts.

Spencer met Margot's eyes in the rear-view mirror. "At least we know where they are in the investigation."

Margot gave a quick nod. "I was shocked to hear they'd talked to Stewart Everleigh already! I mean, it was just a phone conversation, but it surprised me." She gazed out the window, briefly distracted by their surroundings. "I love London."

"It surprised me too, but even more, it worries me," Spencer said. "If Everleigh's been questioned, even just over the phone, it means either Peyton's captors have been tipped off -"

"If he had anything to do with it," Margot interjected.

"Right. Or it means he'll be on high alert, even if he knew nothing about Peyton."

Margot frowned. "But, how could he not?"

Spencer shrugged. "The Detective said he travels a lot;

259

that he's consumed by the business and rarely spends time with the family. At least publicly."

"Hm. We can't know conclusively either way, but you're right. His knowing anything about the police looking for Peyton is worrisome."

Spencer chewed his bottom lip. He glanced sideways at the uncharacteristically silent psychic in the passenger seat. She was facing front, her eyes steadfast on the road ahead.

"Strange that the Detective didn't go to the house," Margot went on. "At least to talk to Constance."

"I've been puzzling over that one. They knew about Enzo's passing," Spencer noted. "It is strange that they didn't seek Constance out, given it was she who was identified by witnesses that night in Halifax."

"Right, but maybe that's exactly why they want to tiptoe around her. They're planning to speak with the uncle – Bertrand? – tomorrow."

Spencer nodded.

"I'm terrible with names," Margot said. "Anyway, they're meeting him in a diner, remember? Not at the house, not at the office. Seems a logical way to get to the source without storming in and spooking the perpetrator."

Spencer's thoughts tried to call up potential end scenarios, should the captor be spooked, but he shook his head, determined not to go down that path. Not now, when focus was so important.

Margot rested back against her seat, her eyes gazing forlornly out the window again.

Spencer cleared his throat, preparing to check in with Charis, but she spoke before he could.

"Your house," she said, her voice low.

"How'd you -?"

"I think we need to review everything you have on the family, like you said."

Margot leaned forward again. "Do we have time?"

"I'm sure we have tonight. Tomorrow is – murky."

Margot and Spencer exchanged a look in the mirror. "Shouldn't we talk to Candace today, then?"

Charis shook her head. "Spencer's instincts are on. But I think we need to drop any intentions of trying to present ourselves as investors or the like." She looked at Margot, then Spencer. "We need to go to Candace Everleigh with our cards on the table if we hope for her to return the favor."

Margot nodded. "I like it."

"I've been questioning myself, though. Why go to Candace when we could go straight to the Estate and confront whatever family member we can get to?" Spencer clenched the steering wheel in a rare show of impatience.

Charis touched his forearm. "We *will* go, but we need Candace to take us."

He cast a questioning glace her way.

"Tomorrow."

"Ugh," Margot sat back in her seat again. "I hate waiting!"

"We need to give this some time to unfold in the way its supposed to," Charis murmured, her eyes on the landscape, again. "Are we nearly there?"

"Yep," Spencer said as he turned into his apartment building's underground parking.

The three were tensely quiet as the elevator took them upward.

"I'd like to make a call to Candace Everleigh, set up the appointment directly, given my relation to Peyton. Maybe she'll have some empathy." Spencer shrugged as they exited the elevator, then dug into his leather satchel for his keys.

"I like your bag," Margot smiled, her hand going absently to her own.

"I think that would be good," Charis said, still on-track. "And Margot and I can look through the information you have."

Spencer pushed the door open. "Please," he motioned them in. "Feels good to have a plan," he muttered, but it felt like he was trying to convince himself.

They got down to business, Spencer leading the women to a coffee table littered with papers and copies of articles.

"My notes are there," he pointed to a sketchpad filled with handwritten musings. He smiled apologetically at the women. "Sorry; I keep far too many notes; helps me get my thoughts organized."

Margot smiled brilliantly, but glanced at Charis and thought better of gushing about her own, similar habit.

"It's fine," Charis kneeled, already drawn to an article. She looked back up at Spencer before she started reading. "Have you a tablet or iPad we can use to research online?"

Margot rolled her eyes and took her own slim laptop out of her bag with a flourish. "Never leave home without it!"

"Perfect," Charis was already flipping it open.

"She's used it before," Margot smiled at Spencer.

His heart fluttered and he turned away, unwilling to let his reaction to being around this woman show. "Uh – I'll set up my laptop, too. I've compiled a set of links in a simple Excel spreadsheet for you and whomever would like to see them in the future. I had the police in mind, you know?" He was walking to his tiny dining area, where a two-person table was cluttered with a stack of what looked to Margot to be books on religion, unsurprisingly, and several empty coffee mugs.

She had to bite her cheeks in an effort not to exclaim over their similarities again. *Focus,* she told herself.

Once the women were set up – which had included Charis raiding Spencer's cupboards and making a snack of cheese and crackers for everyone before he could offer to help – he pulled out his phone and regarded the screen, his nerves jangling. "Do you two mind if I make the call to Candace in here?"

"I'd prefer it, but give us a couple minutes," Charis replied through her mouthful of food, her eyes never leaving the screen of Spencer's laptop.

"Sure," Spencer said, already pointing at the article Margot was reading to tell her the additional information he'd gathered on it. He hadn't a clue why he'd been asked to wait, but something told him to trust the petite woman sitting cross-legged on his floor as though she'd visited many times.

He and Margot had gone through several articles and some of Spencer's notes before Charis spoke again.

"Here," she interrupted them, pointing at the screen. "I managed to dig up the birth announcement for Constance and Enzo."

Margot and Spencer leaned in to view the screen. "Awesome!" Spencer enthused. He'd found it, too, but hadn't recognized any crucial information within it.

"Look;" Charis went on, pointing with one hand while wiping crumbs off her mouth with another. "It says the entire Everleigh family is thrilled that there is finally *an* heir to the Everleigh Enterprises throne, and here," she scrolled down, "here, it mentions Enzo as the heir." She looked up at them each in turn. "Why not Constance?"

"Was he born first, or something?" Margot wondered aloud.

Charis shrugged. "Even then, you wouldn't think that'd preclude her from inheriting the business with her *twin*.

Margot nodded.

Spencer perked up. "Oh! Wait a sec -" he started digging through the papers, then bounded off to the entryway.

Charis smiled at Margot. "How you doing?"

"I'm a little confused about how this is all coming together, truth be told."

"Understandable."

"Eager to get something accomplished, too."

"Mm, hmm."

"I'm really worried about Peyton."

Charis raised one eyebrow. "And?"

Margot gave in. "And he is SO tall! And oh, my God, I can *feel* the energy between us!"

"*There* it is." Charis smirked.

Spencer bounded into the room, paper in hand. "I photocopied this. I couldn't figure the significance at the time, but it stood out to me." He laid the paper in front of the women. "It's an article about a yearly charity campaign the Everleigh company does. It references the founder of the campaign, a woman who'd married into the family, named Gertrude; isn't that a fantastic name?"

Margot felt suddenly as though she were listening to Charis, and laughed.

Charis frowned at her.

"Anyway, they refer to her as 'Gertrude O'Connor,' the *first* wife of the late Everleigh CEO, Edward Everleigh. He was Stewart Everleigh's grandfather; took me a while to piece that together," he sighed.

The women looked at him expectantly.

"Oh! Right, so it references her – here," he pointed as he squatted at the little table, "and then here it notes that the campaign's continuance was in question when she and Edward divorced, given that the act of divorce, regardless of the reason, forfeits all non-blood members of the family's connections with the company."

Margot leaned into the article, frowning as she read. Charis did the same, her chin on Margot's shoulder. Both women gasped at the same time, exclaiming, "- as the result, apparently, of an enduring and mysterious company policy which is quite particular about the rights of family members!"

The two looked at each other, eyes wide, then laughed.

Margot shook her head, going back to the article. "'Yours truly regrets to say it was impossible to eek out any more information about this policy, but I have my suspicions. Consider this: have you ever heard of a female CEO of Everleigh Enterprises? I think not. And if one was compelled to dig, one would find multiple records of failed attempts to claim rights to the Everleigh fortune.'" Margot finished. She looked up at Spencer. "Were you able to find anything more?"

He shook his head. "Nothing but speculation. There are mentions of court cases in the Everleigh history, but nothing that proves anything that reporter said," he gestured toward the article. "I was able to find something of significance, though," he paused, shaking his head. "That reporter was never published in a prominent publication again."

"Holy shit," Charis breathed.

"That's why I had it in my bag. I was thinking of speaking to whatever live family members of the reporter I could find. The whole things struck me as odd, but none of it seemed to be relevant where Peyton is concerned, so I was pushing it to the side to look back into later."

"It might be relevant, after all."

Margot turned to Charis. "How? I mean, sure, it's an indication that Constance won't inherit the business from her father, and I can see how that would cast some suspicion around her brother's death. But assuming she wasn't going to inherit even if Enzo was dead..." she shook her head, thinking. "I just don't see it."

"Not for Constance, maybe." Charis eyed her friend knowingly.

Spencer covered his mouth. "For Candace!"

Margot gasped. "Of course! She's still married to Stewart; we know that, but we also know she doesn't live on the estate."

"And now we know that a divorce would cut her out entirely...unless she was connected to the family in some other way," Spencer added.

Charis nodded. "And I know she was. She was having an affair with Enzo."

Spencer made a face. "Her *stepson!*"

Charis nodded.

"Was she just covering her bases? Sleeping with the prince when the king lost interest?" Margot wondered.

They were all quiet for a moment.

"I don't know," Charis said, finally, "but something

doesn't feel right. From what we know, we can see that Candace has no prospect of gaining from the Everleigh fortune, except, of course, for whatever she's paid for her position within the company."

"So, why would she even stay?" Margot asked.

The three exchanged blank looks.

"Well, we may not know that, but I feel more hopeful she'll talk to us now," Spencer said, eyeing Charis.

She nodded. "Go for it. Set up the meeting"

Chapter 34 – Candace

"Cook!" Candace motioned the small French man at the door into her office. "Come in!"

He hesitated, then took of his beret and smoothed his dark hair. "Madame," he bowed slightly.

"No need for formality with me, Robert. You know that." She smiled. "Please, come in!"

The Estate's former cook – more precisely, the loyal chef of the house for nearly thirty years – entered the office of the Everleigh Winery Museum and sat. His countenance had never been easy, but now he was positively stiff.

"This is a surprise," Candace started, some internal alarm bell sounding. "I'm sorry I've been away. How are things at the house?"

The man pressed his lips together, then sniffed. "I'm afraid I wouldn't know, Mrs. Everleigh. Miss Constance dismissed me early zis week."

Candace laughed first, but there was no hint of humour on the man's face. And his French accent was in full-force - a phenomenon which was known throughout the Everleigh house as a sure indication that trouble was afoot. "Are you serious?"

He sniffed again. "I assure you I am, Madame, but worry not; I don't come to beg to have my position back. In fact, I have realized the parting is for ze best. I come to ask for the two weeks' pay owed to me, and an additional two weeks as agreed in my contract, for dismissal without notice."

"Robert, I knew nothing about this! What happened?"

Candace shook her head, thinking better of her reaction, and picking up her phone. "I'm calling Constance."

Robert reached out, gently staying her hand. "Please, Madame, I don't wish to cause any trouble, but I do need ze money I am owed, as I'm sure you understand."

Candace put her phone down, fully intending to dial her stepdaughter's number when Robert left. "Of course, but – can you tell me what happened?"

Perturbed, the man raised his hands and let them fall. "Things are not the same since – well, you know. Miss Constance is increasingly demanding, despite the diminished family members in need of my services!"

Candace recalled her husband complaining that Constance had been on a firing spree with the staff since her brother's death when Candace had used the state of the house as an excuse to stay away. Just one of many. It had seemed to placate him; he'd gone right back to complaining about his brother. And she'd listened dutifully, like always, her heart on pause. Her emotions on numb. Being in the empty, sad house was unbearable.

Enzo had rescued her when the Stewart Everleigh she'd married grew bored of her. It had happened so quickly, the man's transformation from doting and charming to apathetic – even mean. But when she'd rented a penthouse in the city to gauge his reaction, he'd barely blinked an eye. And when she agonized over how she'd answer questions about her distance that would surely come, it had been wasted energy, for he didn't seem to care.

She still went to business functions and linked arms with him for photographers, but they were strangers in all ways but appearance. And that was good. Enzo's death was a punch that wouldn't be pulled; the slowest blow. The most tragic of stumbles. And she couldn't pretend that part of her hadn't died that day, not for Stewart and especially not for Constance, who'd witnessed it all.

If she'd been smart, she would have rushed to Stewart's side, held him up as he grieved, but damned if the man seemed to barely notice the loss of his son. And she must be sick with grief herself, for she kept thinking she saw something else in her husband's response. Something like relief...and for all the man's flaws (and there were many), she couldn't bring herself to believe her own perceptions.

So, being away from the house was good, but whenever the question of what to do next arose, she shoved it away for later. Cutting all ties would mean such a waste of the years she'd devoted to the family, and with what to show for it? Absolutely nothing.

"Mrs. Everleigh? I can come back later, if you prefer?"

Candace blinked several times, willing herself into the present. "No. I'm sorry, Robert. I got lost in my thoughts, there. It's been a tough time for everyone since Enzo died, but I'm sure you didn't deserve to lose your job. You said Constance has been – unreasonable?" She hoped she'd gotten it right; she couldn't remember what he'd said last.

But he nodded. "I have always been 'appy to oblige the requests of ze family; you know zat!"

Candace nodded.

"But on zat day, as she was leaving, I ask her, because I noticed she did not take ze tea I prepared ze night before. There it sat, untouched and intact, as she fired Ms. Loretta ze day before! So, I ask, 'Do you need ze full tea for tonight, Miss?'"

"Wait. She fired Loretta? She's been staff forever! And –" She shook her head. "Full tea? What do you mean? Like she and Enzo had now and then?"

"Yes, Madame! Formal tea, in ze tearoom, with two of ze

tiered platters full of varieties of sandwiches, fruits and *petits fours*! I assumed you knew?"

Candace shook her head, letting out another laugh. "Are you kidding?"

He smoothed his suit jacket. "I assure you, I make formal tea every day for three months, now!" he replied, his voice escalating as he held three fingers up. "And when she missed it, I figure maybe she does not need it anymore. Maybe she is moving on now zat she iz working at headquarters! But she look at me like I am crazy! I try to explain why I ask, and *boom!* That's it, that's all!" He clapped his hands neatly, then clutched them together in front of himself.

Candace was flummoxed. She gazed out the window to the trees that blocked the view of the estate. "Why would she have you do all that every day? I mean, I know she's lost without her brother, but that just seems…"

Robert nodded, his lips turned down at the corners. "*C'est fou!*" He looked over his shoulder, then leaned toward her. "And zat iz not all! Some months back, she had me stock ze kitchen in ze third floor loft again, and every week since! I haven't done zat since she and ze young master were children!"

Candace nodded, her expression a mask of confusion. "Things have been very – difficult – since Enzo died," she said, her eyes shining with tears. "I guess we're all dealing with it in our own ways." She took a chequebook out of the drawer and wrote one out for him, padding it a bit for his trouble. She handed it over with a look of regret and stood, reaching for his hand. "I'm sorry, Robert. You've been an excellent member of the staff and shouldn't have been treated so dismissively. If I'd known you were slaving over full formal tea for one every day of the week, I'd have done something about it far sooner."

Robert nodded, his expression softening a little. "It iz a

blessing in disguise, Madame. I should be glad to be out of zat house and away from those people." He leaned closer, patting the hand that was still in his. "I never thought you belonged there. Why you still do anything for them is beyond me, and surely none of my business, but if I were you, I'd get out, too."

Candace met his eyes and saw nothing but genuine concern. "Thank you, Robert."

He let her hand drop and turned on his heel, ever-proper. But he looked back as he opened the office door. "It was for *three*, by ze way," he raised his eyebrows at her.

Candace cocked her head. "What? Three months?"

He shook his head. "Ze tea. She make me prepare formal tea every day for *three*, not one."

It was beyond comprehension. Two would have made some sense, if she was missing Enzo to the point of delusion, but *three*? "What? Why?"

The man who'd only ever been referred to as "Cook" by the Everleigh twins shrugged his slight shoulders. "I did not ask. I would have lost my job long ago if I had, with the temper Miss Everleigh has. But it felt strange. And something else – Miss Constance enjoys my cooking, zis has always been true, but – those groceries I put in ze third-floor loft? They are consistently used. I restock at tea time and there are washed dishes on the counter. And Miss Constance is eating what I make for her, too. She cannot cook to save her soul, Madame. I have witnessed her trying. I thought you should know."

Candace frowned, her mind whirling.

The little man gave a subtle bow, and went out.

"What's she up to?" Candace muttered to herself as she went to the window to watch Robert leave. Then went for her phone.

But it rang in her hand.

She nearly dropped it. Her hand on her racing heart, she answered it, despite the unfamiliar number on the display. "Everleigh Enterprises; this is Candace."

"Mrs. Everleigh, my name is Spencer Hale."

She frowned, rubbing her forehead. "I'm sorry; should I know your name?"

"Not mine, but I'm hoping you've heard my sister's – Peyton?"

"What? I'm sorry – Spencer? I'm in the middle of a situation that demands my attention; could you call back?"

"Yes. In fact, I was hoping to come meet with you tomorrow. I have reason to believe my sister, who's been missing since February, was in contact with your stepdaughter on the night she disappeared."

When it rains, it pours.

"I don't know anything about that; it sounds like you should be talking to the police rather than me. Why *have* you called me, exactly?"

"The police are involved, Ma'am, but I'm worried for my sister. She's not the best at taking care of herself in dangerous situations, and I'm hoping to make quicker progress than police process allows. I hope you understand I'm just trying anything I can to make some inroads."

Candace gazed out the window over the parking lot again, the former cook's words about the extra food and preparations echoing in her thoughts. She'd never imagined her continuing involvement with the Everleighs, her marriage notwithstanding, could bring her more surprises than it already had, but here she was.

"Come see me tomorrow at the Berkshire Winery. Early afternoon?"

"What? Yes, of course! Thank you," the man bumbled, clearly grateful.

"I don't know if I can help you find your sister, but if nothing else, I can take you onto the Estate."

"I can't tell you how grateful I am. I didn't expect this, to be truthful."

Candace gave a wry laugh. "Honestly, I don't have much to lose."

Chapter 35 – Escape

Peyton was pacing.

She'd found countless things to be grateful for since returning to the loft the previous evening, but having ample room to pace was the current winner.

That wasn't to say she hadn't taken advantage of her refound amenities. After devouring her sandwich the previous night, she'd indulged in bringing her earlier urge to fruition. In short, she'd prostrated herself in front of the open fridge until she was uncomfortably cold, admiring her bounty with grateful tears. Then, she'd brewed herself a tea and wandered the loft, celebrating her reacquaintance – as brief as it might be - with it anew. *Hello again, and goodbye soon*, she'd thought over and over with an odd surge of melancholy.

She'd taken a bubble bath before bed, too, and had even given herself time to lounge with a book, despite the fact that she'd lacked the focus to read. It had remained open on her lap, a comforting option while she'd watched the evening turn to night.

She'd even slept well. Enzo hadn't reappeared to talk to her before she drifted off, like he often did. Strange, though; on what was to be her last night on the Everleigh Estate, she found she wanted him there.

The seriousness of her impending visit to the stables with Constance – and two ghosts – didn't hit her until she was eating breakfast in the little corner dining nook remembering Enzo's dramatic outburst the night before with some humour.

Could Constance truly mean to set her free today?

And who were the friends whose arrival was foretold by Virginia Everleigh? Could she have meant the police? She frowned at the heavy cloud cover that lingered from the night before. An orchestra of rain and wind had been the soundtrack of her sleep, and though the rain seemed to have let up for the moment, the clouds threatened further release. She hugged her arms to herself as she fretted, her omelette going cold and rubbery as distraction stole her focus.

And as the morning had stretched onward and she'd run out of distractions – she had already packed her knapsack the night before, ensuring her passport and ID were still safely in the front pocket – her previous sense of calm was worn down. Finally, at the realization that Enzo hadn't come to her at all, her resolve shattered completely and, bereft of ways to fill the quiet, she'd begun to pace.

Enzo can't *stay away when he's excited,* she thought. *What if he gained enough peace after the conversation with Virginia last night to feel he could let go?*

She absently chewed at a thumbnail.

What do I do, then? Do I put on a charade in the stables, pretending Enzo is there while Constance confesses the details of his death?

She'd always been a terrible liar.

Then, she'd started thinking about the senior Mr. Everleigh. Constance hadn't shared her plan for confronting him.

Maybe she hadn't decided last night, she reasoned inwardly, but it didn't ring true.

What if she loses patience and goes to him first? What if she confesses everything about me?

This she was good at. Psychologists had dubbed it "catastrophic thinking," unanimously pronouncing her the queen.

Suddenly, there was a muffled *thud* from somewhere

below, followed by a crash. Peyton frowned, but kept moving. She'd heard similar sounds in the house before.

But then there was a male voice, distant but obviously risen in anger, and she stopped in her tracks. A scream came next, and based on her experience since she'd arrived in London with Constance, she knew it was her captor who'd voiced it. She jumped into action, racing to the door. She was dizzy when she reached it, and out of breath. A few little meals hadn't restored her completely. She sank to the floor as stars burst in her eyes, coming to rest on a sharply protruding pelvic bone. Still, she had the presence of mind to put her ear to the door.

She needn't have made the effort. The shot that rang through the air was enough to send her scrambling backward, her vision rushing back with the burst of adrenaline that fuelled her.

The silence that followed was overwhelming. She was unable to move, her eyes riveted to the door, until she realized she could hear her own gasping breaths.

And then she went toward it, her thoughts racing. The image of Constance's gun, then the memory of the stench in the tea room and the realization that Constance may have fired the entire staff, rather than just Cook. *There's nobody to hear it!*

Nobody, that was, except for her.

She stood. "Oh, no," she muttered, and put her ear to the door again. Exhaling when there was nothing, tears springing to her eyes, then scanning the loft, desperate for options.

But then, there *was* something.

She leaned back into the door, her ear pressed painfully tight to the wood. Nothing. Nothing.

A step.

"No!" she whimpered, backing away from the door.

She heard it again: footsteps, louder this time.

Advancing.

"Enzo!" she cried, but quietly, her mind presenting the possibility of the approaching footfalls belonging to Mr. Everleigh rather than Constance.

And then, she was *hoping* it was him to find her. Him to discover his daughter's crime and to revel in how it leveled the playing ground, if all crimes were considered equal. Keeping Peyton alive, so there was proof.

She thought of the abuse of Enzo and the negligence of the business. The absence of the man, even when he was near. The open apathy toward the core elements of his life, and all thoughts of luck finding her dissipated. She whimpered again, still quiet.

When Enzo popped into existence next to her, though, she cried out in relief. It wasn't that she thought he could save her. It was that she wouldn't be alone when she died.

"Shit!" Enzo exclaimed. "She went off the rails!"

Peyton regarded him sideways. "What happened? Was that a shot?"

"I've been watching her. I had a bad feeling after she left last night," he spoke with widened eyes and shock in his features, "but I couldn't stop her when I realized she was going to confront Father first! And it went bad, Peyton, holy *fuck!*"

Peyton grimaced, but said nothing.

"She fucking *shot* him! He's *dead*, I think!" He pressed his palms to the sides of his head and started pacing, like Peyton had been, only his body faded into nothing at mid-thigh. The effect was disconcerting.

Peyton whimpered, but he rushed back to her and

covered her mouth, his hand buzzing strangely. She thought of the red, rough mask he'd left on her lower face the last time he'd done this, but dared not move.

"Don't make a sound!" he hissed in her ear.

"Peyton!" It was Constance, not directly at the door, but in the hallway, certainly, drawing her name out long and high, like a mother searching for her child in a fun game of hide and seek.

She's lost it.

Peyton jerked her gaze to Enzo.

His expression was frantic. "Hide!" A fire blazed behind his eyes as he let his hand drop, then blinked out of existence with that familiar whistling sound.

Peyton lost time in her fear, her feet ignoring her brain's commands until the sound of something heavy shattering in the hallway shook her free and she ran, diving under the bed with a shriek.

She buried her face in her hands as Constance let loose with a rageful scream on the other side of the door.

What did Enzo do?

She peeked over her fingertips, her mind on the paintings in the hallway, and the large, empty vase. She gasped, again recalling his accomplishment with the tea and sandwich the night before. Something sparked in her – pride, she thought – and she smiled.

"I know that's you, Enzo!" Constance accused.

Peyton's smile disappeared.

There were two full seconds of silence, in which Peyton closed her eyes and thought of her mother, and the father of her youth, before he was overtaken with depression. Of her childhood ghost friends – of meeting Jade on her grave and learning just how different she was. Of Lex with his garbled, water-filled speech, of Jerome, whose head had dangled upside-down from the base of his neck and Alma, whose attacker had broken her back with a blow from a baseball bat, effectively paralysing her from the waist down before raping her, then leaving her for dead. Alma had followed Peyton around by dragging herself with her forearms – an army crawl, like Spencer had done as a near-toddler, but with no trace of innocence, no hint at joy.

Perhaps she'd scared Peyton the most, until she realized that Alma was only terrifying because Alma, herself, was terrified, too. Stuck in that state of horror and fear until Peyton came along and figured out how to help her.

There'd been other friends over the years, dead and alive. Margot popped into her thoughts and she smiled. Margot had been special, too. Next, she pictured Spencer, so like her and yet so refreshingly different. She could feel him as though he were near.

She frowned.

Then, there was a quiet knock at the door.

She suddenly felt stupid for hiding under the bed.

"Peyton? Are you still in there?" Constance still sounded out of control, but she wasn't screaming, at least.

Enzo's feet appeared at the edge of the bed, then his upside-down head as he bent to see her. He looked miserable. He looked apologetic. "I couldn't stop her," he lamented.

Then the lock clicked and Constance shushed her way in, her pantyhose announcing her arrival as they rubbed together between her thighs. Enzo flickered into nothing, only to have his visage replaced by Constance's approaching feet. Peyton gasped at the spray of blood on the woman's patent leather pumps and nude-colored pantyhose. Her flesh bulged slightly where the shoes bit into it. Then she knelt, placing the hand which held the gun in front of Peyton's face.

"Found you."

"Are you going to kill me?"

Constance laughed, but it sounded off, like she was caught between humour and terror, herself.

Scents of sulphur and burning came from the gun. "What happened?"

"Father wouldn't listen," Constance replied without hesitation. She swiped a tear away, "I can't believe I actually hoped he would." She met Peyton's eyes.

Peyton was suddenly struck by the surreal quality of the scene and felt again like she might faint.

"He tried to destroy the computer when I told him I knew what was on it! He threw it on the floor and said the only person who'd be found out would be me."

"I'm – I'm sorry," Peyton said.

Constance paused, then stood with some effort. "Get out from under there," she demanded, her voice hardening.

Peyton made her limbs work. She was trembling when she finally stood.

"How did he know about you?" Constance asked, her voice eerily calm now and her gun casually at her side.

Peyton felt her jaw drop at the bit of news, but seemed unable to stop it. "I – I -" she stammered, and Constance rolled her eyes.

"Everything's gone off the rails, I'm afraid," the woman used the same words Enzo had. She raised the gun as though remembering she had it and studied it, her face unreadable. "Well," she looked at Peyton, "come on."

"What? Where?" Peyton was suddenly positive she was being taken to a convenient place for a shooting.

Constance motioned her to the door with her gun. "We have a date at the stables, remember? With Mother and Enzo."

Peyton walked on shaky legs toward the door.

"And then, dear girl, your job here will be done," Constance added. And laughed.

When Peyton looked back, though, the gun was pointed at her, and the face behind it was deadly serious.

Chapter 36 – Strange Meeting

"Wow," Margot breathed as Spencer pulled into the winery parking lot on Monday. She leaned toward the windshield, blocking Spencer's view to the right. He didn't complain. "It's so – *grand.*"

Charis popped her head between the two from the back seat. "And busy," she noted.

It was true; the parking lot was nearly full, and people milled about the front of the building, some with tasting glasses in hand, and streamed up into the vast fields of grapevines that started directly behind the building itself. Margot could see a posted sign at what looked to be the beginning of a trail, and what looked to be a picnic area at the top of a slowly-rising hill. The mostly-naked vines still showed signs of their winter slumber, the gnarled, but well manicured plants only hinting at growth with cheerful bursts of bright green along their lengths.

"Quite the tourist destination," muttered Margot.

Spencer pulled into a recently-vacated spot near the building itself, then leaned forward, squinting up at the impressive structure. "I'm not an expert when it comes to architecture, but I don't think I've ever seen a building so simultaneously rustic and intimidating."

Charis nodded. "It's like they're trying to be quaint and charming, but the 'rich' can't help but shine through."

Margot chuckled. "I couldn't have said it better." She recalled what they'd learned in their research. "But then, it's multi-purpose, right? Museum, gift shop and tasting floor, and of course the upstairs offices for the local Everleigh staff."

"Right; I was impressed with their flexible work policies, actually," Charis piped up from the back again. "They allow work from home, from satellite offices, or employees can travel to headquarters and use the mobile workstations."

"Signs of the times," Spencer said absently, his eyes still on the façade. He pointed, "See that tinted window on the second floor? Bet that's Mrs. Everleigh's office."

Margot inhaled sharply as her stomach flipped. "I hope this goes well."

Spencer relaxed back into his seat, his eyes on her. "She sounded – *nice.* It was weird."

"And you said you got the feeling she was surprised by what you said about Peyton?"

He nodded.

"When I dreamt of her, the only negativity around her was coming from how Constance felt about her," Charis mused.

"Let's hope she lives up to first impressions," Margot said, her hand on the door. "Shall we?"

Spencer nodded, but held a hand up. "I know we agreed I'd do most of the talking, but are we still good with being open about who both of you are?"

Margot glanced back at Charis, who was already halfway out the door.

"I think so," the woman said, "but I think Margot and I will know whether to change things up once the conversation gets going."

Margot laughed. "I think your expectations of my intuition are a bit high, there, fortune-teller."

Charis smiled. "Let's go. Sometimes winging it is the best way to approach a mysterious situation, eh?" Margot and Spencer nodded, but didn't move. Charis sighed. "Guys, we are this close to getting Peyton back," she held a hand up, her thumb and forefinger poised to meet, but not quite touching, "and I believe our timing is really important today. And right now, it's time to *go*."

Margot gave Spencer a short nod, and smiled. He smiled back, creating a secret domino effect of warmth inside her body.

Her thoughts strayed to the night before as the three exited the car and came to stand together in front of it, all eyes on that second-story window with the dark tint.

They'd ordered in for dinner, during which they'd had an animated discussion which covered such topics as ghosts, religion, science, and Peyton herself. All three seemed comfortable and easy with each other – so much so, that Margot was surprised when Spencer commented on the time and asked she and Charis to stay.

In the end, they'd declined, opting to take advantage of their carefully-chosen hotel room, seeing as how they wouldn't get a refund if they cancelled, anyway. But, just as Margot was regretting the choice, her eyes on Spencer as he started bringing empty containers to the kitchen, Charis had asked Spencer to join them at the hotel.

"It makes sense that we stick together between now and when we go out to the Estate tomorrow," she'd reasoned, and her logic was solid. Still, Margot had whispered, "I love you!" in her friend's ear after Spencer had agreed and gone to pack a bag.

The remainder of the evening had been quiet, with Charis dozing off soon after talking to her kids. Margot had already made several calls to check in on work that afternoon, so with nothing left to concern themselves with, she and Spencer had taken advantage of the patio, lounging back with their legs on the railing as they chatted and laughed. When it was time to go in to bed, Spencer had smiled shyly at her and said, "You're nice company, even when my nerves are on edge." Margot had smiled, then they'd separated, Spencer taking one of the queen-sized beds and Margot climbing in beside Charis.

Charis had groaned, then mumbled something about going back to sleep. Margot had giggled at being treated like one of her children and snuggled up to her. Charis had woken, mumbling, "What the hell, woman?" and Margot had replied, "What? Oh, did you want to be the big spoon?"

Charis had laughed as she wriggled away from her quirky friend, and Spencer had snickered into the darkness.

And Margot had drifted off to sleep with a smile on her face.

Now, standing with two people she hadn't even known two months earlier, she counted herself lucky, for she couldn't have chosen better companions for the purpose that lay before them.

Spencer started inside when the doors opened up, guests spilling outward. Margot and Charis lingered behind, Charis whispering, "What'd you two do after I conked out last night?"

Margot grinned. She knew the question was rhetorical. "You know nothing happened."

"But it was nice anyway - the 'nothing' - right?"

Margot only winked at her.

The place was buzzing with activity. Margot found it hard not to be distracted by the gift store shelves, lined as they were with books and knickknacks and of course, a selection of wines.

"There she is," Spencer touched her hand lightly, and she automatically intertwined her fingers through his, then pulled away, mortified.

Spencer was pointing with his opposite hand toward a spiral staircase in the middle of the floor and looking back at her, his cheeks burning a shade of red she could feel reflected in her own.

"Haha – um, that was weird. I'm sorry. I'm weird. Oh! Is that her?" Margot very much wanted to die as her mouth tried to smooth the situation over.

Charis came between them, pushing them both forward and smiling at the beautiful woman on the staircase. "Moving on," she said through clenched teeth, and Margot nodded, mindfully putting her business face on.

Charis reached behind Spencer to press his arm down, as it was still awkwardly pointing at the woman who had to be Candace Everleigh.

"Spencer?" the blonde woman reached for his hand from her perch four steps up.

Spencer eagerly took it. "Thank you for meeting us, Mrs. Everleigh."

"Candace, please," the woman smiled a bit tightly, her eyes touching Margot and Charis briefly. "Come up to the office. We'll finish introductions there."

Margot exhaled as the woman turned and started back up to the second floor. Spencer looked back at them with a shrug and followed suit.

Charis gave her a withering look.

"Did you see that? I'm such an idiot," Margot said, her voice low.

Charis linked her arm through Margot's and giggled.

"You are. It's kind of entertaining, though!"

If the façade of the building had been an impressive amalgamation of two styles, the second floor confirmed it. Exposed wood beams in the ceiling kept the cozy cabin feel, while the grand, open-concept floor (complete with a roaring stone fireplace against the far wall) was fitted with modern workstations in addition to two comfortable seating areas.

Candace smiled as the three slowed to admire the setup. "We have collaboration areas for staff in the corners," she pointed, "and workstations for our mobile staff," she twiddled her fingers daintily at the two workers who'd looked up. "And then we have offices for management, mine being the only permanent one and the others open for visiting employees, or even to use as private meeting rooms," she gestured helpfully to the opposite wall, where several doors stood open. "Mine is here," she gestured over her shoulder at the lone office overlooking the parking area.

"It's really quite lovely," Margot said.

"Nice to have a bit of privacy when needed too, I'm sure," Spencer gestured to the tinted window, grinning sideways at Margot.

Candace stood behind her desk. "I do like to look out as I work, but you're right; privacy is important to me, so I opted for a tint instead of curtains."

"Best of both worlds," Charis smiled, then reached out to the woman, "Let me introduce myself. I'm Charis, a friend of the Hale family."

Candace smiled, her face brightening with it such that Margot could imagine *any* man doing her bidding – husband, staff, and stepson included. She reached out next. "And I'm Margot. Peyton is a long-time friend of mine."

The woman nodded, then turned to Spencer. "And – Peyton? – is your sister?"

Spencer nodded.

"Let's sit," Candace smiled, then frowned at the two chairs opposite hers. She started toward the door again, calling, "Whoops. Let me get a chair. Just a sec!"

"You don't have to -" Spencer called after her, but she was already heading into one of the open offices on the other side of the floor. He looked back at Margot and Charis. "That was nice."

Charis frowned. "Huh."

Once they were all seated, Candace surprised them again.

"I believe you," she said.

The three were silent, first, then Spencer gave his head an almost-imperceptible shake and said, "What?"

Candace smiled, but Margot thought there was sadness in it. "I don't know what you know about the Everleigh family. Much of what is publicly available has been vetted by Headquarters staff. The Everleighs have ties everywhere. It's a family with a long history and a reach farther than you can imagine."

"So, why does that contribute to your believing us? About Peyton, I assume?" Spencer, leaned forward in his chair eagerly, but his voice was calm. Controlled.

"Because I know what's *not* written in public papers," Candace said, her smile faltering, "and while I'm not prepared to go into details about my own position in the family – or how it's been *evolving* recently – I have reason to believe that there is somebody living on the Estate that I haven't met. That no-one has, as far as I know."

Margot glanced at Charis and Spencer, wanting to ask a

thousand questions, but not wanting to steamroll a woman who, in addition to the fact that she seemed willing to help them, had an air of frailty about her that she couldn't quite glean the reason for.

"Would you be able to share what you know?" Charis asked, finally.

The woman looked into the parking lot, but her eyes seemed far more distant. "I don't *know* anything," she said, looking back at Charis. "But yesterday, I learned something about Constance – the woman you mentioned as being identified with your sister on the night she disappeared?" She looked pointedly at Spencer, and he nodded, "Right. Well, Constance has always been a bit of a wild card, and since the death of her brother, she's quickly climbing to the top of the 'Everleigh Eccentrics' list," she gave a wry laugh, then her smile faded. "Please don't repeat that to anyone."

"Of course not," Spencer said.

"Anyway, Constance has been firing staff left and right over the past couple months, and it seems the cook was the final straw. He was in my office yesterday, as he had wages owed, but he told me some strange things, too. Like how Constance has been having formal tea in the tea room every night for the past several weeks."

Margot frowned. "Is that strange?"

Candace regarded her levelly. "Constance, alone, has been demanding formal tea for *three* people, every day, for months."

"Oh!" Margot covered her mouth as soon as the exclamation was out. She leaned to look at Spencer, then Charis. Both nodded, their mouths set in similarly tight lines. Spencer put a finger up before Margot could continue freaking out.

"Is there anything else?"

Candace regarded him. "I assure you, you don't even need *that* to get into the house. I'm still an Everleigh, despite what *some* may think, and after we're through the gates, we have no staff to even acknowledge us, thanks to Constance."

"But what about Constance herself? And Mr. Everleigh?" Margot asked, giving up on biting her cheeks.

"Constance *should* be at the office today, and Stewart -" she rolled her eyes. "God only knows, but if he is at the house, he's likely to take as little interest in our arrival as he does with anything else."

"Ah," Spencer leaned back in his seat awkwardly.

"We're sorry to hear that," Charis said, much more smoothly.

Candace looked at her for a few long seconds. "It's alright. I've been as hurt as I can be by that man. And this may sound surprising to you, but you three have given me the perfect way to close out my time as an Everleigh. I don't mean much to them, but now I can effect some change in how they operate behind closed doors, and hopefully get you your friend and sister back at the same time," she looked out the window again, "I apologize for being more candid than is required," she said, and kept talking even as Spencer tried to reassure her, "but like I said on the phone yesterday, I truly don't have anything to lose." She scanned them all again, eyebrows raised. "And they can't keep getting away with... everything."

"We're grateful for your help," Spencer said.

Candace jumped. "Oh! You asked if there was anything else, and there was. The cook also said he's been stocking the third-floor loft with groceries. Nobody's stayed up there for years."

Charis stood, clearly satisfied. "Can we go now?"

Margot recalled the psychic's words about timing and

pushed her chair back, her heart beginning to race.

"Give me two minutes," Candace said, opening her top drawer and pulling out a few personal items. She tossed them into a box on the floor, which Margot hadn't even noticed when they'd come in. The woman scanned the photos on her desk then, but only plucked one up, and put it into the box as well. "There," she said, a bit breathless.

Margot saw it was a photo of Enzo Everleigh, his hand casually on the reins of the horse he walked beside. His face was lit up as he laughed over something the photographer had said, it seemed. She got a pang in her chest. Regardless of the fact she knew next to nothing about him, it was strange to look at such a vibrant capture of him and know he'd since been dead and buried.

"Does your stepdaughter believe in ghosts, Mrs. – Candace?" Spencer had spotted the photo, as well.

"Pfft," Candace rolled her eyes. "She's been obsessed with them since her mother died."

The three exchanged looks as Candace bent to retrieve her box.

"Let me take that out for you," Spencer offered, already maneuvering it out of her arms.

"Yes, thank you. I won't be returning," the woman said, her pretty features straining against the same emotion that brought tears to her eyes.

"Is there anything else we can do for you?" Charis asked, her brow furrowed.

The woman shook her head. "I think I'm all set. Now, let's go get this sorted."

"I wonder," Spencer stopped them before they could exit, "should I call the police? At least to let them know we're heading over?"

"Not yet," Charis answered, before anyone else could. She looked at them. "Sorry. But trust me. Not yet."

Spencer nodded.

He did trust her.

Margot left the office last, and had to stop in her tracks as Candace paused to look back. "Are you alright?"

The blonde sniffed delicately, then absently placed a hand on the little bump of her abdomen. "I don't know what I've been hoping for – maybe some *purpose* to everything, after all that's happened," she said, her eyes on her office. Then she looked back at Margot. "But women aren't entitled to much in the Everleigh family, especially if they're not blood."

Margot paused, considering her options. It would have been very easy not to acknowledge the simple action of the woman placing a hand on her belly. But she hadn't ever been one for choosing the easy way. "But their children – they have rights," Margot said, making sure her words were low enough for just Candace to hear.

The woman's eyes widened. "I shouldn't have said so much." She turned and went toward the stairs.

And Margot wondered if it was Everleigh Senior or Junior who'd impregnated the woman that was so determined to leave it all behind.

Chapter 37 – A Forked Road

"I don't know what I expected, but it wasn't this." Margot leaned into Spencer to take in the view of the stately gates they were approaching.

"I don't know if it's necessary, but the family's always had the gate, apparently." Candace ducked to view it, too, as though seeing it for the first time.

"You're very kind to do this for us," Charis said again.

She certainly has a sense of how to placate people, Spencer remarked inwardly. Out loud, he said, "Or maybe she's just taking us to throw in the dungeon with Peyton." He knew it was the wrong thing to say as soon as it was out. "Sorry. I'm anxious," he said quickly, rubbing his forehead.

Margot reached over to pat his hand, but this time it was he who grabbed on. When he thought to check her reaction, she was looking out the window, a small smile at her lips.

"I don't blame you," Charis looked back from the front passenger seat, "but we're nearly there, Spence."

He nodded, tears pricking his eyes. He knew he'd been resilient thus far, perhaps to a fault. He'd thrown himself into research, into calming his mother and informing his father, and finally, into willing a positive outcome. But now, as they approached the wrought iron and stone wall that had imprisoned his sister, his emotions would not be held at bay.

What if they were wrong?

What if they should have waited, like the police said?

What if they were too late?

He clenched his teeth and turned to the window. The landscape blurred through hot tears.

"Spencer."

He heard it, he knew it was Charis, but needed a few more breaths.

"The cook stocked the groceries recently, right, Candace?"

"As far as I understood, he restocked the loft just before Constance dismissed him."

Spencer looked forward. Charis met his eyes.

"And the groceries have been consistently used?"

Candace shrugged, but nodded. "That's what he said, though he also mentioned that the last tea he prepared wasn't touched."

Charis flicked her eyes to Candace, then back to Spencer.

Candace hesitated, her eyes going to the rear-view mirror as she pulled into the gate. "Constance is a bit impulsive, and it's true she hasn't accepted her brother's passing yet, but I can't see her intentionally hurting anyone. Do you know why she'd be interested in Peyton in the first place?"

They stopped at the booth, but barely; the guard waved them through immediately. Candace slowed as the roadway narrowed and wound through dense conifers.

Spencer was still trying to decide how to answer the woman's question.

"Peyton is a gifted medium," Margot spoke up from beside him, and the truth felt good. He squeezed her hand.

"That'd certainly catch her attention," Candace murmured. She met Spencer's gaze in the mirror again. "I'm so sorry."

It was several minutes before the trees thinned and then stopped altogether, and the main house still stood a distance away.

"There are the stables," Charis sat up in her seat while Candace frowned in her direction. "I had a dream," she explained, then looked back at Margot. "She's there, I feel her."

"What?" Candace looked between Charis and the stables. "Let me guess, you're gifted too?"

Charis nodded. "Not exactly like Peyton, but,"

Candace raised a hand. "Listen, I have no problem helping you guys find Peyton, but I can't just let you run all over the place. Can we stay together?"

Charis's expression reflected her conflicting emotions.

Candace drew the car up to the front of the house and parked. She eyed Charis. "I'm thinking you're a bit of a wildcard right about now."

"I'll stick with you unless I feel an urgent need to go," Charis promised, her voice tight.

Candace gave a short nod. "That's fair, I suppose." She turned halfway around in her seat. "Ready?"

Spencer had to balance himself with a hand on the car.

"OK?" Margot asked over the roof of it.

He nodded. "I think I forgot to breathe for a while there."

His vision returned quickly and the first thing he registered was Charis's frowning face. She was at the base of the steps to the front entrance, but turned toward him.

"What?"

"You're connected to her. You're feeling what she's feeling."

It made sense before he even considered it. "She *is* here," he wondered, his eyes reflexively going to the stables, which sat perhaps a full kilometer back from the house, a fenced, but overgrown paddock behind it.

Charis sent a pleading look to Candace.

"Just a sec," the woman frowned, then tried the door. "Locked," she muttered, already digging in her clutch.

Margot appeared at his side. "Come on," she said, leading him to the steps with gentle pressure on his elbow.

And that was when Charis bolted.

Candace jumped and dropped her keys, then in one graceful movement dipped to grab them and tossed them toward Spencer and Margot. "Use them!" she said as she descended the stairs, then took off after Charis.

Spencer was frozen in place, staring at the keys in his open palm.

"Call the police!" Charis called over her shoulder, and Spencer saw Margot pulling her phone from her jacket pocket as if in slow motion.

"Unlock the door," she ordered, her voice low and firm, and he finally moved, taking the stairs by two.

"Yes, my name is Margot Francis and I'm calling from the Everleigh Estate in Berkshire?"

Spencer had several keys to choose from, but recognized the Everleigh crest on one. He tried it and it worked, to his great relief. "Margot! I got it!" he called back, then opened the door to demonstrate. A shrill alarm cut through the air and he froze.

Margot had halted at the bottom of the stairs. "Shit!"

He threw his hands up, then turned, calling out through the open door. "Hello? Is anyone home?"

Margot appeared beside him. "The police are coming. Two officers just began interviewing the uncle, so they'll bring him," she shouted over the blaring alarm.

Spencer felt his every tendon tense against the sound and cursed Asperger's Syndrome. He met Margot's eyes, focusing. "Charis's timing," he said, shaking his head. Then he found his palms pressing into his ears; an unconscious act of preservation.

Margot nodded. *Loud,* she mouthed.

He was grateful for her presence in that moment. For her dark, steady eyes on his.

She frowned and looking into the house. "I'm going," she said, and he read her lips.

"We should wait for the police!" he yelled, completely unsure of how loud he was being.

She shook her head, though. "I need to go," she said, and then she was slipping inside. He watched her make a beeline for the staircase, feeling helpless.

The stables, he thought, and though part of him wanted to catch Margot, just to tell her what he was doing, he knew there was no time. He skipped down the stairs and gave a furtive look at the road that headed into the trees. Hoping they were coming in, lights blazing.

And, just as he was turning to run, the alarm bleeped into nothing. Simultaneously, her got the feeling of being watched.

The unmistakeable sound of a rifle being cocked reached his ears.

"Hands up," a male voice commanded. There were no questions or choices in that voice, only the confidence of someone who was used to being obeyed.

Spencer raised his hands.

Chapter 38 – Revelations

Peyton was used to walking in front of Constance. The only difference this time was the lack of restraints.

And the threat of being shot, of course.

She set a pace she knew would please Constance and distracted herself by committing every detail to memory: the shattered vase in the hallway, the familiar portraits on the stairway, the subtle stench of the tearoom that reached her at the landing, where she paused, afraid to assume anything.

A sharp poke in her lower back steered her around to continue downward. The poke had been made with metal. She clenched her fists and concentrated on breathing as they continued to the first floor.

Everything looked unfamiliar here. The only time she'd laid eyes on these surroundings, she'd been in a panic, her eyes only on the control panel by the door. She was in an entirely different sort of panic, now. Still pursued, but at a controlled pace. And with a destination much less clear.

She realized her feet were bare when they arrived at the first-floor landing and the cold marble of the floor sent gooseflesh crawling up her legs. She steeled herself against an outward reaction, determined to avoid any further complications, but involuntarily slowed.

"You know where the door is, don't you?" Constance got her moving again with another poke, courtesy of the business end of her gun.

Peyton moved. The entire atmosphere of the floor felt off, the remains of Constance's argument with her father still hanging in the air. It was impossible not to notice the open door to Mr. Everleigh's main floor office.

Impossible not to look.

And then she was stopped again by a force beyond herself, her eyes first on a puddle of blood, and then on the man it oozed from. She'd never seen his face, except in pictures or online. She'd looked Constance and her family up when Enzo had first started appearing to her, weeks before Constance had shown up in the flesh. But she hadn't spent a lot of energy on the task, figuring she had time. In any case, she recognized the face of Everleigh Enterprises immediately. Only now, his features were slack.

Constance made a sound of frustration as she pushed past Peyton, reaching for the door.

Peyton couldn't look away, though, not until the door blocked the view, because though she'd become accustomed to seeing ghosts, Stewart Everleigh's body was one of very few empty shells she'd ever witnessed in person. And it was nothing like the others. No spirit still hovering over its earthly form, no sure signs on the body that it no longer housed a soul.

All of which was explained when the man's eyes cracked open and met Peyton's, just before the door clicked into place.

"Mind your business," Constance growled, then got in behind Peyton again, the gun poking her in the back, but remaining there, this time. "Move," Constance breathed, and Peyton was glad for the woman's short stature. She didn't think she could stand the feeling of the woman's breath on her ear. Not now.

"I won't tell," Peyton stated, but her words were strained. The pressure of the gun was causing a lower-back spasm that seemed to tighten with every step. She grunted. "That hurts."

Constance tittered. "You'd do well to remember the damage it *could* cause."

Peyton grimaced against the pain as they reached the door. And in her distracted state, she opened the panel and punched in the code before she thought to ask.

"Hm, guess I should have changed that," Constance muttered. Peyton couldn't help but flinch at the dark humour in the woman's words.

"I can forget it just as easily as I remembered it," she said.

"Open the door."

She couldn't have imagined the bliss of the fresh air on her skin. Her eyelids closed as she breathed it in, but she refused to get lost in it. "Should I go down?" she asked, unwilling to make another move without permission. Yet.

Constance only sighed.

Peyton started down, hating the danger implied in her every move.

But Constance followed without a word of reprimand. "Go to the right and around the house. You'll see the stables."

The soles of Peyton's feet protested at the sharp gravel on the driveway. Eyes on the grass, she hardened herself against the bite of the stones and progressed without hesitation.

"Where are your shoes?" Constance finally noticed the omission, and laughed. "Idiot. Did you plan on walking to the road like that?"

"I forgot," Peyton said, dully. It would have done no good to remind Constance she'd forced Peyton from the loft without even her bag. She made a face, realizing she'd need to get it. *If* she made it through this.

"Ugh. How can a person be so gifted and so *dim* at the

same time?"

Peyton focused on the stables and walked.

They slowed as they approached. Everything was just as it had been in her dream, but she made no move to examine anything closely. When they were both well inside, though, she did allow herself a side cast of her eyes. "Where's the horse?" she asked without thinking. She scanned the stalls, unable to stop herself. There weren't any horses, as far as she could tell.

Constance walked past her, then turned. "I sold them," she said, seeming to soften a little. "I couldn't take care of them, and I had to let the stable hands go." She pinned a hard look on Peyton. "You seem familiar with our stables. Why is that?"

Peyton opened her mouth, but nothing came out. "The pictures!" she finally replied, her voice too loud.

Constance eyed her suspiciously, but moved on. "I don't want to be here all day. Are Enzo and Mother here?"

They weren't. Peyton made a show of looking behind Constance. Her heart pounded. "Uh, not that I can -"

"Mother brought me to the stables on the day he died. I thought it was strange from the start, because she usually only came to me at night, but I did what she said anyway." She was looking at Peyton, but her eyes clouded with memory. "I always did. I just wanted her to..." she stopped, shaking her head.

"I understand," Peyton said quickly. Constance had started the story before the guests of honour arrived, and she was entirely unsure how to proceed.

Constance shrugged. "Can you – call them, or something?"

Payton looked furtively around again. "I could try, but

there's no guaran -" she turned on the spot, and was interrupted by a scream ripped from her own throat. Enzo *had* appeared, but not like he'd ever done before. She was aware of Constance saying something, but made no effort to understand.

He appeared to be held in space at first, or affixed somehow to the edge of the hayloft, but soon she could see he was hanging, the trees and overcast sky beyond the open doors framing him in a way that was at once beautiful and macabre. A rope was wound at least twice around his neck, but he did not hang freely. His head was level with the open hayloft, and pulled so tightly to the edge of it that his neck bent at an entirely unnatural angle. She followed the rope with her eyes and found its end tied to a beam that stood amongst the hay bales in the loft. "Oh, Enzo," she murmured, wanting to look away but unable to.

"What?" Constance exclaimed, coming to stand by Peyton.

Peyton realized her hands were covering her mouth and lowered them, "You don't see him?"

Constance looked around, her expression both hopeful and hesitant.

"You don't see him," Peyton said again, and was grateful. Beneath the odd angle of his neck, his skin was as white as the belly of a fish, but above it he was dark purple, his features distorted by swollen flesh. Even the tongue that protruded partway through his lips had been transformed into a massive, dark thing. His eyes were partially open, bulging in their sockets. And finally, he wore nothing but boxer shorts, but it was abundantly clear that the shock of death had misdirected the blood in his lower half to the stiff organ they barely held at bay.

Another whimper escaped her. She'd seen Enzo in a myriad of states, but this was the most disturbing by far.

"What *is* it?" Constance demanded.

"It's Enzo," Peyton cried, and then there really were tears. "He's dead – I mean, he's hanging," she finished, burying her face in her hands.

"It was an accident."

Peyton peered at Constance over her fingertips, avoiding seeing her friend in the state of his demise, but then there was a thud, and she had to look. Enzo's body had fallen to the ground, the untied rope dangling loosely from the loft. "Oh!" she exclaimed as she jumped back. "He fell!" She let her sobs come, uncaring if she was punished for it

"Well, you wanted to know how he died. I guess he just showed you."

Peyton shook her head, then frowned at the woman. She could see peripherally that Enzo was hanging again, though, and her hold on her mental state wavered.

"Like I said, it was an accident."

"But, how?" Virginia's voice startled Peyton such that she collapsed onto all fours, squeezing her eyes shut.

"What *now?*"

Peyton looked up at Constance. Her mother hovered behind her. "Your mother."

"Ah."

"We know he died from a broken neck," Virginia went on, casting a regretful gaze at her son's form, "but this was no typical hanging. *How* did it happen?"

Peyton took a critical look at the scene, now. "Why would anyone hang themselves from a beam at the back of a loft?" Peyton asked, a touch of hysteria in her voice. "And the rope isn't tied at his neck – it dropped him before he could be taken down. It doesn't make sense!"

Constance shook her head "You're talking like he did it on purpose, but I've already told you..." she sighed.

Peyton only shook her head in confusion.

Constance gestured toward the loft. "I can show you."

"You want me to go up there?" A vision of the naked blonde woman flashed behind her eyes. *How does she fit in?*

"What better way than to demonstrate?" Constance said, raising her eyebrows.

Peyton's heart sped up again. "H – how will you demonstrate?"

"Who said *I* would be the model?"

Chapter 39 - The Death Of Enzo, Part 1

Charis ran the last twenty feet toward the stables on her toes, gasping lungfuls of fresh air, then halted, leaning on the building just outside the open doors. Candace was making slower progress, giving Charis the chance to catch her attention and motion for her to be quiet. The woman seemed glad for the option, bending at the waist as she stopped entirely.

Charis squatted as her body recovered from the sprint, leaning toward the voices inside. She heard two.

"I don't want to go up!" a woman cried, and Charis felt the panic behind the words. *Peyton.* She was immediately sure she'd found her, and simultaneously sure she couldn't go in yet if she wanted to bring her out alive.

Waiting had time and again proven itself to be the most torturous aspect of knowing things ahead of time.

"If you want to know, you *will* climb up there. Fast," an accented voice answered. *Constance.*

"Please, Peyton," another voice reached her now, and struck a note of panic in Charis, too, for it echoed as if from a distance, and perhaps it *had* come from somewhere not quite - here. *Virginia.*

Peyton sobbed, making every muscle in Charis's body tense.

"I don't think I can!"

"Oh, for heaven's sake! What is *wrong* with you?" There was a brief scuffle, during which Charis worked so hard to hold herself back she dug half-moons into her palms with her nails.

Candace approached, finally, her eyes on Charis. She waved the woman behind her, and Candace complied.

"OK!" came Peyton's voice again, and there were subtle sounds of - climbing?

Charis sent a questioning look over her shoulder. Candace didn't miss a beat. "The ladder to the hayloft," she whispered. Charis met the woman's eyes with a renewed realization. *Candace was there when Enzo died, too.*

Peyton whimpered, but her words were too quiet to make out. The tortured sounds of her crying were, however, clear.

There were sounds of climbing again, but they were accompanied by grunts and creaking noises. "There!" came the accented voice again. And then, "Oh! I've forgotten the rope," followed by a painful moment of silence. "I guess we don't need it," she added.

Candace placed a hand on Charis's shoulder. Charis shook her head.

"They were up here," Constance started again. "There, to be exact. At first, I could hear them moving, but couldn't tell where they were. I called out for him, but there was nothing. I remember looking back for Mother, but she was gone. I remember wanting to leave. I wish I had -" the woman trailed off.

Peyton said something, again too low to hear.

"Oh, stop *whining!*" Constance yelled. "Just sit, if you don't want to stand! I don't need you yet, anyway. Where was I?"

Charis stood.

"I actually said hello to Oaken; he was Enzo's horse, and

I was about to visit my horse when I heard something from the hayloft. And I knew they were there. I'd known there was something going on with them, but I assumed they were devising a plan to overthrow Father. Enzo was already making headway at Headquarters, and -" she stopped short. Her voice was quieter when she went on, "but it doesn't matter now. What matters is that I *never* thought they were – I mean, when I climbed up here to confront them, the most I'd hoped to accomplish was to be included in their plans!"

"That was my fault," wailed the eerily resonant voice of Virginia Everleigh, and Charis tensed again.

"What is it?" Candace hissed.

Charis only shook her head again.

"Come *on*!" Candace bounced a bit. "This is *my* – I live here, technically! On paper, anyway! You need to tell me what's going on!"

Charis scowled back at her, her finger coming away from her lips. "OK, jeez. It's Virginia!"

The woman blanched.

Charis turned back to the door.

"But when I saw them – well I admit I was confused at first. I actually wondered why they'd taken their clothes off! I was so blind to the truth."

"What did you do when you realized?" Peyton's voice was comfortingly steady.

"If you're asking whether I – if I had anything to do with _"

"That's not what I meant!" Peyton interjected.

"I *was* angry, of course I was! Until that moment, I was still holding on to the fact that I had Enzo. He was all I'd ever had, really! Together, we'd survived childhood, we'd learned piano, and to ride – Enzo was a fierce competitor – and then we'd gotten through Mother's – and Candace! Candace was the worst of it all, or so I thought. A kick while we were down. So, realizing I'd lost him to *her* – it was devastating."

"Why was the rope around his neck?"

Constance laughed shrilly. "Your guess is as good as mine. Some sick sex thing is all I can figure," she spoke with heavy distaste. "That rope was wrapped around his neck countless times when I found him, and he was only just pulling on his boxers! Disgusting. Our stepmother was in an even more shameful state, naked except for the sundress she held up to cover herself." There was a pause. "Our *stepmother!*" Constance's voice had gone up an octave, making Charis jump.

The ghost of Virginia Everleigh began to cry – or cried louder. It was difficult to tell from where Charis stood, but the cadence of it sent shivers down her spine.

Peyton said something that made Constance laugh wryly.

"We argued, of course. I was so – I'd never felt so betrayed! So absolutely alone. I asked him why, and then, I blamed her! It felt good to accuse her of seducing him, of tricking him into submission so she'd have a male Everleigh to latch onto. She and Father weren't – but that doesn't matter, either. The point is that I accused her, and she didn't deny it! It's never made sense to me; that could've been it right there. All Enzo had to do was agree."

"But he didn't?"

"No."

Peyton's next words were muffled.

"Come here, and I'll show you."

Charis looked back at Candace and gave a short nod and the woman jumped into action, crying, "No!" as she burst into the building.

Charis followed closely, but was knocked on her ass by the sheer shock of nearly running into someone hanging from the hayloft. She screamed as Candace ran through him and the body turned slightly, seeming to peer accusingly from bulging eyes at Charis.

Chapter 40 – Margot

Margot hadn't even completed her thought about Charis's sudden mad dash when she'd been overwhelmingly compelled to run into the Everleigh home. And when she finally stopped running, it was only because she'd gone as high and far as she could. She stood, moderately bewildered, in the middle of the only room on the third floor, surrounded by three generous walls of windows and what appeared to be everything one would need to live quite comfortably, even without leaving.

Her eyes went to the kitchen and she was on the move again, checking the fridge and seeing it stocked with milk, eggs, cheese, fresh vegetables and condiments galore. A recently washed frying pan lay upside-down on a drying rack by the sink.

She knew it had been Peyton's home. She made quick work of checking the bathroom and under the bed – where she was suddenly overwhelmed by an odd sulphur smell, but it disappeared as quickly as it had come – and then swinging a knapsack she spotted on the bed over her shoulder.

She cast another look around, her eyes on the trees at the edges of the lot when the alarm stopped blaring. Somehow, the absence of the sound was more disconcerting than the alarm itself had been. She ran to the window. Candace's car remained the only one in the drive, so the police hadn't arrived. Nor could she see anyone outside the house from her vantage point. She wondered briefly if Spencer had figured a way to shut the screeching thing off, then turned to leave. *Timing,* she thought, but still bent to sweep up a pair of flat shoes from beside the door before leaving. Later, she'd say it hadn't been a decision; she just did it, and brought the bag around to stuff them into just as smoothly.

She descended to the second floor slowly, on alert for any indication that she wasn't alone in the house, now that the alarm had stopped. She heard nothing. She stopped on the second-floor landing and was simultaneously hit with two distinct smells: that of smoke and the other of rotting food. She grimaced, but thought little of it. She'd smelled burning on the third floor too, but it had faded before she could even puzzle over it. She decided on a risk and leaned over the railing, calling, "Spencer?" No sound answered her, Spencer's voice or otherwise.

Unwilling to hesitate further, she veered to the right, running with abandon now that she was satisfied she was alone. She ran past the tea room without hesitation, despite the light that poured into the hallway from its open door. But she stopped when the smell hit her, delayed but not diluted. "Ugh!" she put the back of her hand to her nose and turned back, leaning into the doorway before fully entering.

It was magnificent. Even the source of the stench looked magical; an untouched table set for formal tea, just as Candace had described, with platters of sandwiches – though the fuzzy green bits had most likely evolved after their debut – and treats in pastel shades of purple, pink and yellow. Margot clasped her hands in delight, then raised one back up to her nose. *It's pretty, but dear God, it smells horrid.*

She felt a pull back into the hallway, so scanned the setting quickly, then took in the room itself, so dainty in blue, silver and white. So crisp against the windows' reminder of impending rain on the sky's dark palette of greys.

She turned and was running again, perhaps noticing the smell of smoke a little intensely, now, but determined to follow her instincts. Feeling, for the first time in who knew how long, that she was doing what she was supposed to be doing.

Doing what was needed of her.

Both rooms at the end of the hallway felt like valid choices. She paused between them, then opened the door to her right, first.

The hairs on the back of her neck stood on end as she entered. It was dark, but hulking shadows filled her in on its contents. Bed, heavily framed, bureau, no mirror, doorway to a small *en suite,* maybe? A tall wardrobe, and in the corner to her left, a woman.

Margot made a choked sound in her shock, and froze. Her eyes adjusted, but her brain registered the same result. Woman. Corner.

Shit.

She reached to the wall on her left, perceiving an encroaching coldness, but not what she was searching for. She forced herself to turn away from the shape, patting the wall to the right and holding her breath. *There has to be a switch, oh, please let there be a switch.* And there was. Instantly relieved, she flicked it on and snapped her head back toward the corner, where she fully expected to see nothing, but instead a woman in dark bedclothes lunged at her, mouth agape and reaching arms streaming gales of blood.

Retreating so quickly out of the room that she fell against the door opposite, which swung inward, she heard a blood-chilling scream that only registered as her own after laying prone in a new dark room for a few moments, the knapsack which had cushioned her fall becoming an uncomfortable lump beneath her and reminding her that she hadn't chosen her position. She raised her head to check the direction she'd come. No ghosts.

Her sense of urgency, however, did not flag.

"Shitshitshit!" she muttered as she turned herself onto

all fours and breathed, her eyes already going to the corners. Once reassured, she sat back on her heels. There was an open door in front of her. She crawled to it, then stood, her hands feeling along both sides of it simultaneously and her right hand flicking the light on before she realized she'd found the switch. She squeezed her eyes shut instinctively, then cracked them and, satisfied she was alone, let her hands drop.

There was a bang from somewhere in the house, and then a crash. Margot glanced over her shoulder toward the hallway. She sniffed. The smell of smoke again, and that familiar pushing sensation that compelled her onward. There was no time, but she turned back for one thing. One thing which didn't fit in with the frilly dresses and pretty lines of shoes: a bulging black duffel bag, sitting in the middle of the floor.

Another crash from below, and this time her mind conjured a picture of a window shattering, flames bursting forth in newfound freedom.

She grabbed the shoulder strap and lifted, but let the bag fall instantly. "Jesus!" she muttered, imagining stones inside, then remembering the heaviest boxes during her move into the Wolfville house. It was always books in those boxes. She gritted her teeth and inhaled sharply, then pulled instead, exhaling in an exalted *whoop!* when the bag complied and followed her.

She dragged it into the hallway easily, but quickly lost momentum as her jagged breaths pulled in the definitely *not* faded odour of smoke. She was sweating when she passed the tea room, and had switched to walking backward, using her weight to drag the duffel by the time she reached the landing.

She stopped and stood straight, grimacing at the change in temperature. "Fire," she panted, admitting it finally as her eyes found tendrils of smoke weaving their way up the stairs. "Oh, God." She grasped the strap of the bag again but swung it across the landing in an arc, which landed the bag over the stairs descending to the main floor.

"Yeah," she said, happy for the success, but finding herself unable to power a yell of triumph.

She followed the bag to where the stairs stopped and twisted, and paused as she grabbed the strap again. She'd spotted the source of the fire: a room to the left of the door she'd come in through. Smoke billowed out the open doorway and flames chased it, licking the ceiling in the entryway. She couldn't leave that way.

Her heart accelerating rather painfully as her lungs begged for oxygen, she manoeuvred the bag around until she could shove it with a grunt down the final set of steps. It landed heavily at the bottom. Lacking the motivation to stand, Margot slid down the final steps on her belly, feeling simultaneously childish and clever. Wasn't the purest air near the floor, anyway?

She continued in a crouch, pushing against the duffel with straining muscles away from the fire and toward, she hoped, another door. The heat on her back and buttocks intensified steadily, but she refused to look back, for fear she'd lose her nerve and take off at a run, leaving the bag behind.

She did question herself, then, about whether a heavy bag with unknown contents could be worth risking her life, but the question was rhetorical, because her body kept moving as her brain did what it did best. Soon she was going through a doorway, pushing the bag onto ceramic tile. "The marble was slippery-er!" she cried, her voice somehow gravelly and high-pitched at once. She nearly laughed at how she sounded, but decided against it. *Too much work,* her brain said.

She started seeing fireworks behind her eyes just as she caught sight of a door, and rejoiced, because what good timing. And she reached it before she blacked out, even opened it. Shoved the heavy bag onto what appeared to be an outside sitting area with a monumental yell, then, satisfied, collapsed, herself only halfway out.

She thought, just before a hand reached out to her from the overwhelming brightness of the sky, *I saw another ghost! Finally!* And it was his face behind that reaching hand, the one of her first love. The one of a dead boy who'd needed her help.

The face of her Wren.

Chapter 41 – The Death Of Enzo, Part 2

Peyton lunged forward at the sound of Candace's scream, then paused, thinking, before covering the remainder of the hayloft on all fours when a second scream ripped through the air. She peered over the edge carefully, aware of Constance pointing her gun toward the ladder to her left.

A petite woman with an inordinately bold head of curls peered up at her, her scream dying out as her expression changed. "Peyton?"

Peyton frowned. This was Charis, the woman she'd been so excited to learn about. The woman who'd denied her plea for help. "I knew I'd meet you at the right time," she said, smiling.

Charis looked confused for a moment, then relieved. Then she looked at the terrible form of the still-hanging Enzo. "What's happening here?" she asked, and Peyton regarded her dead friend with new eyes.

"Enzo!" she said, and Candace, who'd been mounting the ladder, froze, her eyes darting around the building.

"*You're* not gonna find him," Constance laughed, her gun still aiming at the blonde.

"You're already *dead*, Enzo! Why are you hanging there?" Peyton asked.

She could see his eyes roll upward to regard her.

"See?" she smiled, though Enzo's bulging eyeballs were making her stomach uneasy. "Get down from there!"

He did, but first it was to fall again, the rope unravelling and sending his frame into a roll in midair before it let him drop. It was almost graceful. Peyton watched as Charis crab-walked backward, her eyes on Enzo.

"What's happening?" Candace cried, looking between Charis and Peyton.

Enzo jerked, then rolled onto all-fours. He looked up at Peyton, his skin losing the purple mottling, thank goodness. "Huh. You're right. That was a bit confusing for a while, there."

Charis covered her mouth, but Peyton saw the smile in her eyes.

"Who are you?" Constance looked down at Charis, but her gun remained pointed at Candace.

"I'm a friend of Peyton's," Charis replied, raising her hands, palms out. A sign of surrender. "I just want to take her home."

Peyton rejoiced inwardly, but couldn't relax into it. In her experience, things that seemed too good to be true often proved to be just that.

"That's a shame. She's about to recreate the circumstances around Enzo's death," Constance replied, then smiled at Peyton, making her stomach turn again.

"There's no need," Charis said. Peyton watched as the woman looked pointedly at Enzo, who was sitting cross-legged on the dirt floor now, his eyes on Candace. Charis looked up at Peyton. "I can't see Virginia."

Peyton shook her head. "She's not here."

"I think you've done what you promised," Charis said, looking at Constance again. "Would you agree, Enzo?"

Peyton hugged her arms, revelling in the joy of watching someone else see what she could see.

Enzo, however, wasn't impressed. "Actually, she hasn't told me anything I didn't already know."

"I'm coming the rest of the way up," Candace said, and didn't stop when Constance stepped toward her.

"Don't you *dare!*" Constance cried.

Candace sat on the loft floor, her legs dangling over the edge. "Sorry, I couldn't hang from the ladder anymore!"

"So, it's not just your thinking that's weak, huh?" Constance stated, and Enzo blipped out of existence and then back, this time beside Candace.

Candace looked at Peyton questioningly.

"He's beside you," Peyton nodded.

Candace covered her mouth, tears springing to her eyes.

"Oh, my God! Don't do that!" Constance raged, her face turning red. "Don't pretend you loved him!"

"I *did* love him!" Candace shot back.

Peyton looked down at Charis, who was still watching from her seat on the floor.

"*This* is what I remember," Enzo said. "These two fighting. But that's it." He looked at Peyton. "You owe me nothing, Pey. You can go – leave with her," he gestured with his chin toward Charis, "and never feel you didn't help me. You did more for me in death than anyone ever did for me in life. Don't forget it."

Charis stood. "Peyton?"

Peyton thought that if she held on to the edge of the loft, she could let herself drop to the floor without hurting herself too badly. But she found herself standing, instead. "No. What happened next?"

Constance looked at her as if she had two heads. "I'm

done with this. I can see that everyone's ganged up against me, just like always! What more do you want?" She looked between Peyton and Candace.

Candace cast a glance to her right, where Enzo sat, gazing back at her. "That's fine," she said, "you don't have to tell them the rest."

"Damn right!" Constance said, and looked quite smug.

Candace stood. "I will."

Constance frowned, as though she'd forgotten she wasn't the only one who knew what happened. "You promised!" she said, pointing at her stepmother with her finger now, instead of her gun.

"Enzo was miserable," Candace said.

Charis stood.

"No matter what he gained in money - or cars, or even in me! - he remained unsatisfied, and I think you know why."

"I do! My father abused him. And not just him," Constance was crying, tears running freely down her cheeks, "but many others! When the family threatened him, he started travelling to fulfill his sick desires!" she looked down at Peyton. "He told me more than I wanted to know this morning," she cried, then wiped at her cheeks with the back of her gun-holding hand.

"I was wrong to let it happen," Candace continued, "but I was miserable, too. Stewart was a master of manipulation, but once he got what he wanted, he lost interest. He only needed me to placate the family, but I wanted more."

Constance made a sound and rolled her eyes. "No shit."

"I won't deny it!" Candace stepped toward her. "I didn't love him! But he acted like he loved me! And it felt good, all that attention, and yes, the prospect of never having to worry about money again. But then there *was* more. There was the Winery to run. I found out I was good at something. And there was you! And there was Enzo."

"Me?" Constance laughed. "You must be joking."

"I tried with you, Constance! And when you refused to let me in, I understood. I respected that! But Enzo was different. Enzo had a soft spot for me... and it turned into something more."

"Which brings us right back here, where it all came to a head," Constance gestured around the hayloft.

"That's right. And for once, I didn't let you throw your tantrum and get your way! I defended Enzo. I defended myself!"

Constance turned and eyed Peyton, who had sat again. "As I remember it, you were standing right about where Peyton is, now, screaming a bunch of nonsense at me as you got dressed," she snickered. "Stand up, Peyton."

Candace gasped. "Don't do anything she says." She looked at Constance. "Why is Peyton here, Constance? How *long* has she been here?"

"She was just leaving us today," Constance said, quietly, "but now, since you've crashed our little party, there's no chance of that, is there?"

Peyton stood, her eyes on Enzo, who was watching her. He shook his head. "Don't, Peyton. I can't let her take you, too."

"Thank you, Peyton. Right! Candace was where you are, now, screaming bloody murder, and, -" she faltered, glancing back at the blonde woman.

"And you lunged at me," Candace said. She walked around Constance, her eyes on Peyton, then turned to face the shorter woman. "And Enzo dove in front of me."

"With that stupid rope wrapped around his neck!" Constance screamed, spittle flying as she whirled. "Why? Why? Even *I* can't explain that!"

"Because nothing made him feel good anymore. Not even me. He kept pushing the envelope, just to try and feel *something*," Candace shook her head.

Enzo had come closer as Candace talked. "I remember now," he said. "I blocked Constance from pushing Candace, and I fell."

"Is he saying something?" Candace was watching Peyton.

Peyton nodded. "It was an accident. He remembers."

Constance collapsed to the floor, sobbing. "I told you!"

Candace nodded.

There was a sound from below, and everyone turned to look. Everyone except Charis, whose eyes were still on Peyton.

And then her brother walked in. Peyton gasped, crying out his name, but then she collapsed, too, just as Constance had, for she saw the gun that pushed him forward, and the man who held it.

Stewart Everleigh was not doing well. His blonde hair was plastered in chunks to his skull, slick as it was with sweat. And he was covered in blood from the chest down. While Constance hadn't killed him outright, she'd surely dealt a fatal blow. All that need happen was for the man to succumb to it. But Everleigh was obviously running on determination more than anything else. He was white as a sheet and listing hard to the left as he stumbled forward. Drool hung from his lower lip.

"Interesting story!" he shouted, slurring his words like a drunk. "Too bad it doesn't matter."

"Stewart! What's going on?" Candace turned to look down at her husband, and Constance saw her window. She lunged for her, and this time, Enzo couldn't stop her.

But Candace fell into Peyton, who'd stood to fill in for her anyway, and Peyton fell. She felt it come over her as she did – that familiar acceptance. But instead of hitting the ground, she was embraced by small, but strong arms, which first slowed her, then gave way so Charis could fall with her and cushion the blow.

She'd heard a scream as she fell, but it wasn't hers. After meeting Charis's eyes to ascertain whether the smaller woman had survived, Peyton looked up and saw that Candace had been lucky, too, for the ghost of Virginia Everleigh was holding the woman up as she tilted dangerously over the edge of the loft, and then pushing her back, until Candace could stand on her own again.

"What the hell?" Stewart Everleigh was gazing in wonder at his estranged wife, who, to his eyes, had just defied the laws of physics to beat death for the second time.

Spencer saw his chance and gave a yell, twisting around to disarm the man before Everleigh could comprehend the action. He fell backward, sliding a bit on his behind as he landed, then slumping forward, bubbles of blood mixing with his drool.

"Peyton!" Spencer grabbed her up and held her close, then held her at arm's length to look at her. "Are you alright?"

Peyton nodded, tears swimming in her eyes.

"You're so thin," he noted quietly, then offered a hand to Charis.

"Go," Charis commanded as soon as she was on her feet. He nodded, then ran out of the stables and toward the house, which Peyton could see now was shrouded in smoke and flame.

"Spencer!" she cried as she watched her brother run toward the inferno.

"He'll be alright," Charis put her arm around Peyton's waist and looked up at her. "Hi."

Peyton laughed, a bit wildly. "Thank you."

Charis nodded, then motioned toward the loft. "Think we can leave these two alone?"

Peyton's eyes widened. "I don't know!"

Charis urged her forward. "They won't be alone for long. The police are here."

Peyton looked toward the house. "How do you know?"

Charis smiled.

"Pey?"

The women stopped and looked back.

"I think I can go, now."

Peyton smiled at Enzo, who was dressed and tidied up. "You did good. You're a good guy, Enzo."

He nodded. "Thanks for helping me see it." He lifted his shirt and gestured to his chest, smooth and unmarred. "I think the wound there was metaphorical?" he grinned at Peyton, who could only giggle. "Oh!" He looked up at the loft, then added, "tell them *both* I love them, OK?"

"Hey, you two!" Peyton called, feeling a little giddy. The women looked over the edge. Both appeared stunned. "Enzo wants you both to know he loves you," Peyton called.

Charis giggled at her side. "Well done."

"Bye, Enzo," Peyton waved.

They started through the field. "Where's Virginia, I wonder?"

Charis squinted toward the house. "Oh, good, he's got her."

"Who?" Peyton frowned.

Charis pointed. "Margot. Spencer got her."

Peyton squinted and spotted her brother carrying a woman away from the flames. Her arms were around his neck and she seemed to be looking up into his face. Peyton's heart felt like it might explode. "Is that my *friend*, Margot?"

Charis smiled. "It is." She looked up at Peyton. "And you asked about Virginia – she won't be ready for goodbye for a while. She has some work to do before she can rest."

Peyton's felt her eyes widen again. "Is that what happens?"

The shorter woman nodded, then looked back at the stables. "She got a good start in there, though."

"How do you *know*?"

The woman linked arms with her and it didn't bother Peyton at all. "We have a lot to talk about."

"We do?"

"Yep. Like it or not, you're never going to be alone again."

Peyton smiled, the simultaneous urge to laugh and cry combining into an awkward hiccough.

Charis giggled.

"I can probably teach you a few things too, you know."

Charis gave a laugh. "I'm counting on it."

Chapter 42 – Silver Clouds

"I thought I was dead," Margot rasped, looking up at Spencer as he lowered her to the blanket.

He shook his head, then turned to push Margot's wheelchair away from them. "I'm really glad you're not," he said as he lowered himself to sit beside her. Margot touched his face delicately and they kissed, the world around them fading for just a moment.

"Gross," Peyton remarked from the opposite corner of their blanket, then started opening the Tupperware containers Charis had brought.

"Ah, let them enjoy each other," Charis smiled. She popped a dark red cherry into her mouth. "These are good for you. Eat."

"You say that about everything," Peyton smiled.

"I'm leaving tomorrow, so I have to get my nagging in," Charis exclaimed, but then her face turned serious. "I hate the thought of leaving you two behind."

"You have a whole other life waiting for you back home," Margot said in barely a whisper as she touched Charis's knee.

"So do you," she frowned at her friend.

"But mine can wait. You have little people to hug."

It was such a nice way to describe her responsibilities that Charis smiled, hugging herself as she thought of wrapping her arms around her children.

"At least we're not alone," Peyton said through the sandwich she'd bitten into.

"I consider it a minor miracle that you two are able to room together, considering your very different injuries," Spencer noted as he looked up at the hospital's dull façade.

"I'm not injured," Peyton noted. "I just need to gain weight and get stronger." She grabbed a handful of cherries, offering one to Charis, who gladly plucked it from her palm. "And I gotta say, the prescribed cure is much more fun than Margot's!"

Margot laughed, but it devolved into a coughing fit. When she recovered, she smiled again. "Yeah, you get to eat whatever you want – lots of it – and take frequent naps, while I do breathing exercises and suck on oxygen through nostril straws."

Charis giggled, but Spencer had put a hand on Margot's shoulder, concern on his face.

"Do you need to go back up?"

"And cut short our hospital lawn picnic? Are you kidding?"

Spencer stood. "Alright, but I'm getting your oxygen."

Margot looked at Peyton, then Charis. "In the end, I think we're all pretty lucky."

"Did Spence tell you guys about the Everleighs?" Charis asked.

Peyton nodded, but Margot frowned. "I only know Stewart Everleigh survived, and will likely spend the rest of his life in jail."

"Thanks to the journals you dragged out of a burning building," Peyton jumped in. "Spencer talked to the police again and they said Constance is getting off easy. She's doing an outpatient psychotherapy program."

Margot made a face. "Meaning she can carry on living on the Estate?"

Peyton nodded, then took a bite of a cookie.

"And – get this – Candace is living there with her," Charis smiled.

Margot inhaled sharply through her nose as Spencer placed the oxygen tubes into her nostrils. Her face regained some colour almost immediately.

"You OK?" he asked.

Margot held a finger up as she breathed. "Get tired so easily."

"You need to nap, too," Peyton noted, again through a mouthful of food.

"Would you *stop* that?" Spencer exclaimed.

"Sorry."

Charis barely contained her laughter. She leaned toward Margot again. "Apparently, there was some loophole in the company policy regarding heirs, and once the stepdaughter-stepmother duo had the chance to catch up in the hayloft, they decided to exploit it together."

"Do you remember that man with the red face who came with the police?" Peyton covered her mouth while she talked.

Margot nodded. "The uncle, right?"

"Yep. Or in other words, the heir-apparent, should Stewart Everleigh be stripped of his title. But now – and this is what got him so mad - Candace is the reigning Everleigh. I'm happy for them," Peyton shrugged and went back to chewing.

"Is it because she's pregnant?" Margot asked, recalling her conversation with Candace on the day it all happened.

Spencer shook his head. "Not just that. A child of Stewart Everleigh would be cut off, given the crimes of his father."

Margot's eyes widened. "It's Enzo's baby?"

Spencer nodded.

"It's Enzo's *son*," Charis added, "and there's a neat little clause in the policy that says *any* male descendants at least once removed from the convicted criminal shall *retain* his rights before alternate heirs, like Uncle Bertie, are considered."

"So, the baby resulting from a scandalous affair between stepson and stepmother will inherit the Empire?"

Charis nodded, smiling.

"Holy shit."

Peyton laughed.

"Why did you think you were dead?" Spencer circled back to Margot's earlier comment.

Peyton's phone rang and she stood, digging it out of her pocket. "Mom?" she answered, and walked away from the group.

Margot watched Peyton for a moment, then smiled at Spencer. "I thought I saw Wren just before I passed out, but now I know it was you that dragged me from the patio door to the other side of the deck."

Spencer frowned.

"You saw Wren?" Charis leaned forward.

Margot nodded. "No, it was Spence! But I did see a ghost while I was inside the house: Virginia Everleigh scared the hell out of me! In hindsight, I think she was trying to get me out of there."

Both Charis and Spencer were frowning at her.

Margot inhaled deeply. "What?"

"I didn't drag you to the end of the deck; I *found* you there."

Margot locked eyes with Charis.

"You saw Wren," Charis smiled.

Margot's mouth gaped open for a moment, then her eyes lit up. "And he saved me!"

"You're not going to believe this," Peyton said as she flopped back onto the blanket, already reaching for more food. "Dad's been trying to get in touch."

"With me too, weirdly," Spencer interjected.

"Apparently, he's feeling like a shitbag for being absent for so long."

"Pfft," Spencer said.

"I know, but there's something else. He told Mom he's getting tested."

"For what?"

"He went through rehab for the drinking, and while he was in there, they took an interest in him, recommended he go through the tests to determine whether he's on the Autism spectrum." Peyton sat back on her heels and took a bite of another sandwich, her eyes sparkling.

"No *shit!*" Spencer's eyes looked like they might drop from his skull.

"I love it when silver linings make themselves so obvious," Margot rasped.

"More like silver clouds, huh?" Peyton smiled at her friend.

"Any idea when you'll be discharged?" Charis squinted as the sun came out from behind a cloud.

"Believe it or not, they think I'll be ready to fly back before the month is out," Margot, replied, her eyes on Spencer.

"Don't worry, Spence," Charis poked him with her bare toes, her shoes having been kicked off as soon as they stepped onto the grass. The simple sentiment was anything but simple when it came from a psychic. Spencer grinned.

"There's just one thing I want to clarify about how things went down in the stables," Charis cast a questioning gaze toward Peyton.

"I thought you'd have it all straight, considering -"

"I do, mostly. But I can't figure out what you did to drag things out in the hayloft."

Peyton made a face. "Huh?"

"When we were listening from outside, and Candace was telling you to help her demonstrate how Enzo died, how did you hold her off? I could hear you talking, but couldn't make out what you were saying, and it's been on my mind because of the timing that day. Everything had to happen exactly when it did to make it turn out the way it was supposed to."

Peyton's eyes cleared as she remembered. She put a hand to her mouth as she paused to swallow her food, then said, "It wasn't intentional."

"But I could hear you crying and refusing; I just don't know what was so important that it convinced her -"

"I'm really texture sensitive," Peyton stated, then looked self-consciously around at her puzzled friends. "Uh, I didn't have any shoes on. Margot grabbed my only pair from the loft with my bag. I forget to put things on sometimes."

Spencer giggled. "I can vouch for that. When we were both still living at home, I developed a habit of reminding her to put pants on before she left the house."

The woman laughed.

"It's true," Peyton said. "Anyway, I was dealing pretty well with everything that was happening, considering how overwhelmed I was, but I started losing it when she asked me to go up into the hayloft... because of my bare feet."

"What?" Margot and Charis voiced the questions together.

"I hate the way I feel when I have to deal with two different textures on my skin at the same time, and I knew in the loft I'd have to deal with dirt *and* hay."

Charis shook her head. "So, you were held at gunpoint, weak and nearly *skeletal* from being ignored for nearly two weeks, your dead friend had appeared, *hanging* from a rope, and you were completely unsure if you'd survive the day, but the way hay would feel on your bare feet was the thing that did you in?"

"Hay *and* dirt," Peyton replied, with such conviction that everyone laughed. "What?"

"Ah, you're one of a kind, sis," Spencer put an arm around her shoulders.

"I'm sorry I didn't see it when you first reached out to me," Charis confessed, her smile fading.

Peyton shook her head. "It wasn't our time yet."

"I'm sorry, too. I should've kept in touch," Margot whispered.

Peyton waved it away. "Don't blame yourselves. I could just as easily say none of this would have happened if I'd been better at protecting myself."

"Or at least as good as you are at protecting everyone else," Spencer added.

Peyton smiled, her eyes filling with tears. "I'm glad it

happened. I needed people in my life who could understand. And now I have you," she said in such open honesty that Margot and Charis found themselves welling up with happy tears, too.

The End.

ACKNOWLEDGEMENTS

Thanks as always to my readers for thier kind support and enthusiasm, and to my crazy, wonderful husband and amazing kids for coming along on these adventures with me. Thanks also to my father, Perry Dale, who diligently edits my work, and who inspired me in the first place.

BOOKS BY THIS AUTHOR

Bird With A Broken Wing

A fourteen-year-old girl living in a rural community of Nova Scotia, a group of neighborhood kids, and hours spent exploring or just hanging out in the woods and on the train tracks along the river.

Bird With A Broken Wing brings us back to a time when the best thing about evenings and weekends was heading outside to find your friends - but there is nothing typical about Margot's new friend, Wren. And the new family at the bottom of the hill knows why.

Just as she tries to accept her feelings of being perpetually left behind, Margot discovers some of the different faces of love in the most unexpected way.

That Summer

Twelve-year-old Peyton is dealing with an Asperger's diagnosis and a summer spent away from her parents. Everything changes for her that summer, but it takes some new friends - live and ghosts alike - to get through it all. In the end, she not only learns that being herself is her best option, but that she can make a positive difference in the lives of others, too.

Rose's Ghost

She just wanted her baby back. Rose's Ghost is the first book in a series of three about a family's connection with a tormented ghost, still desperate to gain back the child she lost.Rose remains tethered to her family's property, beseeching those who reside upon or around it to help in her quest. But somewhere between her death and the haunting of Maggie Ridgewood's family, Rose's reality has become darkly skewed, and her efforts to find her child threaten to alter the lives of those whose help she enlists – or end them.

Heather's Grave

Rose is at rest, but the haunting of the Ridgewood family continues in Heather's Grave: Book 2 of the Rose's Ghost series. Maggie is relieved to have found peace in the Ridgewood family home, having solved the mystery of Rose Maplestone. But with the onset of new adventures as she and Jack prepare for their new addition comes more ominous change.Max is forced to admit his anxiety stems from more than regret over his role in saving Alice Ridgewood from Rose's ghost. His body is sick, too.And the tragedies of the Maplestone family didn't end with Rose, for after all, the child she lost was a secret in life – her existence unrecorded and unacknowledged - except by those who'd witnessed it all. And as her desperation to honor her child grows, Rose determines to help Maggie in the strangest of ways – raising questions around her intent. Does Rose mean to help, as she's vowed, or do her methods force an ultimatum instead, wherein the life of Maggie's child depends on the finding of hers?

Dmitry's Shadow

Greyson is grateful for the peace he's found with the help of his friends, but all is not yet well; the questions of his ancestry remain. Why did Viktor Kotova flee his home country? Who was left behind? Amidst rumours of a family connection with the mafia and the suspicious circumstances surrounding his grandfather's death, there are ghosts that linger, insistent on the solving of the Kotova family puzzle. So, Greyson and the property of his family home - once abandoned and then demolished - remain haunted, and like his mother before him, he enlists the help of those who reside upon it.

But Max and Maggie are fighting demons of their own, and Charis finds her world rocked by the dark patches in her vision. Will they be able to pull together and face the truths of a buried past? And will the answers they find bring long-awaited closure to a man whose life is just beginning at the age of seventy-four?

Chrysalis

In Chrysalis, we explore the quiet underworld of an ultra-conservative Canadian city. Our unlikely hero, Trey, is an energy-seeing, cross-dressing sex worker on the precipice of a life or death decision, but when a friend goes missing, he finds himself distracted from the business of self-destruction.

Desperate to find his missing colleague, twenty-four-year-old Trey finds himself part of an unusual group, from a deranged kidnapper to a devoted cop, all focused on a missing girl. And when confronted with these Canadian people, dealing with both human and Canadian issues, we find ourselves suspending our judgement on characters we'd often prefer to look past.Through it all, we witness Trey's chance at transformation – will he be able to set himself on a new direction in life as he finally begins to understand that being different doesn't necessarily mean you don't belong?

Asylum

From the creator of the Rose's Ghost series comes another thrilling tale: Asylum proves to be a ghost story that stands on its own.

We follow Bailey O'Connor on an exciting urban exploration trip across the border to discover the secrets of a long-abandoned institution for mentally and physically handicapped children. But there's more than just mystery darkening the crumbling buildings they discover, and Bailey finds herself lost within them with the help of those who linger.

The search for her is mounted during the day while her own search takes place in the dark. Are the rumors true? The whisperings of experiments performed on the innocent and vulnerable? What secrets lurk within the few impenetrable buildings on the site? Most importantly, can the truth be uncovered before the property is leveled and its secrets are buried forever?

Told in Dale's unique voice, readers both familiar and new will appreciate an engaging cast of characters and a compelling story that is hard to put down.

Rose's Ghost - The Trilogy

The complete collection.

Bird With A Broken Wing & That Summer - Two Sweet & Scary Tales For All Ages

The collection.

Spirit Talker

The first book in a new series from the author that brought you the Rose's Ghost Trilogy and Asylum.

Shya's no stranger to events of the paranormal sort – the women in her family have passed down their strange gifts for as long as they know. But the early loss of her mother has meant far less guidance for Shya than they'd both hoped for, and now she finds herself floundering as she faces darker elements of the spirit world.

She's grateful for her friends in The Seers group... at least they take her seriously, and even provide insight she couldn't have gleaned herself, thanks to their incredible collection of supernatural gifts. But none of them are prepared for the fight that looms ahead, and it's not only a possessed child's life that hangs in the balance – the demon wants Shya most of all.

Will The Seers succeed in saving both souls when Shya's gifts are turned to work against her?

Join Shya and The Seers on an adventure that will have you in its grips and leave you wanting more.